Now they saw the woman; she lay sprawled, unmoving, in a pool of blood. Beside her a small, half-clothed child, thin and dirty but demonstrably alive, screamed hysterically above the sounds of battle.

'The woman's dead,' said Marek.

'The kid isn't.' Michal started forward.

Marek grabbed him. 'Wait!'

Michal shook off the restraining hand. 'We can't leave the poor little bastard there.' He ran, crouched low, dodging and weaving, snatched the screaming child from the ground and ran on towards the shelter of a ruined building. He almost made it. Above the rattle of machine-gun fire in the next street Marek heard the single crack of a rifle shot. Michal stumbled and sprawled, still clutching the child. He lay for a moment among the dust and the rubble, then slowly and painfully he began to crawl.

The Raven Hovers

TERESA CRANE

WARNER BOOKS

A *Warner* Book

First published in Great Britain in 1996
by Little, Brown and Company
This edition published by Warner Books in 1997

A CIP catalogue record for this book
is available from the British Library.

ISBN 0 7515 1297 4

Typeset in Palatino by M Rules
Printed and bound in Great Britain by
Clays Ltd, St Ives plc

Warner Books
A Division of
Little, Brown and Company (UK)
Brettenham House
Lancaster Place
London WC2E 7EN

For Chris

'Although the raven hovers,
happiness is yours if you will.'

EPICTETUS

P_{relude}

I *East Anglia, September 1939.* Stefan

In the chill of an early September morning the dark tide flowed fast and cold, lapping against the mud banks, swirling in the creeks. Dawn was a blood-red line on the sea-horizon.

The young man, shotgun broken and resting in the crook of his elbow, stood poised and still, listening, watching, waiting for the flight, for the moment when the birds whose wings whispered in the darkness above him became visible to the marksman's eye, and the age-old duel between hunter and prey could begin. At his feet, eyes gleaming in the pale morning light, sat a small black Labrador, alert and trembling, head lifted, like her master's, to the sky and to the sound of the flight.

The water ran swifter, filling the fleets; another duel. Even for a man born and bred on these marshes, one who since childhood had known every path, every dangerous, mud-slicked bridge, every flat, rough-grassed island, there could be danger in treating the incoming tide with anything but respect.

And as the water flooded the reeds and mud banks, so, moment by moment, the eastern sky flooded with light, driving back the darkness. By contrast, the sea was still inkily black, unreflective, no sheen yet on its rippling surface.

The dog shifted a little on her haunches, impatient and excited.

There was a rustle, a singing of wings in the air. The gun snapped quietly and came up, steadily and with practised grace. Dark shapes were silhouetted against the brightening sky as a small group of flighting mallard swept in from their resting grounds to the feeding places on the saltings. The man's eyes narrowed a little as the rim of the rising sun lifted above the horizon. Two shots echoed across the flat wetlands.

A bird, mortally wounded, set its wings, gliding into the dazzle of the sunrise. Watching it, the man broke the gun, reloaded, snapped it shut; without taking his eyes off the falling bird he put out a flat, steadying hand to the excited dog who sat, fierce energy pent by discipline and devotion, watching him, tail wagging, waiting for his word.

He pointed. 'Gypsy. Get on.' The words were calm, unexcited, a well-used form that both understood.

Released at last she went, eagerly, into the fast-flowing water, across the creek to the bank beyond, scrambling muddily on to dry ground, the water flying from her coat as she shook herself before bounding on.

The sky was empty. Head tilted back, the man reached into the breast pocket of his battered leather jerkin and pulled out a tin of tobacco and a packet of cigarette papers. The morning was quite suddenly a joyful blaze of light; a breeze blew from the sea, salt-smelling and fresh. Nearby the tide lapped around the skeletal ribs of a small boat, stove in and abandoned to rot. Where there had been mud, now water was everywhere, before, around and behind him. The roofs of the village on the slight rise of land beyond the marshes were catching the rays of the risen sun.

There was movement; a tail wagged, a small, muscular body ploughed through the sharp marsh-grasses. In a moment the dog, Gypsy, was back in the water, swimming valiantly towards him, the kill in her mouth.

He bent to her as, plastered with mud and watching him hopefully, she delivered her prize. For one second he ruffled her wet ear affectionately. Then he straightened. 'Scruffy little tart. Just look at the state of you! What are you like?' The words were wry. The little dog trembled with pleasure; then her head turned suddenly and eagerly, watching the sky. With sure instinct the man turned to follow her bright gaze, and seconds later he saw what she had sensed. Another flight of birds, a bigger group this time, winging their way in to the marshes. Almost he smiled as he lifted the gun again.

An hour or so later, with the sun well up and the smell of woodsmoke on the air, he strode through the village, Gypsy at his heels, waders slung across his shoulder, damp fair hair tousled and unkempt. The village was stirring. Windows were opened. Sunday morning breakfast sizzled in the pan. Dogs barked, and radios played; everywhere, it seemed, the radio played. A man on a bicycle saluted him with lifted hand. A baby cried, and was comforted. A girl watched with longing eyes from her window as he passed, but he did not notice.

'Bin fowlin', then, Stefan?' An old man leaned on an even older gate, pipe in mouth, lined face peaceful.

Stefan grunted, lifted the hand in which he carried three plump duck. 'Looks like it.'

'Good bag.' There was a certain wistfulness in the words. The man's eyes were bright as they rested on the birds.

With no word Stefan produced a knife, cut the string with which he had tied the ducks' necks and handed one of the mallard across the gate. The other man hesitated for a moment. Stefan jerked the hand that held the duck. 'Take it. You're welcome.'

The old man's nod was dignified. 'Good of you, son. Thanks.'

Stefan shrugged, turned to walk on.

'Rum old business this, with the Jerries, an' Poland an' what have you?'

'Yes.'

'You'll be a mite worried, I should think? You havin' relatives out there an' all?'

Stefan said nothing.

The old man swung the duck, watching it ruminatively. The sheened and beautiful feathers glinted in the sunlight, blood shone like ruby drops on a necklace. Gypsy watched the movement, clear-eyed and intent.

The older man lifted his head and gazed at the young one. 'What d'you think? Will there be a war this time?'

'If there's any honour left in this world, then – yes, there will be war.'

The other man shook his head. 'I was in the last lot. The war to end all wars, they called it. Joke, in't it?'

The quirk of the straight, hard mouth could hardly be called a smile. 'That's a way to look at it. Come on, Gyp.' The two men nodded their farewells.

There was an almost unwilling sympathy in the old man's eyes as they watched the tall, broad-shouldered figure turn into the gate of a tiny ill-kept cottage a few yards further up the street. Honour? Perish the thought. Born and bred in the village, young Stefan was still a foreigner for all his handiness with a gun. Well – if he was right and it really was war – it was the young uns' turn this time, thank God. And they'd learn. Oh, yes. They'd learn. He turned and hobbled painfully up the narrow path to the kitchen door. 'Betsy, look here. Young Anderson's brought us a bite o' supper.'

The wireless in the kitchen crackled and buzzed. The cheerlessly sober voice droned on; Stefan could not make out the words. He did not have to. He sat in the sunshine in the untidy back yard of the cottage, his beloved Beretta – his most precious, it might reasonably be said his only, possession – in pieces on a rickety table before him. With care and concentration he cleaned and oiled, pulled through the powdered barrels, polished silver and wood to glowing perfection, emptying his mind, mindful only of the feel, the tactile beauty of the weapon.

There was a flare of atmospherics, and silence.

Stefan fitted the stock back on to the barrels and the forestock clicked into place with satisfying precision. Gypsy, in her run across the yard, came to her haunches, tail going like a windmill, watching him.

He did not even look at her. 'Pack it in, Gyp.'

The dog settled down, sighing.

A woman appeared in the doorway of the kitchen; tall and handsome, with the fair hair and Slavic cheekbones she had bequeathed to her son. 'Stefan,' she said, 'did you hear? It's war.'

'Yes.' Stefan sighted along the barrel, swung the gun a little, quartering the sky. 'I know. It had to be, or all the fine promises would be shown to mean nothing. Not even the optimistic Mr Chamberlain could get away with that.' His voice was dry.

His mother said nothing for a moment. When she finally spoke there were tears in her voice, though her eyes were dry. 'War again.' The words were barely audible, almost drowned by birdsong.

'Yes.'

'Stefan?' She came to him, sat on the rickety chair oppo-site him. Her musical voice was heavily accented. From close at hand the impression of beauty was not so strong; once to be sure it had been there, but time had laid a hand heavily upon her. 'What will you do?'

He was still handling the gun, as some men might han-dle the body of a lover. He sighted again, taut cheek against the smooth wood of the stock; squinting, followed the flight of a pigeon across the bright sky. 'I shall go to Poland, of course,' he said, his voice flat, and pulled the trigger.

II *Early summer, 1944.* Marek

The dim-lit cabin of the Liberator was cramped, uncom-fortable and cold. Of the half-dozen men who occupied it, three, apparently unaffected by the buffeting and shaking of the aircraft, were asleep, their heads on their packs. One, knees drawn up, his back against the cabin wall, steel-rimmed glasses perched on the end of his nose, was immersed in a book and munching his way steadily through a large bar of chocolate. The fifth lay propped on his elbow, his sombre eyes fixed upon the spiral of smoke that rose from the cigarette he held lax between two fin-gers, and the sixth sat fidgeting like a restless child, clicking his knuckles, nibbling at a torn thumbnail, run-ning his hand through already tousled hair. One of the sleepers snored, suddenly and loudly. The smoker, quite casually and with no change of expression, kicked him, hard. The man muttered and turned over. The fidgeter leaned forward and pulled the curtain a little away from the window. 'He's still on our tail.' The words were a lit-tle too nonchalant, and as if to punctuate them there came a sudden rattle of machine-gun fire and a flare of light outside the window as the stream of tracers, fiercely beautiful, tore into the darkness beside them. The reader lifted his head, listening, and a moment later the rear gunner of the bomber sent his reply; a long, sustained burst of fire.

'He's got him! By Christ – he's got him! Look at that!' The German night-fighter that had been trailing them for ten minutes had disintegrated in a ball of fire. The reader, a tall, thin young man with wide shoulders, short fair hair and a square, sensible face, looked up and blinked owlishly over the top of his glasses. The fidget picked at his nails excitedly. 'That'll teach him!'

'Not a lesson that'll do him much good, unless he plans to fly in hell,' the smoker said laconically. 'Anyone any idea where we are?'

'Over the Carpathian Mountains –' the cabin door had opened and a man in the uniform of the RAF with the insignia of the Polish Air Force smiled down at them – 'and heading towards Cracow. As long as the elastic doesn't break, it looks as though we'll make it this time.' He smiled at the well-worn joke. 'Not long now, gentlemen. I'll be back in ten minutes or so and we'll just check through the procedures again.' The door shut behind him.

'Thank Jesus and His mother for that!' The fidget, small, dark and lean-faced, reached for a pack of cigarettes. 'This is my third try. God, if we'd had to turn back again!' He shook his head as he extracted a cigarette from the pack, and left the sentence hanging in mid-air. 'Mind you – I suppose there's been something to be said for a couple more weeks in *bella Italia*! Bit different from the camp in Scotland, eh?' The other smoker calmly ignored him. The reader, courteously recognising a need to talk, sighed, marked his page precisely with a slip of paper, closed the book and laid it aside, took off his glasses and waited.

'And now – here we are.' The dark man drew deeply on

his newly-lit cigarette. 'Oh, sorry – want one?' He held out the pack to the man with the book.

Marek Anderson shook his head. 'No, thanks. I don't smoke.'

'Jesus! A Pole who doesn't smoke? I didn't think there was any such animal!'

Marek had heard variations on this theme so often in the past weeks that he simply smiled a little and did not reply. Very precisely he unwrapped the last square of chocolate.

The other man laughed. 'Something to be said for eating it now, I suppose. If the old 'chute doesn't open, at least you won't have wasted it!'

Again, politely, Marek smiled. 'Yes. That would be a shame, wouldn't it?' He took a long, steadying breath.

The fidget was looking out of the window again, peering downwards. 'Look out. Bit of ack-ack –'

Marek pulled his knees to him, hugged them with long arms, hunched his shoulders a little. He knew what he was doing, and he knew how silly it was; no matter how small a target he made of himself it did not, in the brilliance of the moonlight, make the bomber any less visible to the gunners on the ground. The plane shook, and steadied, the engines droning monotonously.

'OK. We're through it. We're through the mountains, too. We must be nearly there. Let's hope we find the dropping zone without any trouble. And let's hope that whoever's organised this little show is ready and waiting for us.'

'Oh, he will be.' Marek could have bitten his tongue out.

The other man picked it up immediately; lifted his head sharply. 'You know him?'

'I – yes. Yes, I do. As a matter of fact we're –' he hesitated – 'we're cousins.' He stopped. The other man watched, steadily enquiring. 'On our mothers' side,' Marek added, maniacally aware that he was talking as if in a drawing-room in London.

The dark man was tapping his teeth ruminatively. 'Code name "Janek". Half English, isn't he?'

Marek said nothing. He glanced sideways, longingly, at the book of poetry he had laid aside. He knew he could not take it with him; he had hoped, for these last few minutes, to read his favourite just once more.

'A hard man, they say.'

Marek blinked himself out of reverie. 'Sorry?'

'This "Janek" – he's got himself quite a reputation, hasn't he?'

'I – don't think we're supposed to talk about it, are we?'

The other man laughed.

The smoker had straightened, sat with his head tilted back against the wall. 'His reputation is deserved,' he said, and turned his head to look directly at Marek, his curiosity and surprise undisguised. 'You're cousins, you say?'

'Yes.' Marek knew as surely as if it had been voiced what lay behind the question. As he had struggled through the training for this unwanted mission, as he had battled his fear, his lack of physical co-ordination – to say nothing of aggression – his complete inability, even in face of the brutally exhausting regime they had been put through, to share the camaraderie that seemed to come so naturally to the others, it had become a matter of torment to him. No one knew better than Marek himself that he had no place with these men. Handed a gun, he had handled it so clumsily that his instructor had – profanely – despaired. P.T., cross-country runs, tuition in hand-to-hand fighting had been a torture of physical pain and of ridicule. The team to which he had been attached on the sabotage course had, to their often and fiercely expressed chagrin, themselves been sabotaged by his ineptness. In

vain he had protested that he was an engineer, not a soldier; over and again he had had it hammered into him – a
man who was a danger to himself was a danger to others.
His special task notwithstanding, the Polish military
authorities were not about to send an untrained, unfit
civilian into Occupied Poland on active duty.

The other man, who had, early in the flight, noticed the
poetry book, was looking at him in mild amusement.
Marek felt himself flush. He folded his glasses, slipped
them carefully into their shatterproof case. There was, he
knew, another bar of chocolate in his pocket. With inordi-
nate willpower he resisted the temptation to break into it.
'If the old 'chute doesn't open, at least you won't have wasted it.'
He took another deep breath and tried to quieten the terrible thumping of his heart.

'You'll be looking forward to seeing him, then, I
expect?'

'What?'

The other man smiled gently. 'Your cousin. You'll be
looking forward to seeing him again.'

Marek did not so much as blink. 'Yes,' he said. 'Of
course.'

'Right, gentlemen – we're over the dropping zone – are
you ready?' The so-called chucker-out, whose task it was
to see them safely on their way, had reappeared at the
doorway. 'If you'll take your places, please?'

The smoker dipped his fingers into his pocket, produced a small flask and took a long swig. He did not offer
it to anyone else.

The fidget glowered.

In something close to a dream Marek stood and followed the others to where the trapdoor covered the hole
from which they were to jump. As they passed him, the
chucker-out solemnly kissed each man on each cheek and
wished him luck; a small, personal tradition and as such

they all accepted it. Every man in this business had his superstitions, and the worst of luck was to deny it. Once in their places, he hooked the parachute straps on. They were, as always, to jump in twos. Marek found himself assigned the smoker as partner. They were to jump second.

There came the crackle of orders on the intercom, and the chucker-out opened the trapdoor. A cold wind blew in their faces. Through the hole Marek could see lights far below, in the shape of an arrow, marking for the pilot the direction of the wind.

As it turned sharply, approaching the dropping run, the Liberator's searchlights glared, sudden and perilous, lighting the countryside.

'Action stations!' A short pause, then a green light flashed. '*Go!*'

The first pair jumped. Marek, to his own surprise, found himself praying. 'Jesus, Mary and Joseph, protect me. Jesus, Mary and Joseph –'

Beside him, his partner was swearing in a low, monotonous voice. Even in this extreme, Marek could not but admire his creativeness.

'Next.'

Marek manoeuvred himself to the hole, and the familiar resignation settled on him like a shroud. This was it. There was nothing he could do about it now. If his time had come, it had come. Precarious fate had taken over. 'Jesus, Mary and Joseph, protect me. Jesus, Mary and Joseph –'

The thought occurred; what in hell's name was he doing? Did God listen to the prayers of an atheist? Mightn't it be just a little counter-productive? Damned if I'd listen to someone who's told the world he didn't believe in me, he thought, and for an idiotic moment he almost found himself smiling.

His companion, against the roar of the wind, was still cursing inventively.

Dark emptiness, the horrifying gap between earth and sky, yawned beneath them.

Before he shut his eyes, below him Marek saw the billowing grace of two parachutes drifting towards the ground.

'Action stations!'

The green light blinked.

Somewhere below, Stefan, code name 'Janek', waited.

Stefan, brother and cousin.

Stefan, who hated him. Who had always hated him.

'*Go!*'

PART ONE

Marek

Chapter One

'They're coming!' Danusia Zofia stood with her head thrown back, listening.

A man stood beside her, tall and broad-shouldered, a huge, rawboned black dog seated at his heel. He nodded, hearing as she had the sound of the Liberator's engines as the distant thunder of ack-ack died in the south.

'Light the flares.'

Two men disappeared into the darkness, and a moment later the guiding hurricane lamps were lit.

The small group stood in silence as the sound of the plane's engines grew steadily louder. Then, 'Everyone set?' Stefan asked. 'Jas? Alex?'

'Ready.'

'Danka?'

The girl, tall, long-limbed, dressed in a man's trousers and shirt, opened her mouth to reply, but stopped, her attention caught by light and movement below.

They all saw it. 'Trouble,' someone said softly in the darkness.

The dropping area was located in the rolling wooded

countryside south of Cracow. Beneath them a narrow lane
snaked along the valley.

'Shit,' Stefan said conversationally. 'Sodding Boches.'

In the distance a string of headlights had appeared,
moving slowly, flickering in and out of the trees.

'They've heard the plane,' Danusia said. 'They must
have.'

The Liberator was overhead now. 'Action stations!'
Stefan snapped, and in that moment the plane's searchlight came on, sweeping the open ground of the hilltop,
momentarily blinding them. Stefan raised his voice above
the sound of the engines. 'Fast about it, now. The Boche
won't hang around once they see that.'

Above them the parachutes were opening, one by one,
shining in the moonlight, floating like thistledown on the
dark air.

'We don't have time to get the equipment away. The
men are more important.' The words were crisp and calm.
'Alex, take Michal and his boys and hide as much of the
stuff as you can. You know the places. The rest of you –
there are six men to collect, and quick about it.' The small
column beneath them had rolled to a halt. Even above
the sound of the plane they could hear shouts, and the
revving of motor-cycle engines. A distant shot echoed
from the valley, too far away as yet to be threatening.

Stefan hitched the rifle he carried higher on to his
shoulder. The pilot of the Liberator had banked, turned,
tilted his wings once in greeting and farewell and was
gone. The first parachute, expertly handled, was heading
for the clearing. 'Danka, you hid the cart well?'

'Yes.'

'It's a bloody nuisance, but we'll have to take a chance
and leave it. The bastards are coming too fast. Jas, I'll have
to leave you to cover us.'

'Right.'

'And be careful. No heroics. You hear me?' The words were harsh. Danusia glanced at him. The lines of his face, the set of his mouth, were grim in the shadows. The disaster of the night before had left its mark on all of them.

The German column had spread out and left the road. Motor-cycles were weaving between the trees, coming uphill towards them, slowly on the difficult terrain, headlights glaring, lighting the forest and peopling it with the sweeping, jagged shadows of a nightmare. A small detachment of horsemen, however, was making faster progress.

In the last endless and terrifying moment before he crashed into the rocky ground Marek saw it all; the group standing by the flares, the steadily approaching lights, heard the sound of rifle and machine-gun fire. He made a bad landing, as he had known he would, the shock jarring painfully through him and sending him sprawling, but at least he had landed on the open ground of the hilltop and not, as he had feared, in the tangle of the treetops. As he struggled to his feet and to free himself of the cumbersome parachute, he saw someone running towards him. The password. What in hell's name was the password? His mind was a blank.

Competent hands untangled the lines and straps and he was free. 'Is Aunt Martha's cat still lost?' a light voice asked in Polish.

Relief flooded him. 'She found it yesterday.' He used the same language, easily and with no accent. Automatically he had begun to gather in the voluminous silk of the parachute.

'Leave it. There's no time.' To his astonishment there was a glint of laughter in the girl's voice. 'Pity. There goes my next party dress. Come on.' He stumbled as he followed her, one of his knees almost giving way. She turned, concerned. 'Are you hurt?' From the forest came a sustained burst of gunfire.

Marek flinched, more at the sound than from pain. 'No. I'm fine.'

'Right. Follow me. And stay close. I'm sorry; this isn't quite the reception we had hoped to give you.'

He was aware of figures around him, shadows in the moonlight, moving quickly and quietly about their allotted tasks. One of his companions from the plane had landed nearby and was being helped out of his harness. The containers full of arms and ammunition that had followed them were drifting into the forest. The sound of the German patrol's motor-cycles was coming nearer by the moment. Shouted orders rang through the woodland.

'All safe?' A quiet, authoritative voice beside them, a tall figure, face in shadow, long rifle slung across his shoulder, a silent black shadow at his heels.

'Yes,' Danusia said.

'Then go. I'll see you back at the camp as soon as you can make it. I don't have to tell you to be careful.' Stefan had neither greeted nor glanced at Marek. Now he turned his head and the moon shone full in his face; a face leaner and harder than Marek remembered. 'I'm sorry about the –' Stefan stopped as he realised to whom he was speaking. There was a moment's precarious silence, broken by a shouted command and a sudden vicious burst of gunfire nearby. Stefan slipped the rifle from his shoulder. 'That's Jas doing his stuff. Go. I'll see you later.' He was moving before he had stopped speaking, the dog, with no command, loping beside him.

Danusia laid an urgent hand on Marek's arm. 'This way.' She turned and ran, heading away from the noise and violence of the action behind them, and towards the deeply shadowed edge of the forest on the opposite side of the hill to the road. Marek, pack bouncing uncomfortably on his back and with every step jolting into his injured knee like a knife-point, followed her into the darkness.

They were well into the forest before the girl dared to use the small torch she carried; twice Marek tripped, arms flailing, and all but fell. At last she slowed her fast pace and reached for his hand to guide him. 'I'm sorry. But we must hurry.' Behind them the fierce, sustained sounds of a gunbattle split the darkness. Marek had no breath to talk. With absolute confidence the girl led him through the trackless woodlands; he could do nothing but trust her, and follow. He lost all sense of time, and of distance. His knee ached abominably. At last she stopped by a fallen tree. 'All right. We can rest a while if you'd like. No one's following.' The distant sounds were sporadic now; the odd shot, a brief rip of machine-gun fire.

Wordlessly he swung the pack from his back and leaned against the tree, legs shaking, his heart pounding in his chest as if it would burst.

'Do you have a cigarette?'

He felt in his pocket, handed her an unopened packet, heard the sounds as she opened it, took out a cigarette. 'Thanks.' She handed the packet back.

He shook his head in the darkness. 'Keep it.'

'You're sure?'

'I don't smoke.' He smiled wryly at the surprise in her silence. 'I eat chocolate,' he added in deprecating self-mockery.

She laughed a little. Her laughter, like her voice, was light and attractively musical. He wished he could see her face. 'You might as well get rid of that flying suit. We can hide it under the tree here. Then we'd better get on. It'll be dawn in a couple of hours.'

The sky had indeed just begun to lighten as they entered a clearing on the edge of the woodland in which stood a hut and a small barn. The scent of woodsmoke hung on the still air. A dog barked, and Marek jumped. 'Best we rest here for a while.' Danusia led the way to the barn. Inside, it was warm and heavy with the smell of the cow and her calf who occupied it.

'Is it safe?' It was a stupid question, and he knew it the moment he uttered it.

She took no offence. 'It's safe,' she said simply. 'You go on up into the loft. I'll be back in a minute. Are you hungry?'

Suddenly, and to his own surprise, he realised that he was. 'I am a bit.'

'I'll see what I can do. It won't be much.' She left him.

He heard the dog bark again, and quieten to the soft sound of her voice. Wearily he clambered up the ladder into the hayloft. It was very warm. Slipping the pack from his sore shoulders was the greatest relief he had ever experienced. Thankfully he threw himself down in the straw. He had never felt so exhausted in his entire life.

He wakened, startled, to her hand on his shoulder. A small oil lamp threw gaunt shadows upon the rafters. Her face – spare, strong-boned, tired-looking – was lit by it; heavy, straight hair, brown with the gleam of chestnuts in it, cut to a bob but at the moment scraped back untidily behind her ears, a wide mouth, eyes that in the shadowed light could have been dark blue or brown. 'Breakfast,' she said, smiling a little. 'And then you can sleep, for a couple of hours at least.'

She had brought milk, sausage and black bread. A feast.

They ate at first in silence. She watched him with frank curiosity in her eyes. 'You are, I think, some relative of Stefan's?'

'Yes.'

'You look rather like him.'

'I – suppose I do.'

'You're here because of the rockets?' She shrugged at his quick glance. 'Oh, I know we're not supposed to talk of such things. But –' she shrugged wide shoulders, grinned like a child – 'everyone knows.'

He said nothing.

The smile widened. 'In a couple of days – as soon as things quieten down – I'll take you to Warsaw. I am your liaison.'

'I'm glad.'

Her laughter was warm. 'It's surprising, isn't it, how quickly friends can be made in such circumstances?'

'Yes, it is. Tell me – what's your name?' It seemed purely ridiculous after the camaraderie of the past perilous hours to be asking such a question.

'Danusia. My friends call me Danka. And you are Marek.'

'Yes.'

'We all have code names, of course. Stefan is "Janek", I am "Ola". But – between ourselves –' Yawning, she allowed the words to trail to nothing.

'And the people here?' Marek indicated with a movement of his head the small house beyond the barn. 'They're part of the Underground movement?'

Danusia had finished eating. She took a drink from the jug of milk, wiped her mouth with the back of her hand in an unselfconscious way that was oddly endearing, lifted suddenly serious eyes to his. 'All Poles are part of the Underground movement, Marek. Poland lives. She has not surrendered. She will never collaborate. To do so would be to die. Wait and see. Wait and see how the people fight. Wait and see what the Occupying Forces do to our country. We are to be slaves. We are not to be educated. Our culture is to be eradicated; our theatre, our music, our poetry, all are outlawed. Our universities are closed, our law courts illegal. We are to be denied our birthright, our culture, our language. But already they know. They have found that Poland fights on. Nothing they can do will stop us. Not unless they kill every last one of us.' Her wide, full-lipped mouth quirked to a small, bitter smile. 'And they try. Oh, they try. Our hosts had three sons. It's a common enough story. One lost to the Russians in '39, one to the Germans two years later and the third caught in a roundup in Cracow, deported to a slave labour camp in Germany and never seen again. Do you doubt them?'

Marek shook his head. Yawned. 'Sorry.'

'Don't be silly. Get some sleep.' She went to the end of the loft where a small unglazed opening looked down on to the clearing, settled herself cross-legged on the floor, reached for her cigarettes. 'I'll watch. Just in case.'

'Wake me in an hour or so,' he said, blinking, heavy-lidded, 'so that you can get some rest.'

Danusia smiled.

Marek slept.

As the sky lightened and dawn crept through the forest the girl watched him, curiosity in her eyes. She would not quickly forget Stefan's reaction when he had learned the identity of the expert being sent to them. 'Marek,' he had said softly, just the one word, and smiled. It was a smile that Danusia knew; one of the few things in this world that still had the power to frighten her, and it fitted well with the contempt with which he had spoken the name. She moved now a little closer, studying the face of the sleeping man. What lay between these two? That there must be some close blood relationship was undeniable; the man who lay before her, arm flung above his head as he slept like the dead in the rustling straw, could almost be taken for Stefan. Almost, but not quite. She had noticed it from the fraught moment that he had landed, stumbling, in the clearing. Their build was the same – tall, lean, wide-shouldered, yet Marek gave none of the impression of strength that Stefan did, nor did he move with his sure-footedness and grace. On the contrary, sometimes his movements were positively awkward, positively unco-ordinated, like a schoolboy whose growth had outstripped his ability to cope with it. And his face, too; the high cheekbones and the sharp line of jaw were the same, but the fierce and vivid life that drew the eye to Stefan's face was missing in Marek's. Instead, to be sure, there was a shy kindness, a quality almost of innocence; these, unquestionably, he did not share with Stefan. Danusia remembered that smile and nibbled her lip. She had seen Stefan smile like that as he had killed. In war, as in love, the rules of acceptable behaviour could so easily be bent to breaking point. Stefan could be kind. No one knew that better than she. Stefan could be the most delightful and civilised companion if he willed it. But – a vision of the savage fury in his face the night before when they had had to stand helplessly by and watch the death of a comrade rose in her mind and a small chill raised the hairs on her arms. Stefan could be brutal too, mercilessly so if the need arose. From what she had observed, it seemed that this man – Marek stirred a little and muttered in his sleep, almost as if aware of her intent regard – this apparently inoffensive man had somehow incurred Stefan's enmity. Danusia did not envy him.

Her heavy hair swung about her face as she bent her head to light another cigarette.

With any luck at all the two men's paths would not cross often enough to encourage conflict. The orders were to deliver Marek to the Underground laboratory in Warsaw and to keep a supportive eye on him until the job was done and he was airlifted back out. Stefan and his partisans would stay in the mountains. Unless either man went out of his way to challenge the other, there should be no trouble. She looked back at Marek's still form. His thick fair hair, again so like Stefan's, was exactly the colour of the straw in which he lay. Asleep, long lashes curled against his cheek, he looked younger, and somehow very vulnerable.

She shook her head sharply, and again her hair swung about her face.

We're all vulnerable. This is war. He'll have to take his chances like the rest of us.

She went back to her vigil at the window.

Chapter Two

When they arrived at the camp in the forest the next day it was to find Stefan in savage mood.

Marek was weary and in considerable pain; it had been a long and difficult trek over uneven terrain, and by the time they reached their destination his knee was bruised and swollen. To his mortification Danusia had insisted on carrying his pack, swinging it with practised ease upon her back, brushing off his protests.

'That's all we need,' Stefan said in English, eyeing him, the words a lot closer to scorn than sympathy. Their greeting had been strained.

Marek answered in the same language, 'I hardly did it deliberately.'

They were in a crude, camouflaged wooden hut, one of several in the clearing where the Partisan camp was situated. Stefan sat behind a rough wooden table piled with papers. A tin lid overflowed with cigarette ends, and a small handgun lay half-concealed under a tattered, spread map. A long rifle was propped to hand by the chair, and the great black dog that Marek had noticed the night before was lying beside it. Stefan, like many other young men that Marek had seen as he had walked through the camp, was dressed in an approximation of uniform – the high black boots and field grey jacket which had obviously been those of a German officer, with the Nazi insignia removed and replaced by the red and white armband and Polish Eagle badge of the Home Army. A well-worn forage cap lay on the table next to the pistol. Marek could not help thinking that he looked as much a brigand as a soldier. In the poor quality civilian suit provided for his sojourn in Warsaw, he felt, in this setting, rather less than adequate. A memory surfaced; one of the few times that he and his mother had ever visited Stefan's home on the marshes; Stefan in ancient leather jacket, muddy corduroys, heavy, battered boots, himself in smart school uniform, shining, inadequate shoes. Wrong again.

Stefan leaned back in his chair, surveying Marek with chill eyes. The dog's eyes followed his every movement. 'As I remember, that was always your answer to any cockup you found yourself in. And it always worked. Didn't it?'

Marek's heart sank. Here it was again. Nothing had changed. Nothing. He spread conciliatory hands. 'Stefan –' he began.

Unexpectedly, Stefan flung himself from the chair so violently that it teetered a little. Before he could speak, however, the door behind Marek opened and Danusia came in, her face sober. If the atmosphere was as charged as Marek thought, then she was too preoccupied to notice it. 'Is it true?' she asked abruptly of Stefan. 'We lost two of them?'

'One for certain. They used him for target practice on the way down. He was dead before he hit the ground. The other? I don't know. He drifted into the forest. He may be OK, he may not. We'll just have to wait and see. The peasants will bring him to us if they find him.' He smiled grimly. 'The Germans won't.' Effortlessly Stefan had slipped into Polish.

It took a moment for Marek, still thinking – still feeling – in English to catch up on what they were saying. Then, 'You mean –?'

Stefan shuffled through some papers on the desk, not even bothering to look at him. The dog, on seeing Danusia, had sat up, and was watching her expectantly, feathered tail thumping on the wooden floor. 'Pack it in, Donna,' Stefan said quietly, and then, as the dog settled down again, glanced at Marek. 'The last two parachutists. They didn't make it. And we haven't found the blasted transmitter that was dropped, either. Danka, I've a report here to be taken into Warsaw when you go.'

Marek turned and limped to the window, stood looking out into the clearing. Even though he had been told of the existence of such camps it was a strange sight to see the casual, commonplace normality of it, here in the middle of Occupied Poland. Stefan's was a small unit, the core being these young Home Army soldiers, perhaps twenty or twenty-five of them, augmented when necessary by volunteers from nearby villages and from Cracow. In a makeshift shed on the far side of the clearing – camouflaged, as were the rest of the buildings – a couple of men had their heads under the raised bonnet of a truck – captured, Marek saw from the markings, from the occupying army – the engine components of which, together with various tools, were spread out on the ground around them. Another youngster groomed an elderly-looking but still sturdy horse. Two girls in incongruously pretty summer frocks were the centre of a laughing group. A small field kitchen was set up near the shed. It all seemed quite bizarrely calm and everyday; apart, that was, from the weapons that these hard-faced young men carried so casually, the bandoliers of bullets strung around waists or across shoulders; apart from the fact that one, possibly two, of his companions on the flight from Brindisi was already dead. He tried to remember the order in which they had jumped, but his mind was a blank. All he knew was that – guilty though it made him feel – his predominant reaction, after shock, was one of relief, of thanksgiving that it had not been he who had been ripped to shreds by machine-gun fire as he swung vulnerable and helpless in mid-air. It had always been one of his nightmares. One of them. He became aware, suddenly, of a raised voice behind him.

'Danka, will you get it into that damned thick head of yours that when I give you a bloody order, it's just that – a bloody order! Not a polite request! Not a civilised suggestion, but a *bloody order*! And if I catch you anywhere near that bunch again –!'

Marek turned in surprise at the violence of the words, and as he did so caught Danusia's eye. She flushed a fiery red and turned back to Stefan, her chin high. 'But, Stefan, they're old friends, and –'

'I don't care if they're your brothers and sisters! I don't care if they're your maternal grandmother! *Stay away from them!* For Christ's sake, girl, can't you see? You put us all in jeopardy for the sake of a few bloody newspapers –'

'A few bloody newspapers!' Danusia's temper flew to match his. 'Do you hear what you're saying? A few bloody newspapers? These people risk their lives to publish and distribute the best Underground newspaper in Warsaw, and –'

'And you risk ours – and theirs! – by getting anywhere near them!' Stefan reached and caught her wrist, jerking her sharply towards him. She flinched, catching a quick, painful breath. Marek, with an exclamation, stepped forward, and his damaged knee buckled under him. His yelp of surprise and pain drew the attention of both of them.

The dog sat up and watched him interestedly. There was a moment of complete silence. Marek had the feeling that, in that instant of temper, both had forgotten he was there.

Stefan let go of Danusia's wrist. It was welted with the marks of his fingers. She put it behind her.

Marek steadied himself, down on one knee. Neither of the others moved as he grabbed a chair and pulled himself upright.

'You had something to say?' Stefan asked grimly.

'No.' It was Danusia, not Marek who answered sharply. 'No, of course he didn't. Stefan, why don't we talk about this later? Marek needs some attention to that knee. He can't go on to Warsaw like that.'

'There's nothing to talk about. I've told you; I will not have you putting us all at risk by delivering a clandestine newspaper. They don't need you. They have their own networks. Danka, you're playing games! Unless you know what you're doing, you're a danger to everyone. The Underground presses are prime targets for the Gestapo, you know they are. You have a job. Stick with it, or leave it. There are plenty of others who'd jump at the chance to join us. You want me to find someone else?'

It was deliberately brutal, deliberately humiliating; even Marek could see it. The girl bit her lip. 'No,' she said.

'Then do as you're told.' The words were harsh, measured.

She tried just once more. 'Stefan, you don't understand! I get stuck in Warsaw sometimes for weeks at a time, and I feel I'm doing nothing –'

'So for the sake of relieving your boredom,' he said, savagely precise, 'you risk being spotted, shadowed –'

'I'd know,' she said.

He shook his head, wearily scornful. 'You know better than that, Danka. Yes, you might know – the first time, perhaps even the second – but there's always someone better than you at this game, you know it. And the third, the fourth time? You'd lead them straight to our door. Or you'd be arrested. Tortured –' He let the word hang on the air.

Marek watched them both.

'That could happen anyway,' she said, stubbornly. 'To any of us. At any time.'

'Yes.' He was suddenly, precisely, patient. 'But don't you see? By messing about with the papers you double the risk. OK – I do know how important the clandestine press is, of course I do. But you're playing at it. Which makes you a danger to them and a danger to us. I mean it, Danka. Stay away from them. And that's an order. Obey it or you're out.'

Her colour was still high. There was a long moment's silence. Then 'Yes –' she said, and then added with a bitter emphasis – 'sir.'

Stefan's eyes met hers, blazing with a quick and perilous anger that was as quickly controlled. Then with an abrupt movement he turned from her, dropped back into the chair and hauled the map towards him, frowning, tracing a route with his finger, instantly and dismissively absorbed. Almost absently he jerked his head towards Marek. 'You'd better get something done about that knee,' he said, the words addressed not to Marek but to the girl. 'We've got to get him to Warsaw and he's sure as hell nothing but a liability the way he is.'

Danusia regarded his bent head with furious eyes for a long moment before turning to the embarrassed Marek. 'Come on. I'll show you to the First Aid hut.'

They crossed the clearing in a difficult silence, Danusia slowing her long stride to Marek's awkward gait. She pushed open the door to one of the huts. 'Krysia? Irene? Anyone here?'

There was no reply. Marek, entering behind her, found

himself in a tiny, well-ordered, white-painted room containing a bed, a large scrubbed table, a couple of sinks and a variety of medical equipment. 'Krysia?' Danusia called again, opening another door and putting her head round it. Several more neatly made beds were ranged against the wall. 'Anyone here?' She turned back, 'They must have gone over to the kitchen for lunch –' she began, and then stopped. Outside a whistle had shrilled, twice. Marek jumped. Danusia ran to the window, peering up into the sky. Outside, people were running for cover. The man with the horse led it quickly under the shelter with the lorry. Within seconds all movement in the little clearing had stilled.

Then Marek heard it: the drone of an aeroplane's engine.

At the window, Danusia was tense, neck still craned. 'Boche,' she said, the word loaded with contempt.

'Looking for us?'

'They're always looking for us,' she said, 'or others like us.'

The plane approached, low – almost, it seemed to the nervous Marek, at treetop height. He held his breath, resisted the desire to duck under the sturdy table. The sound increased to a roar, and then diminished. 'Missed us,' said Danusia with calm satisfaction. 'Again.'

He joined her at the window. He saw now that stationed around the still and quiet clearing were men carrying rifles. 'Rifles?' he asked faintly, 'Against an aeroplane?'

'It can be done,' she said, 'if it gets close enough.' She grinned, a little wryly. 'Ack-ack guns are pretty hard to come by around here.'

He turned towards the door. She reached a hand to stop him. 'Not yet. It'll be ten minutes before the all clear goes. There's probably another of the bastards around, or that one will come back. Might as well make ourselves comfortable. If I were you I'd sit down and ease that knee. Once I can get out, I'll go and find the girls.' She watched him as he lowered himself gingerly on to the bed, eased herself up on to the table and sat, legs swinging, regarding him with sympathetic eyes. 'Does it hurt much?'

'No. Not much.' It did, but he was not going to say so to this bright, beguiling girl.

She put her head on one side. 'Do you mind if I ask you something?'

'Go ahead.'

'You and Stefan –'

'We're cousins,' he said, before she could go on. 'Our mothers are sisters.'

'Polish?'

'Yes.'

'And your fathers?'

'English,' he said, after the briefest of hesitations.

'You're very alike,' she said. 'Physically at any rate.'

'And that's where it finishes, I'm afraid.'

'Why be afraid? We're all different.' She reached into her breast pocket for the cigarettes he had given her, made to offer one to him and then, remembering, smiled a little and extracted one for herself. 'You aren't good friends,' she said quietly.

'No.'

She looked at him, faintly enquiring, waiting for him to go on. He said nothing. The girl shrugged. 'Sorry. I didn't mean to pry.'

'No, please – it's just – it really isn't worth talking about, that's all. It's always been so. Even as children we were never able to be friends.' Her eyes were the darkest blue, her chestnut hair shone in the light as she moved. 'As you say, we're all different.'

'And Stefan's most noteworthy quality isn't his tolerance?' she suggested, gently wry.

He shrugged.

She jumped from the table, leaned on it, long legs crossed at the ankles. 'He isn't always as bad as he was just now, you know.'

He looked at her in silence, trying not to think that he had never seen anyone or anything more beautiful. Trying not to notice the way her full breasts swelled beneath the rough material of her shirt, trying not to imagine – he pulled himself up sharply. The stress of this damned business had obviously completely unhinged him. He cleared his throat awkwardly.

'Last night was bad enough,' she said, tilting her head back to blow smoke to the ceiling. Marek could see the shadowed bruises developing on her wrist where Stefan had held her. 'He hates to fail. You know him well enough to know that.'

'Yes.' He watched her, aching, suddenly, to touch her, to have her look at him – really look at him. To talk about something other than Stefan.

'He takes it personally.' She turned her head, listening, for a moment, and Marek heard it too; the drone of an engine. 'Here comes the bugger again,' she said conversationally, and then continued, 'It wasn't just last night that went wrong. The night before was if anything worse.'

'What happened?' He didn't really want to know, but neither did he want her to stop talking; it gave him an opportunity to watch her without embarrassment.

She took a moment to answer, bent her head, sombrely studying the drift of smoke from her cigarette. 'Four of them blew a railway bridge north of Cracow,' she said at last. 'Stefan and his friend Kazik from here in the camp, and a couple of guys from the city.' The sound of the plane was growing louder. She tilted her head again, listening for a moment. 'It's OK. He's over to the west.' She fell silent. The roar of the plane's engines diminished.

'What happened then?' Marek asked, interested in spite of himself.

'They blew the bridge as a train was going across it – it's always best to wait for a train if you can, as it causes more damage and wrecks the system for longer because they have to clear the wreckage. Unfortunately only one of the charges went off. Even more unfortunately the train turned out to be better guarded than usual. Kazik didn't move fast enough. He was shot, and captured. The others couldn't help him.' She shrugged. 'The Boches didn't waste any more bullets on him. They clubbed him to death with their rifles.'

Marek swallowed.

'He was a good friend,' she said softly, after a moment.

'I'm sorry.'

She shook her head. 'We're at war, Marek. These things happen. I only told you to explain why Stefan is in such a foul temper. They were in the forest only a hundred yards away, but they had to lie there and watch it happen. They couldn't do anything. To make things worse, the pigs took the body with them –' She caught Marek's frown of puzzlement. 'We never leave them our dead if we can help it.'

A whistle blew shrilly. Danusia stubbed out her cigarette. 'There we go. All clear. You stay here, I'll go and find the girls. I'll find us something to eat, too.' She flashed him a smile. 'It'll almost certainly be bread and sausage again, I'm afraid.'

'I like bread and sausage,' he said truthfully, and was amply rewarded by another smile.

She left the hut. He limped to the window and watched as she walked across the clearing with her long, swinging stride, lifting a hand in greeting to the men who were back tinkering with the truck.

Marek had had a forlorn love affair two years before –

desperately, and he supposed pathetically, he had tried to convince himself that the girl who had taken his virginity in a dirty, blacked out room in blitzed London had loved him, and he her. That he could hardly remember her face now gave the lie to that. Since then, immersed in work and fearful of making a fool of himself again, he had steered clear of anything but the most Platonic of relationships, although in the dangerous, almost feverishly emotional, atmosphere of the embattled capital opportunities had certainly presented themselves. It was the norm to be in love in war-torn London; several of his friends had managed it three or four times in a year. As was his habit, he had analysed and rationalised his own attitude; however much he might wish it otherwise he knew that he could not indulge in casual affairs, it was not in his nature – for how could a lover not be a friend? And how could one use a friend in such a manner? On the other hand, recklessly to fall in love, actively to look for love, in such circumstances was surely to court nothing but hurt.

Watching Danusia as she stopped for a moment to talk to one of the other girls, pushing her chestnut-gleaming hair back behind her ear in what he was coming to recognise as a characteristic gesture, he suddenly realised that while he still believed that, it somehow did not seem to matter any more.

Mildly alarmed, he returned to the bed, stretching his painful knee out in front of him; the rueful thought occurring to him as he did so that he really had no need to worry. What chance could there ever be that Danusia, surrounded as she was by these fierce and fearless young men, would ever look at a short-sighted, milk-and-water non-combatant of an engineer? The thought almost made him smile.

Almost, but not quite.

*

They were sitting at a small table under a tree eating the predicted bread and sausage, washed down by a home-made brew that Marek suspected a little worriedly was a lot stronger than he was used to when, distantly, there came the stuttering sound of a motor-bike. Heads turned, movement stilled. 'It's Alex,' Danusia said after a moment, 'come from Cracow. I'd recognise the sound of that old thing anywhere.'

A moment later an ancient motor-cycle bumped along the narrow track and into the clearing. It was ridden by a cheerful-looking young man with hair the colour of carrots. Danusia and Marek watched as people gathered about him, talking, laughing, slapping him on his back.

'A popular young man, from the look of it,' Marek said.

Danusia's laughter was warm. 'Yes, he is.'

He watched her as she smiled and waved to the new-comer. If nothing else then at least, perhaps, he would become part of this; part of the friendship, the cama-raderie. Perhaps at least sometimes he might earn that smile?

And – *for Christ's sake!* he found himself thinking, close to anger, *what the hell's got into you?*

The red-headed young man had gone into Stefan's hut. Some minutes later Stefan emerged, Donna as always shadowing his steps, Alex beside him. They came directly to the table.

'How's the knee?' Stefan asked Marek brusquely.

'Oh – well, much better – one of the nurses –'

'Good.' Stefan turned his attention to Danusia. 'Danka, I want you to go into Cracow. I've some errands for you.'

She pushed away her uneaten food. 'Of course. What is it? Something happened?'

'We've found out where Kazik is. They've buried him in the prison cemetery. We need –' he paused, thinking – 'perhaps another dozen men. Tonight.'

'Right.' The girl stood up.

Marek was looking from one to the other in puzzlement. Catching Danusia's eyes he asked, almost without thinking, 'What for? What can you do?'

It was Stefan who answered. 'We can go and get him,' he said, 'and we can take him home, where he belongs.'

Kazik Kowalski was buried a few nights later with full military honours in the churchyard of his native village. It was a warm and scented summer's night, more suited to lovers than to the business of death. While Stefan's Partisans guarded the roads and set up outposts about the small community to prevent any surprise attack, Stefan himself, Donna as always at his side, and in company with Kazik's mother and three young sisters, walked behind the cart that carried the flag-draped coffin. The women, proud and tearless, held candles that flickered in the warm darkness. In front of the cart a small detachment of Home Army cavalry rode, both guard of honour and added protection for the population should Stefan's precautions prove inadequate.

The village priest was waiting at the gates of the cemetery to escort the cortège to the grave. The entire population of the place was gathered for the ceremony. The coffin was lifted on to strong shoulders and carried at a measured pace to the spot prepared for it. Stefan watched as it was lowered into the ground, stood in silence through the prayers and responses, his hand resting upon Donna's rough head. There was no consolation for him in the ritual and the promises; on the contrary, it constantly astonished him that in a country that for the past five years had been systematically and deliberately brutalised, where rape, torture and murder were commonplace, where there was neither safety nor justice even for the youngest and most innocent, so many people held

to their faith and gained comfort from it. He often felt
that it was a blessing not to believe, for if he had, it was a
certainty that by now he would have hated the God in
whom he believed. All he felt at this moment was rage;
rage at the butchers who had so casually beaten to death
the jaunty, likeable, occasionally infuriating young man
that Kazik had been, rage at himself for not having been
able to stop it happening. It was time, he thought grimly,
to arrange another 'accident'. A life for a life; and if only
he knew that a German drowned in the Vistula, or killed
in a motor-cycle accident was payment for the death of a
friend, it did not matter to him, and it ensured that there
would be no reprisals against the civilian population. He
looked at the candlelit faces about him; the proud, quiet
faces of Kazik's womenfolk, the haunted but equally dry-
eyed face of Halina, the liaison girl who had loved and
quarrelled with Kazik for as long as Stefan had known
them both. The grim faces of his own comrades. Danka,
her wide mouth set against tears. And – Marek.

The hostility that the mere sight of the man invariably
caused stirred.

Marek.

Clever Marek. Lucky Marek. Legitimate, likeable Marek
with his bloody mild manners and his tentative, good-
natured smile. Christ, I hate him. I still do.

He had not been surprised to hear that Marek was one
of the scientists chosen to help in the vital operation con-
cerning the secret weapons the Germans were known to
be developing; how many skilled radio engineers were
half Polish, spoke the language like a native and had
spent a good deal of his young life in the country? Not
many, he would guess. The choice had been an obvious
one. No, what had surprised Stefan was his own reaction
on hearing the name after so many years. He had truly
believed himself indifferent at last, and had discovered he

was not. The slights and injustices of childhood haunted him still. Odd that the ties of blood should deepen rather than lessen the animosity.

The priest had turned to him. 'Captain? You wish to say a few words?'

Stefan stepped into the circle of lamplight, looked about the circle of faces turned to him. 'Kazik is dead. We can do nothing for him but to ensure that he did not die in vain. Poland lives. She will never surrender. In some societies a warrior's weapons are buried with him; we cannot do that for Kazik and he knows why; those weapons will pass into other hands and be his revenge. For every man or woman that falls, another will take up the fight. Kazik knew the risks he took; we all know them. But we take them gladly, knowing that our comrades will never betray us, never betray our too-often betrayed country. Long live Poland!' He slipped the rifle from his shoulder. The pallbearers joined him, their own guns held ready, pointing to the dark sky. As the last salute was fired, someone in the crowd began to sing. '*T'was on the green field he fell –*' – the Partisans' Song composed by a Home Army lieutenant, the singing of which was punishable by death. '*Sleep well as you have fought – to make Her free –*' Everyone was singing. Tears at last were running down Danusia's face, shining in candlelight. Before the grave was filled Halina stepped forward, erect and graceful, and dropped a cornflower, the national flower of Poland, on to the coffin; and still she did not cry.

As the singing died, Stefan bowed over the hand of Kazik's mother. 'Poland has another martyr,' he said gently.

Her rough hand tightened on his. 'I thought he was my only son,' she said, dignity in every line of her lined, peasant's face, 'but now I find that I was wrong. God has made you all my sons. I pray that He blesses you.'

Stefan stepped back and saluted her.

Marek, watching him, could find no trace of emotion in the hard face. Beside him Danusia scrubbed at her wet cheeks with the heel of her hand, sniffing like a child. He wanted to put an arm about her shoulders, but did not dare.

The next day they left for Warsaw.

Chapter Three

Although he had thought himself prepared, Marek was cruelly shaken by his first sight of Warsaw, a city with which he had been very familiar before the war and of which he had been extremely fond. He had, of course, known that the place had been subjected to relentless aerial and artillery attack in those twenty-seven days of invasion and siege that had, in September 1939, been the trigger for a war that had speedily engulfed the whole of Europe. He had even himself experienced the brutal destruction of the German Blitz on London. But nothing had prepared him for the shattered skyline, the window-less, bomb- and fire-scarred buildings and the grimy, ruined streets, squares and monuments of the city he remembered as the proud and graceful capital of a free Poland.

Warsaw had been punished mercilessly for her stubborn resistance to the invader; many of the shell-blasted buildings had been abandoned, left as a stark and deliberate reminder to her people of their defeat. Even her status had been stripped from her. Medieval Cracow, a hundred and fifty miles or so to the south, from where

Marek and Danusia had that day travelled by train, was
now the Nazi capital of what little was left of Poland – of
that region known now as the *General Gouvernement* – no
great area to be sure, since, in pursuit of Adolf Hitler's
declared aim to eradicate the country from the map of
Europe, great swaths of Polish territory to the east and to
the west had been annexed to the Third Reich. And
meanwhile the terrorised, gallant and ravaged city of
Warsaw still suffered. Though Danusia had done her best
to prepare him, the sight of the gutted buildings, of
streets, parks and gardens filled with the makeshift
crosses and headstones of the dead, of the places of pub-
lic execution with their pock-marked walls, their Nazi
placards openly proclaiming the names of those innocent
civilians rounded up and arbitrarily shot in reprisal for
Underground activities, their offerings of flowers left by
the still-defiant inhabitants of the city shocked Marek to
the soul. Swastika-decked flags and banners draped
walls, buildings and what few memorials the Occupying
Forces had not destroyed, and the streets were full of
propaganda posters – attacking the Jews, attacking the
Allies, attacking Poland herself – though in many
instances these had in their turn been boldly and sometimes humorously defaced or were countered by slogans
scrawled on walls and pavements by youngsters of the
Underground movement. For the best part of five years
the invaders had done their utmost to turn Warsaw into a
German city – even the names of her main streets and
squares had been changed. Schools, universities, muse-
ums, libraries and theatres had been closed down. Polish
literature and music had been outlawed; indeed, one of
the first casualties of the invasion had been Warsaw's
lovely memorial to that most passionate and Polish of
composers, Frederic Chopin. In these years of
Occupation, just to listen to the man's music was a

transgression that could lead to imprisonment, possibly to transportation and, at the worst, as always and apparently on a whim, to execution.

In these past years, Danusia had told him with an ironic shrug, it often seemed that in Warsaw simply to be a Pole was a crime punishable by death.

And now things were deteriorating even further; tension was high, the war was not going well for Germany. The Eastern Front was moving steadily nearer as the Soviets advanced, and in the West it was an ill-kept secret that plans were afoot to invade France. Here in Warsaw tanks and armoured vehicles patrolled the shattered streets, ploughing with a deliberate and ruthless lack of care through the bicycles, carts and improvised rickshaws of the indigenous population, and there were jackboots and field grey uniforms everywhere. As Marek and Danusia made their way through the crowded streets they were accosted by undernourished children, ragged and barefoot, some straightforwardly begging, some anxious to trade – cigarettes, black-market food, clothing and other goods that if not smuggled were as likely to have been stolen as not. There were adult street traders, too, men and women, young and old, desperate to augment a meagre income in a city of massively spiralling costs and taxes and where for the duration of the Nazi Occupation subsistence wages had been enforced by law. Later Marek was to discover that it was virtually impossible for a Pole to earn any kind of reasonable or legal living in Warsaw. Understandably, for this was a simple fight for life, people did anything that came their way. The Varsovians lived a hand-to-mouth existence. They sold or bartered the last of their prewar possessions, they let out rooms in their already overcrowded houses, they worked, perhaps, in a factory all day and in a bar or café virtually all night. They grew their own vegetables in any spare space they could

find. And, if worst came to worst – or if necessity over-
came scruples as it understandably often was bound to –
they stole, if possible but not always from the Germans, or
they smuggled – despite draconian punishments – or they
sold their bodies. It was the harshest of environments,
and for those who had thus far survived the brutalities of
the Occupation there were two paramount priorities; the
one survival, and the second the burning desire for freedom. Warsaw had fought once; she would fight again.
No one doubted it. Meanwhile the struggle merely to stay
alive went on.

Danusia led him to a tall, narrow house in the Stare
Miasto, the Old Town. At one point, above the bustle of
the streets, distantly they heard the sound of whistles and
gunshots; faint screams. For an instant all heads were
turned, alert, listening. 'A roundup,' Danusia said. 'Down
by the river by the sound of it –' She stopped abruptly as
an armoured truck lumbered and bumped round the corner at the end of the street. A child-beggar near them
rapidly dived for cover, sliding through a grating into a
nearby basement like a skin and bone sewer rat. A tremor
of almost tangible fear ran through the crowd. Danusia
caught Marek's arm and edged them both towards an
open doorway. Then the vehicle picked up speed and
lumbered down the centre of the road, cyclists, rickshaws
and pedestrians scrambling out of its way. Marek fancied
he could actually hear the collective sigh of relief as it disappeared. With a certain bravado Danusia grinned at him.
'You'll get used to it,' she said.

Marek, his heart still thumping in his throat, took silent
leave to doubt that.

The house where he was to lodge was in Brzozowa
Street, one of the narrow, precipitous streets that ran
between the old Market Square and the Vistula River. The
house, crowded by its neighbours, its pale, flaking paint

pockmarked by shrapnel and seared by fire, had miraculously escaped the bombardment comparatively
unscathed and was three and a bit storeys high. His room
was a gabled attic at the top of a dangerously worm-eaten
flight of open wooden steps, at rooftop height with an
absolute minimum of facilities. The one window not
boarded up looked out over the battered roofs of the Old
Town to the east, and the river. He was thankful indeed at
having been sent on his mission to observe and assist the
Underground Research Committee at this comparatively
pleasant time of the year; in the sub-zero temperatures of
a bitter Warsaw winter the cursory patching of the gar-
ret's bomb-damaged roof would have been bad enough –
the lack of window-glass at this height would have been
a severe disadvantage. As it was, a makeshift blind had
been contrived that looked as if it would keep out the
worst of the summer rain. He possessed a large and not-
uncomfortable-looking bed, a rough pine table and chair,
an oil lamp, a pot cupboard complete with pot and a sink
with neither plug nor water. Despite the obvious perils he
felt at home in the city as he had not done in the mountains. There was a job to do, a job he understood. He was
no Stefan – put a gun in his hand and he honestly
doubted his ability to pull the trigger – but to help the
Polish Underground unravel the secrets of Hitler's newest
and potentially most devastating weapon, there he could
hold his own ground, and enjoy doing it. He looked forward, too, to meeting in person the courageous and gifted
scientists with whom until now he had been in contact
only through others.

'A penny for them?' Danusia had joined him at the window. Tall as he was, still her smiling face was level with
his shoulder. He wondered if she knew the effect her
closeness had on him; looking into her dark, guileless
eyes was certain she did not.

'I'm looking forward to starting work,' he said, simply.

'I'm sure you must be. I've set up a meeting for tomorrow afternoon. I'll come to fetch you at noon. We'll have to be back before the curfew, of course.' She indicated the bag she had dumped on the bed. 'There are supplies for the next couple of days. I'd advise you to go out as little as possible until you have become –' she shrugged a little, smiling again – 'shall we say acclimatised? Oh, I know about the training, I know how good it is – but believe me, until you have actually lived in Warsaw –'

He nodded. 'I'll be careful.'

'Come.' She laid a hand on his arm. 'I have something to show you.'

She led him back out on to the tiny landing. Beside the door of the room was what looked like a small cupboard. Danusia opened it. Marek found himself looking into the dappled sunshine of the ill-repaired roof space.

'If the house is raided, this is your escape route,' the girl said. 'It leads into the attics of the house next door. If the Germans should come – and one can never be sure they won't, they make random house checks all the time, looking for smugglers and black-market dealers as well as for our people – don't take any chances. I know your papers are in order, I know your story is more or less watertight, but until you have been here for rather longer it's best to take no risks. If they should come, go through to the next house and go to room three, on the second floor. Two sisters live there. The arranged password is "Crossbow". Don't go near them unless it is absolutely essential. Is there anything else you need to know?' She closed the small door and led the way back into the room.

'What about the rest of the people in this house? Do they know who I am?'

'No. And they won't try to find out. They are trustworthy to a point; they are Poles, and they hate the Nazis.

But this is a hard city to live in, Marek, and trust is just another luxury that is in short supply. Most of the population would do anything to assist a member of the Underground or the Home Army; a few would not. It's best not to find out the hard way. Now –' briskly she walked to the bed and picked up the bag, starting to unload its contents on to the table. 'Here you are.' Marek's heart turned over at her sudden, open grin, 'your favourite meal! Bread and sausage. Or would you prefer sausage and bread?'

'That'd be nice.'

'And –' she reached into the bag again – 'a special treat.' A bottle of vodka joined the food on the table. 'Don't drink it all at once! Oh, and a bottle of water. If you need more, I'm afraid you'll have to go to the street tap for it. I'm sorry there are no cooking facilities – there's a shared kitchen on the landing below, but I think for now it's best if you keep yourself to yourself.'

'That's fine,' he said.

She turned, stood, head on one side regarding him thoughtfully. 'I can't think of anything else. Just be careful and keep your head down until you've got your bearings.' She reached for her small shoulder-bag. 'I'll see you tomorrow.'

She was wearing a shabby, flowered summer dress in faded greens and yellows, her legs and arms were bare and brown. The thought of her leaving was like lead on his heart. He picked up the vodka. 'Won't you stop for a drink?' he asked.

She shook her head briskly. 'I really have to go. My sister is expecting me, and she worries.' She stepped to him and planted the lightest of kisses on his cheek. 'I'll see you tomorrow.' She turned, and was gone. Marek heard her quick footsteps on the stairs. He went to the window. In a moment she had stepped out on to the pavement and set off up the hill towards the Market Place with that swinging, fluent stride he would recognise anywhere. She did not look up.

He stayed at the window for a long time after she had disappeared, looking out over the town, watching the early summer sun glint on the waters of the river.

The tram swayed, rattling and clanking, through the busy streets towards the Kierbez Bridge that led across the river to the suburb of Praga on the Right Bank of the Vistula. Danusia rubbed at the grubby window, watching but hardly seeing the familiar scene as it passed. As always the sunshine of early summer was making her restless and unhappy. It was always the same; this time of the year, no matter how she tried to fight it, brought the nostalgic memories flooding back; memories of home – the lovely, shabby farmhouse, the woods and the fields, the horses, the dogs. The family. The days with her father helping him to train the latest colt, the glorious gallops across the plain, the exhilaration as she set Black Baron at a fence and he took it, soaring like a bird – She blinked a little and sucked at her lower lip. The tram had stopped. The conversation around her had died. Someone shouted an order in German. Another damned spot-search. She leaned her head back and closed her eyes for a moment.

She had heard somewhere that an amputated limb could still give pain. She was certain it must be true. For how could one feel such agonising homesickness for a home that no longer existed? The farm had been reduced to ashes, her parents were dead, Adam, her brother, had disappeared without trace into Russia. The horses and the dogs were gone. She and Czesia were the only survivors of those tranquil, happy years; if indeed Czesia could truly be described as a survivor, which Danusia often doubted. Her frail, highly-strung young sister had never been able to adapt to their new circumstances as she herself had. Danusia had long ago realised that the way to survive – to win – was not to look back, not to allow what had been destroyed to hold you. The only way to stay sane was to close the door on the sweet, enchanted past and live in the present, however bleak, however perilous. For if one didn't – if one allowed oneself to remember the picnics by the lake, the magical music of Chopin drifting across from the open windows of her mother's music room to the stables, the warm, comforting breath of the animals as they nuzzled affectionately at ear and neck, Father's smile as he watched her put a difficult hunter through his paces for a prospective buyer – if one remembered all of that, then hard on the heels of those memories came others. The arrival of the Russian troops in 1939 – rapacious allies, then, of a German regime whose avowed intention was to see Poland enslaved, erased from the map of Europe, as so often before. Adam taken, sixteen years old, standing fierce and proud and refusing his mother's farewell kiss. The flight from the farm when the deportations had begun; Danusia's father had fought against the Russians eighteen years before in the war for independence; the family were marked. They had watched from the forest as their beloved home had been put to the torch, the horses taken.

Then had followed the dreadful days on the road, part of a human river of misery, hungry, thirsty, sick, the long columns of refugees strafed by the machine-gun fire of the fighter planes that harried them from the skies. Day after day they had toiled westwards, away from the ancient enemy, away from the Cossacks, away from the streaming red banners that spelled slavery. Towards the advancing German war machine. Towards death. Towards rape.

'*Papiere.*'

The brusque word snapped her eyes open. The young

German soldier clicked his fingers impatiently. The old woman sitting opposite scowled at her. It did not pay to antagonise them. Reprisal for lack of total co-operation – real or imagined, deliberate or accidental – did not necessarily fall only on the culprit. Hastily Danusia reached for her papers, handed them to him. Boredly he scrutinised them. And even though she knew they were perfectly in order, still her heart was in her mouth for a moment. Somewhere in the back of the tramcar someone was arguing, protesting loudly. 'But I tell you it's true – my papers were stolen – I reported it – I did!'

There came a brisk command, sounds of a scuffle, of a blow. A girl cried out.

The soldier handed the documents back, moved on, his pale blue eyes not even flickering to the scene of the disturbance. Danusia watched through the window as an elderly man, blood streaming from a wound on his head, was dragged from the tram. He was accompanied by a young girl, who pleaded desperately with his captors, tears running down her face. The officer in charge of the patrol shook his head and made a threatening, dismissive gesture. Still she tried, catching him by the arm as he tried to turn away. One of the soldiers gripped her shoulder, swung her round to face him and slapped her, twice, across the mouth, as coldly and as casually as he might have swatted a fly or kicked a stray dog. The last of the German patrol jumped from the tram; the vehicle began to move. The last Danusia saw of the girl was a slight, sobbing, blood-smeared figure watching helplessly as the elderly man, stumbling, was marched to a nearby truck.

'Pigs,' said the old lady opposite, a deadly rancour in her voice. 'Filthy pigs.'

Tiredly Danusia closed her eyes again. Such scenes were run-of-the-mill, everyday affairs; that never stopped the boiling fury, the rage of frustration at having to sit

and watch it happen. And, invariably, to see those uniforms, to hear those harsh voices brought back personal
memories so strong, so painful, so bitter that they made
her feel, as now, physically sick.

Think of something else.

Her father, that proud man, pleading on his knees, not
for himself, but for his wife and daughters. The blow with
a rifle butt that had finally silenced him for ever. Her
mother's screams –

Think of something else!

For a moment her mind was a pit of darkness, inhab-
ited by monsters.

Think of something else!

Marek. Think of Marek, with his quiet voice and slow
smile. What a very nice man he was.

The screaming in her head had stopped. And almost –
almost – she could erase the recollections of what had
happened next. Except for Czesia's cries of pain, her desperate, hysterical tears. The way she had begged. The way
they had laughed.

Marek. She was thinking of Marek.

He found her attractive. She knew it. If she were honest,
she rather enjoyed it. She wouldn't let it go any further, of
course; that would be unfair. But – what a change it was to
be treated with such self-deprecating gentleness in this
increasingly barbarous world. It came as something of a
jolt to realise that there were still worlds other than this
one, places where one's every step, one's every breath
wasn't dogged by danger, by the need to be on guard, by
the possibility, in some cases the certainty, of capture, torture and death. Places where a knock on the door was no
threat, where to walk the streets of a city on a sunlit afternoon involved no menace. Though he had not yet realised
it, Marek came from such a world, and it showed. He
really was a darling. And an innocent to boot. She sensed

that her work would be cut out keeping him safe in the perilous jungle that was Occupied Warsaw.

The tram swayed and clanked across the bridge. The wide, willow-fringed river was peaceful beneath a vast, pale sky. Danusia got up and pushed her way towards the door.

Stefan and Marek. What exactly was their relationship, and why did Stefan hate his likeable, inoffensive cousin so? For hatred was not too strong a word; Danusia had seen it in Stefan's eyes – eyes she knew well. Eyes that were used to hatred. Stefan had been in Poland since the beginning. Like the rest of them, the ability to hate had become second nature.

But why Marek? What could he possibly have done to attract such hostility? Her feminine curiosity was aroused. She would get nothing from Stefan, that was certain; but Marek? There was a softer target. And they were going to be thrown much into each other's company in the next couple of weeks. A little artless probing might not come amiss. Danusia had always been the same, even as a child: if there were a secret, she wanted to be part of it.

As always, her determined stand against her memories had defeated them. She was even smiling a little as she swung down from the high step and set off into the drab, overcrowded suburb that was Praga.

The apartment she shared with Czesia was on the second floor of a bomb-damaged house in a cul-de-sac not far from the river. Part of the street had been completely razed during the September '39 siege, and had never been rebuilt. She greeted a couple of familiar faces, ran lightly up the rickety staircase and fitted the key into the door.

'Czesia? Hello? It's me – I'm back –' Czesia worked in a bar-cum-café opposite the Saski Gardens and because of the curfew never arrived home until morning. Her days, mostly, were spent sleeping. But at this time in the afternoon she was usually pottering about, frail, lovely and sleepy, in her dressing gown, drinking the awful ersatz coffee that was all that was available and chain-smoking the cigarettes that had been her tips from the night before. Danusia did wonder, sometimes, whether she ever ate at all. Czesia must be one of the only people in the city who never complained about the stringent, not to say starvation, rations set by the conquerors on the citizens of Warsaw. 'Czesia? It's Danka –'

There was no reply. Danusia shrugged and threw her shoulder-bag on to the battered sofa. Unusually for her, her sister had obviously gone out. A nuisance, really; though she loved the times she spent in the mountains with the Partisans she always looked forward to coming back to Czesia. She could talk to Czesia.

She went into the kitchen. There must surely be *something* to eat?

Chapter Four

Marek did not sleep well. The bed was fairly comfortable and the night was warm, but the strangeness of the surroundings and the fact that for the first time in months he was entirely alone unsettled him and made him restless. Even when he did doze he found himself jumping awake at the slightest sound. At two in the morning he resorted to Danusia's vodka, but even that did not work, and since the last thing he wanted in the morning was a hangover, he gave up. Dawn found him standing, tired and impatient, by the window watching the sunrise and the awakening of the battered city. He would have given blood for a decent cup of coffee, and more for a bar of chocolate.

Today was the day. Today, at last, he would stop being a liability to those around him and come into his own. He felt the familiar excitement that anything connected with his work always brought. He knew it amused people, the idea that radio technology could be exciting. He knew that his enthusiasm for his chosen metier had in some circles given him the reputation of being an eccentric of the less interesting kind, a dry young boffin. In a time of peace he would perhaps have settled into the obscurity of some university or research institute and never come close to consequence or adventure. But the war and the aptness of his background had decreed otherwise; now, for once, his proficiencies and knowledge were as important as – possibly more important than – the courage and fighting skills of men like Stefan.

It had long been known that the Nazis were developing a secret weapon, a 'revenge weapon', they called it – a so-called 'flying bomb', with which to attack Britain. The first experiments had been held in northern Poland, at Peenemunde, on the island of Usedom at the mouth of the Oder River. Thanks to the resourcefulness and daring of the Polish Home Army Intelligence, London had been informed and in July 1943 six hundred Allied bombers had attacked the base and wiped it out. The experiments, however, had gone on, and this time out of range of such an attack, here in south-eastern Poland, at Blizna, near the town of Rzeszow, a hundred miles or so east of Cracow. And the project had become more ambitious, more menacing. With the winged 'flying bomb', the weapon known as the V1, already in production, experiments were now going on to develop a rocket – the V2. The possibility of radio-controlled rockets raining down on British cities was a terrible one. In the east and in the west Hitler's armies were slowly but inexorably being driven back. The Russians were advancing in the east, most of Italy had fallen, it could only be a matter of time before the Allies invaded mainland Europe. Such a weapon could dramatically alter the balance of power, alter indeed the whole course of the conflict.

The Poles, however, in what he was coming to think of as typical fashion, had been for some time one jump ahead of the enemy. Each time an experimental rocket was fired a race was on to recover it; a race between the well-equipped, well-armed motorised or mounted German patrols and Polish partisan units. If the Occupying Forces apparently held the advantage with their radios, their armaments and their freedom of move-ment they were not by any stretch of the imagination always the victors. The great weapon that the partisans wielded was the co-operation of the people of the countryside. Many a time a German patrol would spend wasted hours searching for the site of a landing long after the crater had been filled in and ploughed over and the salvageable parts of the rocket hidden. In Warsaw an Underground committee of engineers and technicians had been set up to attempt to reconstruct the missile and unravel its secrets. It was with this group that Marek had been working, through couriers and through radio con-tact. The breakthrough had come a few weeks before; while the Home Army had been planning a daring but hazardous raid to steal one of the rockets in transit, the goddess of fortune had taken a hand. A rocket had landed on a sandbank in the River Bug, and had not exploded. The local villagers had hidden it by the simple expedient of pushing it into the river. A complete weapon had fallen into Polish hands and within days had been dismantled and transported, under the very noses of the Occupying Forces, piece by piece to Warsaw, where it was now being studied by the Polish engineers. Within the next few weeks the plan was to airlift the most crucial parts back to Britain. Marek, together with any information that had already been gleaned from the prize, would with any luck be going with them.

He yawned and stretched. The Vistula was a blaze of light as the sun rose. He looked at his watch. Six or seven hours before Danusia was due to pick him up. Danusia. Danka. Would she mind if he called her Danka? Almost everyone else did. Should he ask her?

He wandered back to the bed and threw himself down on it. There could be little doubt that he was in desperate danger of making a fool of himself over the girl. He could only suppose it was some kind of circumstantial hazard, something like a patient falling for his nurse, or a pupil having a crush on a favourite teacher. The thought made him smile a little.

Danusia. Danka. Would she mind?

He slept.

He woke to the sound of harsh voices and revving engines. For a moment, bemused and disoriented, he could not remember where he was. When he did, and when the significance of the shouted orders, the voices raised in protest, clicked into his sleep-clouded mind he was off the bed and at the window in one movement, shaking with terror.

His first feeling, shamefully, was of relief. It was the house next door that was cordoned off. An armoured personnel carrier and a camouflaged covered lorry had pulled up outside the door. Heavily armed soldiers were posted on the pavement. The street, which shortly after dawn had been the scene of some busy activity, was deserted. Through the wall he could hear shouts, the hammering of rifle-butts on doors. He drew back a little, pulled down the blind, leaving a space to observe without being seen. Moments later a small group emerged on to the pavement: two frail-looking, elderly women surrounded by the field grey uniforms of their captors, who hustled them towards the truck. As Marek watched, one of the women stumbled. A rifle-butt swung. He turned from the window, sickened. When he looked again both vehicles were pulling away, engines roaring. Within moments people were slipping from doorways and alleys, back on to the street. One shining head, one long-legged stride caught his eye. Danusia. God Almighty – what was the time? He looked at his watch. Ten minutes past midday. He had slept the morning away.

Danusia tapped on the door a couple of minutes later. 'Was anyone taken?' she asked, the moment he opened it.

'Yes. Two elderly ladies. Small, grey-haired. What's the matter with these bastards? What harm can two frail old ladies possibly do them?'

She walked to the window, stood looking down into the street. 'A pity,' she said softly, then, 'We'll have to move you. They may break. And they know you are here.'

He stared at her. 'You mean – they –?'

She nodded. 'The sisters from room three, yes. Bring your things when we leave. You'll have to come home with me until we can relocate you.' She turned, and for the first time he saw the excitement in her. 'I have news,' she said, simply. 'News we've been waiting for.'

'What is it?'

'The Allies have landed in France. At last.'

He stared at her. 'Are you sure?'

'Oh, yes, I'm sure. The reports have been coming in all morning. They've landed in Normandy. It's started. Europe will be free. The end is coming, Marek. It will take time but the end is coming.' She turned back to the window. 'And Warsaw will not wait much longer, of that I'm sure. Warsaw will free herself. She will not wait for another invader, another slave-master. We'll fight, and we'll win. Poland will live again. You'll see.' She looked at him over her shoulder, smiling, gently caustic. 'But don't worry – we'll get you and your precious rocket away first. Come on. Time to go.'

The Underground laboratory to which Danusia took him was in the basement of a building not far from the old University. He was greeted warmly and made welcome,

and for a few engrossing hours Marek all but forgot the
difficulties and dangers around him. Here were like-
minded people, people who shared his own knowledge
and enthusiasms; here he was at home. When Danusia
returned to pick him up he was amazed at how quickly
time had flown. So involved had he become that stepping
back out into the streets of the city was a renewed shock.
Despite the strange surroundings the past few hours had
been so absorbing, so near to normal, that he found the
sight of the battered buildings, the uniforms, the weapons
of war more grotesque than ever. They climbed aboard
the crowded tram that was to take them across the river.
Danusia had not wasted her afternoon.

'I've got someone looking for a room for you. And I
managed to swap some of your cigarettes for a tin of meat
and some potatoes. We'll have a feast tonight, providing
the electricity doesn't go off again, that is. You can stay
with me until we find you somewhere of your own.'

Marek, standing beside her, studied her strong, viva-
cious face with some curiosity. Ever since she had first
come to his room that morning with her momentous
news it seemed to him that there had been about her an
odd, overexcited edginess that he had never seen before.
She was speaking rapidly, not giving him a chance to
answer or comment.

'I met a friend of mine this afternoon. She says that while
I'm in Warsaw I can work with her in the soup kitchen she
runs. It's one of the PKO kitchens – used mostly by writers
and artists – it's just for a couple of hours a day, but perhaps it'll keep me out of mischief. Not even Stefan could
object to my feeding a few starving artists, could he? Oh,
and she's invited us to a party. On Sunday. I said we'd go –
I hope that's all right? Her boyfriend distils the best vodka
in Warsaw. They're a friendly bunch, I'm sure you'll enjoy
it –' She ran out of breath.

'I'm sure I will,' Marek said, amused.

'I haven't got a thing to wear. I told you I should have salvaged your parachute! What a waste that was! Never mind, I'll just have to ask Czesia if I can borrow –' She stopped.

Marek looked at her enquiringly, waiting.

She laughed a little. 'How silly of me. I can't ask Czesia anything. She's staying with a friend for a few days. I'll just raid her wardrobe anyway.'

'Czesia – that's your sister?'

'Yes.'

'The one you live with?'

'Yes.'

'She won't mind? My staying with you, I mean?'

'Of course she won't. Don't be daft.' She turned her head, hair swinging, to look out of the window. 'We're nearly there.'

Once in the safety of the small apartment Marek asked if she had heard any more news of the landings. She shook her head. 'Only that they've definitely taken place. There's heavy fighting.' She was peeling potatoes into a chipped enamel bowl on the kitchen table. Her sun-browned hands were strong and deft, the fingers long, the square nails clean and sensibly short. With her head bent, her face was veiled by the heavy chestnut hair that had swung forward to reveal the pale, silky skin of the back of her neck. Had he been standing any closer to her he feared he might not be able to resist lifting a hand to stroke that small, somehow vulnerable spot.

Not for the first time it occurred to him that the next couple of days were not going to be easy.

He turned away from her and walked to the window. In the street outside a radio-detector van – an all too common sight in the city, as Marek had already noticed – drove slowly past, its deadly, eavesdropping sensor turning slowly. He watched it to the end of the road, was relieved when it turned the corner and disappeared. He had already learned that operating a clandestine radio was one of the most dangerous of roles in the never-ending battle between the rebellious Poles and their Nazi overlords. The radio link with the Government in Exile in London was the artery for the lifeblood of the Home Army's continued defiance; operators were ruthlessly hunted out and as ruthlessly exterminated if found. The mere presence of a radio transmitter in a house or apartment block could mean the rounding up of all residents, young or old, innocent or guilty, to be thrown into the notorious Pawiak prison, prior to transportation or execution. Pawiak, the main Gestapo prison in Warsaw, was a name to strike terror and despair into the bravest of hearts; not many survived its grim walls unchanged or unbroken.

'Supper will be ready in half an hour or so.' Danusia had come to stand beside him. A small detachment of soldiers goose-stepped past beneath them. Danusia watched them with narrowed eyes. 'Pigs,' she said with calm contempt, and turned away to lay the table. 'One day,' she said quietly, 'we'll show them. One day Warsaw will have her revenge.'

Marek propped himself on the windowsill, one leg swinging, watching her. 'Word in London was that the Rising will be in the east, as the Russians advance. That Warsaw shouldn't take part at all.'

She smiled grimly. 'Word in London is not word in Warsaw. Yes, we've heard that too. But those in London, high and mighty as they are, haven't lived for five years with persecution. With terror. With death. They haven't lived cheek by jowl with an enemy intent upon destroying them. Nor have they seen men, women and children beaten, tortured and shot for no crime other than being in the wrong place at the wrong time. They have not felt the hatred – the deadly hatred – that unites the citizens of this city. I don't believe that Warsaw will allow herself to be delivered from the enemy by anyone but her own people. And besides –' she smiled one of those occasional, caustic smiles that were so unlike her usual open grin – 'those in London invest too much trust in the Russians. There are rumours that already the Soviets are disarming units of the Home Army wherever they find them. And what does London say to that? They are still urging us to contact the advancing Reds. It's lunacy, and most of us know it.' She had wandered back to the window again, her arms folded around the plates she had been about to put on the table, stood looking down into the street with unseeing eyes. 'They should ask those of us who know. They should ask those of us who come from the east. They should ask those who have fought the Russians before. Those who were deported to the slave camps of Siberia. Those who saw their homes burned, their families murdered – oh, yes –' she turned back to the table, laid the plates precisely upon it – 'they should ask those of us who know never to trust a Russian any further than you could throw a Panzer tank. They're as bad as the Nazis. No – they are worse. And they, too, will never let Poland be free if they can dismember her and gobble her up, as they have done before. To be "liberated" by the Soviets would be no better than to remain enslaved to the Gestapo and the SS. No – Warsaw must free herself. Stefan has always said so, and he's right. It's the only way we'll have any say in our own destiny. And if they won't give us the weapons, then we'll fight with our bare hands. Sooner or later.' She lifted her head, smiling again. 'Supper's ready. I do hope you remembered the vodka?'

Over supper he asked, 'You said you came from the east?'

She nodded. 'Yes. We had a small stud farm not far from the Russian border.'

'Your family is still there?'

She lifted her head, answered briefly. 'No.'

The obvious inference did not pass him by. 'I see. I'm sorry.'

'Czesia and I are the only ones left. My young brother was taken by the Russians – God alone knows what's happened to him. And my parents were killed by the Germans. Czesia and I –' she hesitated – 'managed to escape and came to Warsaw. It was at the beginning of the war. It all seems very far away now. Another life.'

They fell silent. Curfew time had come and gone; the streets of the suburb were quiet.

'When will your sister be back?'

She shrugged. 'Oh, not for a couple of days. You can have her room until we can get you settled somewhere else. It shouldn't take long. Do you play cards?'

'Not very well, I'm afraid. "Snap" is about my standard.'

'Good,' she said round a mouthful of potato. 'Then I'll slaughter you at poker after we've eaten. It'll make a change to play with someone who isn't a cut-throat gambler and a bad loser to boot.'

'Stefan?'

She leaned over and picked up his empty plate. 'Stefan,' she said. 'Wouldn't you know it?'

He was right in thinking that the few days he spent in Danusia's apartment would be difficult; or to be more exact, since their days were spent apart – he at the Underground laboratory and she at the soup kitchen – that the evenings of companionship forced on them by the curfew would be pain and pleasure mixed in fairly equal parts. Yet later he was to look back on that interlude as a happy one. They listened to the BBC on Danusia's tiny – illegal – battery-operated radio, following day by day the desperate battle that was going on to liberate northern France. They read the clandestine news sheets that the paper-seller on the corner of the road conveniently folded into the official Polish-language German-sponsored newspaper. They played cards with a pack so scuffed and dog-eared that it was like playing with linen squares. Danusia smoked almost all of the rest of his cigarettes, and acquired another bottle of vodka, which they drank in two sittings. Above all, they talked, they laughed and they argued; and in doing these things became friends. He finally plucked up courage and slipped into calling her Danka, and tried not to brood upon how often Stefan's name cropped up in her conversation. When on the Friday morning she told him that a room had been found for him on the edge of the Zoliborz district near the Gdansk/Danzig station, she sensed that he received the news with less than wholehearted enthusiasm. She touched his hand.

'I'm sorry – it's hard to be alone, I know. But you knew it had to happen. Czesia needs her room back. And as a general rule it's best that we aren't too obviously friends. One never really knows who's watching. Besides – we'll see each other often, I promise. Don't forget the party the day after tomorrow. If I have no reason to contact you beforehand I suggest that I call and pick you up. Oh, and next weekend, God and the Gestapo willing, there's a wedding in the forest –' She stopped at the look of surprise on his face. 'I'm sorry. Didn't I tell you? The message came through yesterday. Alex – the redhead, remember? – he's marrying Irene, the nurse who saw to your knee. He and I have been friends for a very long time; I won't let Irene make an honest man of him without being there to see it. You'd like to come, wouldn't you? A Partisan wedding can be quite an affair, believe me.'

'Of course, I'd love to.' He hesitated, hating to ask. 'Is it safe?'

'Why wouldn't it be? We both have cover to travel backwards and forwards to Cracow. And –' She looked away and stopped speaking.

And it's been a week since you've seen him, the commander and brother-in-arms you speak about so often?

'– and –' she resumed brightly, 'it'll give me a chance to steal another of Czesia's frocks. Even if they are all too short for me.'

The room that had been found for him was in a relatively new district of the city, north of the Old Town and of the dreadful, haunted wasteland that was all that was left of the Jewish Ghetto, razed to the ground the year before with murderous ferocity when its inmates, pushed to the end of their endurance, had erupted into last-ditch, hopeless revolt. Marek's journey to the laboratory each day took him past that grim memorial to murder, and the great, glowering Pawiak prison with its huge metal gates and barred windows. His room was a semi-basement with a view of nothing more exciting than the passing ankles on the pavement outside, but it was marginally better equipped than the other one, having a small tap and a gas-ring. As in the rest of the city, that did not necessarily mean that there was always water or gas, but sometimes the supplies were there and that was better than nothing.

On Sunday afternoon Danusia called for him as she had promised, to take him to the party. She looked ravishing in a dark green dress as well worn as it was well suited to her, designed to emphasise the fullness of her breasts and the slimness of her waist and flaring to swirl about her legs as she moved. When he told her so, she kissed him, light-hearted and delighted, on the cheek. 'Thank you.' She was carrying a basket containing food, cigarettes and a small newspaper-wrapped present.

He took it from her. 'Do we have far to go?'

'Wladek and Helenka live in the Old Town. You won't mind sleeping on the floor tonight, will you?'

'Of course not.' He was all too aware that he wanted to tell her that he'd sleep on burning coals if it meant being near her, but he dared not.

'It's the curfew, you see. It's such a pity to let it break up a good party – and Wladek and Helenka's parties always are good – so we usually stay the night. Hey – run for it – there's a tram.'

It was, as Danusia had predicted, a surprisingly good party. Everyone had brought what they could of food and drink, most had managed to rustle up a small present of some sort – anything from a packet of cigarettes to a precious, outlawed prewar book, treasured and much thumbed. Best of all was the tiny wind-up gramophone and the much scratched but miraculously whole records of 'twenties and 'thirties dance music that were Helenka's pride and joy. Wladek, whose birthday it was, was an extrovert and popular young man to whom Marek took an immediate liking.

Arriving with Danusia he found himself accepted without question, drawn into the chattering, laughing group as naturally as if he had known them a lifetime. There were a dozen or so people crowded into the little apartment – any greater number might have drawn unwelcome attention and suspicion – and Marek watched them with some admiration, marvelling at the resilience of the human spirit. Undernourished, shabbily dressed, there could not be one of them who had not lost family and friends in these past grim years, and they themselves lived still in constant danger and privation, yet they threw themselves into the business of enjoying the afternoon and evening with a verve and cheer the more remarkable for being totally unforced. The furniture was pushed back against the wall to make a minute dance floor. In the tiny kitchen Wladek's bootleg vodka flowed and a discussion on the politics of postwar Poland was fast becoming a highly enjoyable and impassioned argument, reminding Marek of the oft-quoted adage that where any two Poles met there were inevitably at least three opinions. He danced with Danusia a couple of times, then relinquished her to a slim, doe-eyed young man and went to find a drink and to observe the battle in the kitchen. To his astonishment he was accosted on the way by a pretty young woman in a red dress, who introduced herself as Janina and enticed him back to the dance floor. Danusia, dancing next to him, winked over her doe-eyed young man's shoulder.

Marek began to enjoy himself.

It was three hours later, and an hour after curfew had fallen, that the Gestapo arrived.

Chapter Five

Danusia saw them first.

She was standing on the tiny balcony taking a breath of air when the lorries, the motor-cycles and the cars swept around the corner and screeched to a halt outside the house. Behind her the strains of Bing Crosby's 'Some of These Days' rose above the laughter and talk.

'Quiet!' She pushed her way to the gramophone. The needle screeched across the record and there was silence.

'Danka!' Helenka began, startled.

'A raid,' Danusia said. 'This house, I think.'

There was a second's total silence. In the street, the shouts, the slamming doors, the revving engines told their own story.

'They may not be coming here,' someone suggested, half-heartedly.

'They are.' The words were grim. Wladek had pushed his way out on to the balcony. He turned. 'There's a way out, but only for a couple of us. There's no time for every-one. Who needs most to go?'

'Marek,' Danusia said immediately. 'Essential. And

Michal.' She looked at the slim young man with whom she had been dancing earlier.

He shook his head, put his arm round the girl who stood beside him. She looked terrified. 'You go. I'll be all right. I've fooled them before.'

Beneath them the all-too-familiar sounds of booted feet on the stairs, of rifle-butts hammering on doors were getting closer. Orders were shouted. '*Halt! Hände hoch!*'

'Put the music back on.' Wladek pushed through to Danusia and Marek. 'It's a party, remember? A birthday party. We're doing nothing wrong. You two – come this way.' He led the way into the little kitchen, opened a cupboard door, hastily pulled out the paraphernalia of brooms, tools and old newspapers it contained and leaned into it, his hands feeling along the back wall. Behind them Crosby was crooning again. There was a thunderous knocking on the door. 'There.' A section of wall had come away, leaving a small dark hole. 'I'm sorry – there's no time to find torches. It's a bit claustrophobic, but it isn't far. It leads through the roof eaves to the house next door but one. It was badly bombed. It's deserted, but there's a safe cellar. Try to be quiet as you go through next door – you'll be over someone's ceiling. And hurry. *Hurry!*'

There was need for his urgency. The music had stopped again; and again, clearly, came the sound of hammering on the door.

'Go!' Wladek said. 'Quickly.'

Danusia, followed by Marek, pulled herself into the hole. The roof sloped steeply from left to right, there was barely room to crawl on all fours. As Wladek hastily closed the secret entrance behind them they found themselves in a darkness black as pitch. It was very hot. Faintly they heard a girl scream. Danusia gritted her teeth and began, slowly and carefully, to inch forward, mentally

cursing the full-skirted dress that she had donned with
such pleasure and which now as she tried to crawl caught
about her knees and hampered her movements. Spiders'
webs brushed and clung to her face. There was a scuttling
sound further along the passage. A hand touched her foot
and she heard Marek's quiet voice, a mere breath, behind
her. 'Perhaps we should wait for a moment? Until our
eyes get used to the darkness?'

She stopped. It was true that even after these few
moments a few gleams of light could be seen filtering
through the wood-lined roof. It was very quiet; indeed the
loudest sound seemed to Danusia to be the hammering of
her own heart; terror parched her mouth and her throat,
while perspiration slicked her face and pooled her spine.
What if Wladek were too slow in rearranging the contents of the cupboard to disguise the entrance to the
passage? What if the Germans suspected something and
instigated a thorough search? The simple fact that they
were trying to escape would be more than enough to
incriminate them. She strained her ears, but could hear
nothing of what was going on behind them.

'OK,' Marek whispered. 'Let's try again.'

'Just a second.' Danusia hauled the spare material of
her skirt up in front of her and tucked it awkwardly into
her belt. Under the circumstances being ladylike had to
come a poor second to surviving.

The next party I go to – she found herself thinking,
grimly amused – I'll wear a boiler suit. Just in case.

They inched their way onwards, mindful of Wladek's
injunction to silence. Danusia desperately wanted to clear
her dry throat. Sweat ran from her hairline and burned in
her eyes. She could hear Marek's breathing behind her.
Something ran over her hand, and she stifled an exclamation. Dimly now she could see; somewhere ahead there
was a gleam of light. Safety – at least comparative safety –

beckoned. A few minutes later her hand touched the bricks of a wall. For a moment her heart almost stopped; surely not? The passage couldn't have been bricked up? If so, they were well and truly trapped. Then, feeling along the line of the bricks she realised that they were loose; there was no mortar between them. They had simply been carefully stacked to disguise the entrance to the tunnel. Very, very gingerly she began to remove them. Once the first few were out it was a matter of moments before she had cleared a space large enough for them both to scramble through, filthy dirty and streaming with perspiration, to the rubble-strewn floor of a roofless room. Thankfully Danusia straightened, shaking out her skirt, taking gulps of cool air, wiping her wet face with the back of her wrist.

The room they were in was a shambles; doorless and windowless, it was difficult to tell what might have been its original function since all the fittings and fixtures had long since been torn from the walls; in these past hard years in Warsaw nothing could be allowed to go to waste. The roof of the building had been destroyed by fire; a few charred rafters stood black against the pale evening sky.

Marek went to the open doorway. A passage outside led towards what had once been the front of the building but was now a ragged gap open to the street. There was a narrow staircase leading downwards. Brickdust and debris were everywhere.

From outside came the sound of harsh voices, and of engines. Marek and Danusia dropped to hands and knees and crawled to a viewpoint at the end of the landing, where they stretched out flat on their stomachs to look into the street.

The young people who just a short half-hour before had been celebrating Wladek's birthday with such gusto were lined up in the road under the guns of a dozen or so SS men. The men had been separated from the women. Michal's girlfriend was sobbing; Helenka, her own face very white, had a comforting arm about her. Michal himself, his face so battered and bloody that it was barely recognisable, was held upright by two of his friends, his arms about each of their necks; patently he had taken such brutal punishment that he could not stand alone. As Danusia and Marek watched, the two groups were pushed and prodded towards separate lorries. Michal's feet dragged behind him on the ground; beaten almost senseless he was totally incapable of the effort of climbing the tailgate. One of the SS men moved threateningly forward. The two young men who were holding him heaved him unceremoniously aboard, and climbed into the lorry themselves. In moments they were followed by half a dozen armed guards. The women were climbing into the other lorry, those already aboard reaching down to help those behind them, refusing the proffered help of the German soldiers. The engines roared. The motor-cycle outriders with their sidecars and machine guns moved into place and the column drove off.

The sounds of the engines died. The street was deathly quiet. Danusia, tiredly, laid her face on her folded arms and closed her eyes. She had known and worked with Michal for over three years; had once, indeed, half fancied herself to be in love with him, as had most of the other girls at one time or another. With his beguiling doe eyes and thin, handsome face he had always been one to charm the birds from the trees. And that was far from the sum of the man; she well knew that the slight frame and boyish smile had disguised a tough and dedicated fighter of great courage. She closed her eyes, trying to blot out the picture of that bloodied face, the knowledge that it was unlikely she would ever see Michal again. So many times it had happened; so very many times.

'Danka?' Marek, beside her, turned his head, still lying flat. 'What should we do? Would it be safe to go back to the apartment, do you think?'

She spared herself one more moment to take leave of Michal, then cleared her mind of everything but the immediate concern of survival. 'No,' she said firmly. 'They sometimes come back. And you never know if there's an informer in the building. Best to stay here. Wladek said there was a safe cellar. He must have hidden people here before. There's no point in breaking the curfew and trying to get home. Come on.' She wriggled backwards until she felt it safe to stand without being seen from the street. Marek followed. The sky was darkening now and the air had chilled. She led the way down the rickety, banisterless staircase.

The cellar was small, lit by a tiny, metal-shuttered grating at the top of one wall that looked out at ground level on to what once had been the garden of the house but was now a weed-grown heap of rubble. Someone had done their best to make the room at least half-way habitable; there was a pair of bunk beds with two musty blankets, a small hurricane lamp and a box of matches and in one corner a bucket behind a wooden screen. Even in the dimming half-light it could be seen that there were rat droppings on the floor.

'Home from home,' Danusia said, looking round. 'Do you want top or bottom?'

Marek smiled, shook his head. 'Take whichever you want. I don't mind.'

'Thanks. If you really don't mind I'll get as far away as possible from the floor.' She kicked her shoes off, surveyed the dirty skin of her legs and arms, the crumpled dress. 'My God, look at the state of me! I look as if I've been down a bloody rabbit hole!' She put a foot on the bottom bed and swung herself easily up on to the top one, sat, bare legs swinging, rubbing her face tiredly. 'We'll have to take a chance and nip back into the apartment before we leave tomorrow. We can't walk the streets in this state. Oh, blast it!'

'What?'

'Cigarettes. I didn't get a chance to pick them up. I'd murder for a smoke. Preferably several bloody Germans.'

'Here.'

Danusia looked up in surprise. Marek was holding out an unopened packet. 'I always carry them with me. They're better than money.' He tossed them to her, reached for the matches.

She tilted her head, smiling suddenly. 'Remind me under no circumstances ever to leave your side!'

He smiled at the flippancy, and said nothing.

She threw herself back on the thin mattress, opening the cigarettes. Marek perched on the lower bed, elbows on knees. A match flared. There was a long silence.

'Poor Michal,' Danusia said at last.

'He was in the Underground?'

'Yes.'

'Was it him they were after, do you think?'

'It certainly looked like it.'

'What's likely to happen to the others?'

'It's hard to say. If they're lucky they could be interrogated and let go. If they're not –' there was a small, expressive silence – 'anything could happen. There's never any telling. There are simply no rules in this game; or at least, if there are, the Gestapo make them up as they go along and they're all in their favour. I wouldn't be surprised if most of Wladek's friends were involved with the Underground in one way or another. It just depends if they can keep their nerve.' She drew deeply on her cigarette. 'I was taken a couple of years ago. I got away with it. It does happen.'

He stood up, leaned on the beds watching her. 'You were arrested?'

She blew smoke pensively to the ceiling. 'Yes. I got caught in a roundup at one of the cafés we were using as a contact point. It wasn't me they were after, but as always they took us all. I was in the Pawiak for nearly three months.'

'How did you get out?'

'They let me go. When they finally got round to interrogating me – there were so many people in the place it took weeks – I pleaded ignorance, innocence and all but insanity and I convinced them. I told you – it does happen. The worst of it was the fact that I had to give up my liaison work for a year or so. I hated that.'

'Why? Why did you have to give it up, I mean?'

She sat up, cross-legged and regarded him with mild patience. 'Because after you've been in the hands of the Germans you have to stay away from all former haunts and acquaintances until it's certain that you're not being used as a decoy – or worse, that you haven't been coerced into collaboration. That doesn't often happen, but it has been known.'

'I see. Of course.'

She drew on the cigarette again, half-closing her eyes against the smoke. 'It's a pretty awful place, the Pawiak.'

'I've heard so. You were badly treated?'

She shrugged. 'I've survived worse.'

'When you first came to Warsaw?' he asked at last, after a long quiet moment.

She nodded, not looking at him.

'Danka, do you mind if I ask what happened? You said your parents were killed – that you and your sister escaped –'

She lifted her eyes to his, hesitated; shrugged. 'Why not? The simple fact is that Czesia and I didn't escape.

Not then. We got away later.' She paused again, but only for a second. 'After they'd raped us,' she added. 'There were six of them – six brave upstanding young men who'd been told that all Polish girls were whores and who intended to take full advantage of that fact.' She was watching his face intently, her full mouth straight and sombre. 'You're shocked?'

'Well – of course I'm shocked!' Marek stared at her. He had begun very slightly to tremble, and could not control it.

She shook her head with a bleak half-smile. 'It isn't such an unusual story. Not here. You'll find the shock wears off when you hear it often enough.'

Marek reached a hand to touch hers. Gently she detached her fingers from his light grip. 'Father tried to defend us,' she said, her eyes distant. 'They cracked his skull like an egg. Mother tried to go to him as he lay dying. So they shot her.' Her voice was nervelessly collected. 'And then they took us – Czesia and me – into a field beside the road –' Her voice trailed to silence. 'It was raining. A pity. I always used to like the rain.' She glanced at him. 'Oh, Marek, poor Marek, don't look so horror-stricken. It was a long time ago. It happened to another person.'

'Five years.'

She nodded. 'Yes. As I said. A very long time ago.'

Marek was fighting the most murderous rage he had ever experienced. 'How did you get away?' he asked calmly.

'They put us in a camp. It was absolute chaos. There were so many people, so many refugees. Not even German efficiency could cope with them. One night a couple of weeks later some of us simply cut through the wire and left. Czesia and I walked for four days to get to Warsaw.' She stubbed out the cigarette on the metal of

the bunk and tossed it on the floor among the rat droppings. 'Czesia was unwell,' she added. 'For quite a long
time.'

'I'm not surprised.'

'She's always been – delicate.' She pushed her hair
behind her ear and, amazingly, smiled her sudden, flash-
ing smile. 'Unlike me.'

Marek was fighting several different compulsions. He
wanted to roar with anger. Shamingly, he wanted to cry.
Most of all he wanted to hold her. To kiss her. He turned
away abruptly and sat down on the bottom bunk. The
stub of her cigarette was glowing a little on the dirt floor
between his feet. He ground it out with his heel.

'Your turn,' she said, her voice disembodied in the gath-
ering darkness.

'I'm sorry?'

He heard the rustle of the blanket as she settled down
above him. 'Your turn,' she repeated. 'Since we're likely –
indeed certain – to be here until morning we might as
well at least get to know each other.'

He did not reply. Then, 'I thought we'd already done
that?'

'So we have. But there's something we haven't talked
about. Isn't there?'

'Is there?' he asked, after a moment, carefully.

'I think so.'

'What is it you want to know?'

'Why do you and Stefan hate each other so much?'

'I don't hate him.'

'– but he hates you.'

'Yes. Or perhaps despises is a better word, though it
certainly started as hate.'

'Why? What on earth did you do?'

Marek sighed, ran his hands through his dusty hair.
'It's nothing I did.'

'What then?'

'Why don't you ask Stefan?'

'Because I know he wouldn't tell me.' The answer
came, prompt and honest. 'He never talks about himself,
so I'm asking you. You say it was nothing you did – that's
odd. Stefan may be hard, even cruel sometimes, I suppose. But I've rarely known him to be unjust.'

She heard his movement in the darkness. There was a
flare of light as he struck a match and set it to the wick of
the lamp.

'Cover the grating,' she said. 'We don't want anyone
coming to investigate.'

The metal cover clanged shut. The lamplight cast a
strangely comforting glow about the little room.

Marek sat down again.

'Well?' Danusia asked.

He sighed. 'You don't give up easily, do you?'

'No.' She was composed. 'You might as well tell me. I'll
keep on until you do.'

'It's to do with our mothers.'

'The sisters.'

'Yes.'

'Polish sisters.'

'Yes. They came to England just before the last war.'

'So you and Stefan are first cousins.' Danusia's voice
was puzzled. 'What's wrong with that?'

'Nothing. What was wrong was –' he hesitated – 'was
that we're brothers too. Well – half-brothers at least.'

She sat and puzzled at that for a moment. Then light
dawned. 'You mean –' She stopped.

'We have the same father. You may not have realised.
Our surname is the same. Anderson. The difference is that
my mother was married to him. Stefan's mother was not.'

'I – see.' There was a sudden understanding in the
slowly spoken words.

Marek stood up and leaned against the bunk again, his face almost on a level with hers. 'Father was an extremely attractive man. Feckless, but handsome and rather – I suppose dashing is the word, when he was younger. He was a captain in the Guards, a crack shot and a brave soldier. He met Stefan's mother while he was on leave – she was only eighteen at the time – courted her and within a couple of weeks was engaged to marry her. These things happened then.' He flicked a glance at her, colouring a little. 'I suppose they're happening now. One of the consequences of war.'

Danusia watched him intently. 'Your father was engaged to marry *Stefan*'s mother?' she asked.

'Yes.'

'What happened?'

'My mother had been away staying with friends in Scotland. She came back, and father met her. She was two years older than her sister. A very determined woman. She still is. And in her youth she was very beautiful. The moment she met him she decided he was hers. She's admitted as much to me.'

'So he ditched Stefan's mother and married yours?' The words were faintly incredulous.

He shrugged a little. 'I suppose, put simply, yes, that was what happened. He was infatuated, and so was she. And, as I said, my mother is a very determined woman.'

'And Stefan –?'

'Stefan was born exactly a month before I was. Father acknowledged him, of course. He bought a small cottage on the Essex coast and made an allowance to Isadore, Stefan's mother. Not much, but enough for them to live on and to salve his conscience. Understandably, Isadore was terribly bitter. She truly hated my mother and brought Stefan up to do the same. I suppose it must have been a very small step from that to hating me too. The problem was that our father used to insist that we met occasionally, God alone knows why. It was murder. Stefan used to terrorise me. You can't blame him, I know. I apparently had everything, and he had nothing. The only thing that Father ever bought him was a gun. It was a beauty, even I could see that. I was there when he gave it to him. Stefan wanted that gun so much, but, by Christ, he didn't want to accept it. It was the one and only time I ever saw him swallow his pride. It's probably the one and only time he ever has. That I was there to see it is one of the things I don't think he'll ever forgive me.'

'It was hardly your fault.'

'I know it wasn't. But you know Stefan –'

'Oh, yes. I do.'

Marek folded his arms on the bunk and rested his chin on them. 'He threatened me with that gun once. I'll never forget it. For a moment I truly thought he was going to shoot me. God, I was scared.' He stared into space for a moment before resuming. 'And then, of course, there were the times when we used to come here, to Poland. When it became safe, after the Russians were defeated, Father used to pay for both sisters to come to see the family once a year. He never came, of course. There was a serious danger that the Polish uncles might have killed him.'

'I'm not surprised.' Her words were dry. 'We're talking about Poles.'

'My mother always tried to avoid being here at the same time as Isadore and Stefan, but inevitably some-times the visits clashed. Then there was hell to pay.' He laughed a little, wryly. 'And me to pay it.'

'Poor Marek,' she said, softly.

'That's the second time you've said that.'

'Yes.'

He raised his eyes to hers. 'Tell me something. Have you ever called Stefan "poor Stefan"?'

'No.'

He looked away again. 'I thought not.'

There was a moment's thoughtful silence. Then, 'You're jealous of him, aren't you?' she asked softly and by no means without sympathy.

He answered with no hesitation. There was no point in denying the truth, and he knew she had guessed it. 'Yes.'

'But why? As you said – you had everything, and he had nothing. I understand now why he dislikes you, but how can you possibly envy him?'

'Because he's everything I'm not. Because he's strong, and brave, and confident, and doesn't give a damn for anyone or anything. Because no one's ever pushed him about and no one ever will.' He lifted his head again, looking directly into the dark, cornflower eyes. 'And because you love him. Don't you?'

He regretted it the instant he said it, but the words could not be called back. To his mortification he saw the glint of pity in her face as she answered.

'Yes,' she said, 'I do.'

There was a very long moment of silence. Then his mouth twitched into the shadow of a smile.

'Poor Marek,' he said lightly.

She raised her eyebrows, pulled a small, self-mocking face. 'Oh, no,' she said. 'In this instance I think "poor Danka" is rather more appropriate, don't you?'

Chapter Six

Danusia and Marek did not see much of each other in the week between the raid and the wedding in the forest, being busy about their own separate concerns. Arrangements had been made for them to travel together to Cracow on Saturday. They met briefly midweek, when Danusia came to his room with travel documents and a cover story, and news that the Allies still had not broken out of Normandy, and that the first V1s – christened immediately, and with apt London humour, 'buzzbombs' – had fallen on London.

'It's always hard to tell exactly what's happening,' Danusia said, sitting cross-legged on his bed, the inevitable cigarette between her fingers. 'According to the official German radio it's as bad as the Blitz and Londoners are terrified and demoralised. According to the BBC the city's defences are coping and the people are thumbing their noses at Hitler. I suspect the truth is somewhere in between.'

'They need to capture the launch-sites.' Marek longingly fingered a small block of chocolate she had given him. 'Danka, it really is awfully good of you to bring me this.'

'I remembered,' she said, smiling. 'And I owe you for the cigarettes.'

'When the V2s get off the ground – *if* the V2s get off the ground –' he corrected himself – 'then the RAF – any kind of airborne defence – is going to be useless. These are rockets, Danka. Rockets. One day they'll conquer space. One day they'll change the face of warfare. Radio-controlled – well, we think they must be, though we still can't work out how – and with an explosive warhead – what can stop them? Barrage balloons? I don't think so.' He unwrapped the chocolate and looked at it.

'You're supposed to eat it,' Danusia said, amused, 'not make love to it.'

'I can't decide whether to eat it all at once or bit by bit.'

'All at once,' she said, immediately and crisply. 'You save it for tomorrow, and tomorrow might not come. Or someone else might get it. That would be a pity, wouldn't it?'

'It would.'

There was a long and contented silence.

'Nice?' Danusia enquired.

'Wonderful.' Marek licked his fingers. 'Where did it come from?'

She grinned. 'Don't ask.'

Marek lifted his head to look at her, rubbed his eyes.

'What's the matter?' she asked.

'Nothing. Just – these past few days my eyes have been playing me up. I've glasses to read with, as you know, but – I don't know –' He shrugged. 'I've been doing a lot of close work lately. Just a bit of eye-strain, I expect.'

She swung long legs to the floor, picked up her bag. 'I'd better be off. I'll see you at the station on Saturday morning.'

'Does Stefan know I'm coming?'

'Yes.'

'You've seen him?'

She hesitated a moment. 'Yes. He's here in Warsaw for a few days.'

And where is he staying? With you? Where is he sleeping? In your bed? He could not bear to ask. 'I see.'

'He's going back on Friday.' She kissed his cheek lightly. 'I'll see you on Saturday.'

'Take care.'

'I will.'

In fact it was the next day that he saw her again, unexpectedly and in such strange surroundings that he wondered at first if his capricious eyesight were playing him tricks; though he would have sworn that he would have recognised the swinging, shining hair and the leggy stride anywhere. When, dodging bicycles and rickshaws and an oncoming tram, she crossed the road in front of the stationary tram in which he was sitting, he was certain it was Danka. But what in the world was she doing coming out of the grim gates of the most notorious prison in Warsaw? Puzzled, he watched for a moment as she disappeared into the crowded street. Then he shrugged and went back to his newspaper. There must be an explanation. Perhaps she had had news of Michal and the others. He'd ask her on Saturday.

They were on the crowded train that crawled at snail's pace across the flat plain south of Warsaw when he mentioned it. Beyond the window the small farms and the villages with their clustered wooden cottages and steepled churches lay quiet beneath warm June sunshine. Peasants – mostly old men, women and children – worked the narrow strips of their fields, the women in long black skirts, aprons and shawls. The orchards and woodlands looked cool and shady. The train stopped and started, was often shunted into a siding to make way for a military train, a seemingly endless snake of flatcars and coaches laden with tanks, artillery, armoured cars and men. Danusia had already warned him that the tedious journey would take at least twice as long as it used to in peacetime, longer if there had been any recent Partisan activity along the line. At what seemed like every stop papers were demanded and checked; Marek wondered if he would ever get used to the uncomfortable surge of adrenaline that stretched his nerves taut as piano wire and brought his heart into his throat every time he handed his forged papers to a steel-helmeted soldier, and came to the honest conclusion that the answer was probably no. He simply had to hope that he did not look as guilty as he felt. It was during one of the stops, as a train carrying tanks and guns clanked past the window, that he mentioned Michal.

'Do you know what's happened to him or the others?'

Danusia, her eyes on the passing train, shook her head. 'No.'

'I thought –' he stopped, shrugged a little as she turned her head to look at him – 'I saw you coming out of the Pawiak the other day. I thought perhaps you'd gone to visit them –' He stopped. Every vestige of colour had drained from her face and her eyes had widened.

'Don't be ridiculous! Visit the Pawiak? Do you think I'm crazy or something?'

'But, Danka – I saw you.'

'You most certainly didn't. I tell you I haven't been near the place!'

He sat in uncertain silence, his eyes holding hers. Colour began to lift in her face. 'Your eyes,' she said after a moment. 'You told me yourself that your eyes were bad.'

'Not that bad.' He was gentle. 'I did see you. On

Thursday. I was on a tram. You came out of the gate and you crossed the road. Danka, I saw you. If you don't want to tell me what you were doing there, that's fine by me, but I do know that I saw you.'

She ducked her head, picking at the worn material of her skirt with a strong, square nail. Then after several long, still moments she lifted her chin a little defiantly. For the first time it came to Marek that what he had taken for anger was actually fear. 'All right,' she said very quietly, the words almost lost in the clatter of the passing flatcars, 'I did go there. And yes, I was enquiring about Michal and the others.'

'Did you find anything out?'

She shook her head. 'They wouldn't tell me. So it was a wasted trip anyway.' She put out a hand, touched his arm. 'Marek, I hate to ask – but please – please! – don't mention this to anyone?'

'Of course not.'

'Stefan would be so angry. It's strictly against all the rules to get anywhere near the Gestapo even on such an errand as that. He's already mad with me – you heard him the other day. I couldn't bear it if he got me posted somewhere else, I truly couldn't.'

'I've said I promise. I won't mention it.'

'Not to anyone.' She was insistent.

'Not to anyone,' he agreed.

She smiled her most dazzling smile. Her hand was still upon his sleeve; he could feel the warmth of her fingers on his arm. With the strangest combination of elation and something close to terror he realised that had she asked for every last drop of his blood he would have given it gladly. The train started with a jerk and she was thrown close to him. He put out a hand to steady her. She took it. 'Thank you,' she said. 'Dear Marek.' She did not release his hand.

They reached Cracow just before five o'clock in the afternoon, were met, by arrangement, in the lovely old medieval Market Square, one of the largest in Europe, by a boy of perhaps eleven or twelve, whom Danusia introduced as Jerzy, Alex's young brother. As she and the child spoke, Marek glanced around the square. He remembered it well from before the war, with its great arcaded Cloth Hall in the centre of the open space, its huge brick tower, the only remnant of the original thirteenth-century town hall, its graceful Gothic mansions and the wonderful soaring towers of the church of St Mary. The square now was crowded with German soldiery, both officers and rank and file, taking their ease at the pavement cafés and bars, every one of which displayed the prominent notice '*Nur für Deutsches!*', drinking the coffee or the beer that was too, at least officially, 'only for Germans'. The place was a hubbub of loud voices and laughter. Marek thought of the shattered streets of Warsaw, remembered the walls of execution, the mass murders, the persecution and suddenly felt the stirrings of an almost blinding rage. How dared they, these thieves and jackals? How dared they steal, and slaughter and rape and wantonly destroy without justification and without conscience? How dared they pursue a declared aim of the obliteration of a country, of a culture, of an entire people, and believe themselves right in doing it? Small wonder that Poland fought on. Small wonder that men, women and even children like the one who stood talking so earnestly to Danusia risked torture and death every day to stand against them. The terror these invaders inflicted worked, in the end, against their own interest; it served, in the end, only to unite their victims against them.

Quite suddenly the hubbub died. Faces were turned towards the church tower as the clocks in the square struck five. In the silence a trumpet-call echoed, eerie in the quiet. These towers had once been the city's watch towers. This bugle melody, abruptly interrupted, never finished, was a centuries-old tribute to a trumpeter killed by an enemy arrow as he called his fellow-countrymen to arms. As the last note hung hauntingly on the air there was a murmur of voices, a smattering of applause.

Danusia took his arm. 'Come on. We've a fair way to walk before we find our transport.'

'I'm surprised the trumpeter still plays,' he said as they made their way from the square.

'Only twice a day, at midday and at five. It's one of our quaint little customs that the Nazis actually enjoy.' There was a trace of bitterness in the words.

'And the altar?' The dazzlingly beautiful gilded wooden altar-piece, world famous as a masterpiece, had been the jewel in the church's crown since the fifteenth century.

'Gone,' she said briefly. 'Shipped to Germany. What would you expect?'

They continued on their way in silence for a while.

'I think,' Marek said at last, 'that I'm actually learning to hate.'

She glanced at him. 'Good. You'll survive longer that way.'

It was early Sunday afternoon and Stefan Anderson was becoming quietly and pleasantly drunk; though no one who did not know him very well indeed would have guessed so. He sat at a table beneath the trees, his gun and his dog in their accustomed places beside him, a bottle of home-brewed vodka with his pistol on the table in front of him, watching the preparations for the wedding. A small flower-decked altar had been set up for the cere-mony and two long trestle tables laid beneath the trees for the festivities that were to follow. A young man dressed in high boots, slim dark trousers and a full-sleeved white shirt was leaning against one of the tables playing snatches of melody on an accordion. Young women in patched and shabby but colourful Sunday best moved between the field kitchen and the tables, talking and laughing. He watched Danka as she carried a tray of bread in those slim, strong arms that he knew so well, chattering to one of the other girls as she walked, throwing him a sudden lovely open smile as she caught his eyes upon her. A few children ran shrieking about the clearing and not far from where he was sitting two young boys wrestled in the grass.

It was a scene so far removed from war, from Occupation and oppression, that even Stefan found himself seduced by it. For a short while at least he could relax. Could stop thinking of the next move, stop planning the next raid, forget for a moment the stresses and tensions that drove him and let himself be carried by something other than hatred, than the need to fight, the desire for vengeance. His few days in Warsaw had not been ill spent – Kazik could rest easily in his grave. Two lives for one, and no reprisals. Stefan was well satisfied with that. His eyes were still upon Danka. She had come to him last night, after the camp was asleep. They had made love in the woods beneath a sky that had glittered with stars. Remembering it now he shifted a little in his seat, reached for his glass. Stefan had had many women; life for the past five years had been a chancy and perilous affair; a bright eye, a shapely leg, love – or what passed for love – freely offered had been hard to refuse. But that had been before Danka.

He sipped his vodka.

Damned girl. He almost smiled at his own sudden and he knew probably vodka-induced vehemence. Bloody little nuisance.

Danka waved to him as she walked back with the empty tray. He did not return the wave.

Beside him Donna wagged her tail. A short, heavily built man with thick, scruffy dark hair and eyes like black buttons was walking towards him, grinning widely, showing a mouthful of stained yellow teeth. 'Stefan, by God! How are you, boy?'

Stefan stood up to receive a bear hug and several slaps on the shoulder that would have sent a lesser man flying. 'Well, Leon. Yourself?'

'Oh, as usual, lad, as usual.' Leon reached for the bottle, tilted his head, poured a stream of the raw liquid straight down his throat, smacked his lips and wiped his mouth with the back of a huge, dirty hand all in a matter of a moment. 'God, that's good.'

'Help yourself,' Stefan said, straightfaced.

The other man grinned again, threw himself down in the chair next to Stefan. 'How goes it?'

'Not bad. Though we lost Kazik last week.'

The other man uttered a fierce profanity, picked up the bottle again. Danka came back out into the clearing, called and waved. Leon waved back energetically, watched her with a wistful eye as she went to the table. 'Now there,' he said, 'is a woman I'd know what to do with.'

Stefan cocked a sardonic eyebrow. 'There's one somewhere in the world that you wouldn't?'

Leon chuckled. Watched his companion for a moment, head cocked, bright, black eyes curious. 'Word is –' he said.

'Yes?'

'– that you've got a piece of it?'

'That so?'

'True?'

Stefan raised peaceful eyes. 'Mind your own business.'

'Fair enough.'

They drank again in tranquil silence. Leon surveyed the activity around them. 'So. Poor old Alex has got himself well and truly snared.' He shook his head gloomily. 'I do hate to see a good man put his head into the noose.'

'She's a nice girl.'

Leon nodded. 'They're the worst kind.'

Stefan turned the glass in a perfectly steady hand. 'Leon?'

The other man halted the movement of the bottle to his lips and looked at him.

Stefan waved a hand, taking in the clearing, the activity, the small flowered altar. 'Seriously. If you met someone – fell for her – would you? Marry, I mean?'

The other man sat transfixed, the bottle still half-way to his mouth. 'That's the stupidest fucking question I've ever heard in my entire life,' he said conversationally, and this time the bottle made it.

Stefan shrugged. 'I just wondered, that's all.'

'You know what would happen the first time you left her? The first time you went out thinking about someone other than yourself? The first time you weren't concentrating on the job in hand? You'd cop it. Bang. Finished. Fat lot of good that'd do either of you.' He frowned, suddenly concerned, all banter gone from his voice. 'Christ Almighty – you aren't thinking of it, are you?'

Stefan threw back his head and laughed aloud. 'Of course not, you silly bastard! Can you see it?'

The little eyes watched him for a moment, and then the lined face relaxed into a sudden, relieving smile. 'Thank God for that.'

'God,' said Stefan, 'has absolutely nothing to do with it. In fact in my book God has very little to do with anything in this –' he stopped. 'Oh, shit. Here he comes.'

Leon turned his head. A tall figure had emerged from one of the huts, stood running his hand through tousled fair hair, blinking myopically in the sunshine.

The boot-button eyes opened wide. 'Christ! It's you!'

Stefan laughed again. 'No, it's Marek. My cousin.' He lifted the glass, crooked his little finger in parody of elegance. 'Come for the wedding.' He leaned back in his chair, and there was amused malice in his eyes. 'I'm afraid he's feeling a little the worse for wear. In fact this is the first we've seen of him today.'

The other man regarded him with knowing amusement. 'You bastard!'

Stefan's smile was dangerously peaceful. 'How right you are.'

They watched in silence as Marek walked across the clearing towards them, stopping to have a word with Danusia on the way, shading his eyes with his hand. When he got to the table, Donna growled. Marek prudently approached Stefan from the opposite side, acknowledged the introduction to Leon with a careful smile and as carefully sat down. 'What in hell's name were we drinking last night?'

Stefan smiled charmingly. 'Vodka.' He prised the almost empty bottle from Leon's fingers and held it up. 'Want one?'

Marek flinched. 'No. Thank you.'

'Hair of the dog, old boy,' Stefan said in English.

'Fuck off,' Marek said in the same language, and rubbed his face tiredly.

There was an interesting silence.

Stefan's eyes, quite deliberately, wandered over Marek's shoulder, to the girls by the table. 'By all means,' he said quietly, still in English.

Leon watched, intrigued, as pale blue gaze clashed with pale blue gaze. Marek looked away first.

Stefan reached beneath the table and, like a magician conjuring a rabbit from a hat, produced another bottle. He banged it on the table firmly. Marek winced. Stefan smiled amiably, turned back to Leon. 'What news?'

'Apart from the business in Warsaw, all's well.' Leon accepted the fresh bottle, tilted it.

'What business?'

Leon turned, surprised. 'Didn't Danka tell you?'

Stefan shook his head, his eyes intent. 'What should she have told me?'

'The *Chronicle* got raided. Bagged the lot of them, equipment as well.'

'Perhaps Danka doesn't know?'

Leon shrugged. 'Perhaps not.'

'She'll be upset. They were her friends.' Stefan glanced at Marek. 'Did she say anything to you?'

Marek opened his eyes. 'Sorry?'

Stefan eyed him with amused patience and a graceless smile. 'Did Danka mention that the *Chronicle* had been raided?'

Marek shook his head; and instantly wished he hadn't. 'No.'

Leon picked up the bottle. 'My advice to you, son, is either to have a large one of these or go and get yourself something to eat,' he said, not unsympathetically.

Marek buried his face in his hands. 'I don't think I could face anything.'

Leon laughed. 'It must have been quite a night.'

Marek lifted his head, his face rueful. 'To be absolutely honest, I don't remember most of it.' And what he did he would rather not. He looked at Stefan, whose eyes were on Donna as he played with the dog's shaggy fur, a small smile on his lips. What in the world, Marek wondered – not for the first time today – had possessed him to accept his half-brother's unspoken challenge to drink him under the table? As an exercise in infantile behaviour his actions last night could hardly be bettered, and he knew it. He had no head for drink – he didn't even really like it that much; certainly not in the quantities he had consumed last night. But that infuriating, sardonic smile, the inference that Marek should go to bed and let the men get on with the business of the evening, on top of the fierce emotions the sight of the German troops strutting about Cracow had aroused, had proved too much for him. Obstinately he had stayed. Obstinately he had matched his half-brother drink for drink, despite Danka's attempts to stop him. And what had he gained from it? A sick stomach, a blinding headache and a feeling – a certainty – that he had made a fool of himself. In front of Danka. He flinched at that.

'Marek? How are you?' As if his thought had conjured her, there she was at his shoulder, eyes sympathetic.

'I'm fine,' he lied.

She nibbled her lip, trying not to laugh.

'No, really – I'm just a bit –' he pulled a face and shrugged – 'dying. That's all.'

This time she could not stop her laughter. 'Poor Marek.'

Marek sighed.

Stefan lifted his eyes from the dog. Danusia turned. And for a split second, as pale eyes met dark, they might have been alone, naked and alone; as they had been last night beneath the starlit canopy of the sky. 'No need to ask how you are,' Danusia said lightly, after a moment.

'No. No need.' He regarded her with lazy eyes.

Deep colour had risen in her face. 'I came to tell you that Father Franek has arrived. The ceremony will be starting in about fifteen minutes.' She shook her finger at Stefan. 'I should stay out of Irena's way if I were you. Marek isn't the only one with a fat head this morning. Alex isn't feeling exactly himself either.'

Stefan stood, reached for his gun and slung it on his shoulder in a movement so habitual that it was hardly noticeable. 'What else would you expect? The condemned man is surely at least entitled to a good send-off?'

'Yes, Stefan.' She was sweet patience personified, and her eyes glinted mischief. 'But it's nice if he can keep the proverbial breakfast down the following day, don't you think?'

Stefan shrugged innocently. His eyes flickered to Marek and back. 'Perhaps the boys shouldn't drink with the men?' he suggested gently, and left them, Donna padding at his heels.

Leon reached for the bottle. 'I'll say one thing for that lad,' he said after taking a long, noisy swig, 'he doesn't change. Oh, no. Our Stefan doesn't change.'

Danusia looked at Marek. Opened her mouth to speak.

He shook his head. 'Leave it,' he said tiredly. 'Leave it. It doesn't matter.'

But it did. As always, it did.

The ceremony was simple, moving, and safe by dint of the fact that Stefan had armed guards posted at all approaches to the camp. The bride and several of her friends cried happily, the groom managed manfully to disguise his hangover. Stefan, his eyes as much on the dangerously clear skies as on the ceremony, his ears tuned to the tell-tale growl of an aircraft engine, stood at the back with Donna, rifle still slung across his shoulder, his face expressionless. Again, as at Kazik's funeral, he watched the faces around him and was confounded. The congregation consisted mostly of young men; young men he knew to be as tough as they came, veterans, most of them, of five years of guerrilla warfare, five years of being hunted like wild animals, of losing friends and family, of killing in their own turn. Yet still they held faith with their God and their Church, a faith almost as important to them as their faith in their country. He found it incomprehensible. He stood aloof and immobile, one hand on the dog's head, the other thumb hooked into the leather strap of his rifle, as they knelt for the last prayers and the blessing. Heads were bowed and hands moved to make the Sign of the Cross. After a moment's quiet there was a surge towards the newly-weds; backs slapped, hands shaken, kisses exchanged. Then, with the accordion playing a gay mazurka and escorted by their guests, the couple led the way to the tables and the serious business of eating and drinking began.

It was, one way and another, an extremely lively afternoon. For the space of a few short hours the danger, terror and oppression with which they lived were forgotten. The girls, overwhelmingly outnumbered, were danced off their feet, the vodka bottles were emptied at a prodigious rate, there was much laughter and no little ribaldry. The bridal pair were sent on their way in an ancient but flower-decked cart drawn by an equally ancient and flower-decked horse and, reluctantly, those who had to get back to the city in time to beat the curfew went too. Those that were left settled back to enjoy the rest of the long June evening. A card school was set up. The accordion-player sat on one of the tables, his foot on a chair, his glass – as had been the case for the entire afternoon – never allowed to empty, and played those outlawed songs of Poland, old and new, that would never cease to stir a Polish heart. At his friends' urging, a young man stood and sang in a clear and lovely tenor voice.

Slowly, silence fell, broken only by the singer's voice and the murmur from the card-players' table. Stefan sat in the shadows, his chair tilted back on two legs, his booted feet on the table. Danusia sat on the grass beside him, with a Marek who looked at least a little less the worse for wear than he had earlier stretched out beside her, hands behind his head, eyes closed, listening.

Stefan watched him from the corner of his eye. Once, in that life that now seemed more and more removed from reality, he had listened to Marek sing this very song. Was he remembering? Was he regretting the loss of that golden soprano voice he had possessed as a child? Did he recall that day in the house in Warsaw when, protesting – surely? – too vehemently he had at last allowed himself to be persuaded to sing? Did he remember the applause, the praise, the petting that had followed? Did he remember then turning those earnest and much too innocent eyes upon Stefan and saying in a voice that rang to the ceiling, '*Stefan must sing for you now –*'?

'*Oh, no, darling. Don't be silly.*' Stefan could hear the words now as clearly as if they were being spoken. '*Stefan can't sing.*'

'*Yes, he can. Can't you?*' Again the pale, artful, bewilderedly innocent gaze.

He had shaken a surly head.

'*You can! I know you can! I've heard you.*'

Stefan could remember now the blinding rage. Could remember too his pride in his control of it. He tilted his head back and closed his eyes; saw clearly the small, tousle-haired boy dressed in his Polish cousin's too-large hand-me-downs step forward in the surprised quiet that had followed Marek's words, stop a foot from the other boy. Heard the quiet, precisely-spoken stream of obscenities with which he had answered him. Every foul or profane word he had ever heard – and even then he had heard a fair few – he had utilised. A woman had shrieked theatrically. A huge hand had grabbed him by the collar and hauled him from the floor, feet dangling. '*Little savage! Little brute!*' The words were with him still, spoken in his uncle's gruff voice. And '*What else would you expect from a bastard?*'; the venom of his mother's sister, Marek's mother. His own mother's distraught tears. Her begging as his uncle had picked up the leather belt. His own young voice, shaking a little, '*Stop it, Mother. Go away. Go away!*'

The beating had been the most vicious he'd ever been subjected to, and he'd had a few in his time. Despite himself, towards the end the pain had become unendurable and he had screamed, once. His back still bore a scar.

Marek's fault.

How many scars did the exemplary legitimate son carry? Precious few, Stefan was ready to bet.

The song was finished. There was an enthusiastic shout of applause, a call for more. Stefan opened his eyes, leaned forward to pull the bottle towards him.

Marek had sat up, was talking quietly to Danusia, his head close to hers. Danka laughed softly, and covered his hand with hers for a second.

Stefan drank.

The challenge was inevitable, despite Danusia's efforts to head it off. Leon, by now drunkenly maudlin, was the unwitting trigger.

'Here's to poor old Kazik.' He raised a glass unsteadily. 'To Kazik. And Jerzy. And Adam. And Jurek. All of them dead. All of them heroes. Polish heroes. As we all are.' He waved the glass drunkenly, saluting the small group that were left sitting at the table.

'Dead?' Stefan asked interestedly, 'or heroes?'

'Heroes, you fool.' Leon eyed the glass in sober speculation, the problem being the small difficulty of actually getting it to his lips.

Stefan's eyes flickered round the circle of faces. Came to rest upon Marek's. 'Oh – I don't think so,' he said gently.

Marek's chin came up sharply and warily.

''Course we are!' Leon gave up trying to find his mouth with the glass and slammed it down on the table. 'Heroes all!' He followed the glass with his fist. 'Ouch!'

Stefan's gaze was steady on his half-brother. Marek held his eyes. Danusia looked uneasily from one to the other.

'No,' Stefan said, his voice still soft as velvet, 'I don't think so,' he repeated.

Leon leaned forward, scowling aggressively. 'You tryin' to pick a fight?'

Stefan laughed. 'No, of course not. I have my fill of fighting. I don't need to pick on my friends.'

'Well – tha'ss what I mean!' Leon was triumphant. He thumped the table again, and the glass jumped. 'Heroes. Old-fashioned heroes! You can't tell me that there's a man around this table that hasn't shed blood for his country –'

'Oh yes, I can,' Stefan said, very gently, and directly to Marek. 'Can't I?'

Marek blinked.

'Stefan –' Danusia began, and stopped.

Stefan was smiling, eyes veiled and innocent. 'Can't I?' he asked again.

Marek linked hands that had begun to tremble and to sweat upon the table in front of him. Here it was again. Always the hatred. Always the need to torment. 'Yes. I suppose you can,' he said calmly. 'Unless you can count sticking a staple in my finger while I was writing a report.'

Stefan appeared to consider that. 'Better than nothing, I suppose,' he said after a moment.

Danusia stood, leaned both hands on the table, looking fiercely at Stefan. 'Will you stop this? There's no need. For goodness' sake, why can't you leave him alone?'

Stefan's eyes flickered from her face to Marek's, eyebrows raised, the look a comment in itself.

Marek flushed fiercely. 'Leave it, Danka. Please.'

A slightly perplexed silence had fallen. Leon frowned ferociously. 'Wha'ss going on?'

'We are establishing,' Stefan said, all patience and sweet reason, 'whether Marek is a hero. Or not.'

'You know I'm not.'

Leon laid his head upon the table. 'All heroes,' he muttered. 'All bloody heroes.' He snored once and was silent.

'Would you like to be?'

'What do you mean?'

'What I say. Would you like the chance to prove me wrong?'

'*Stefan!*'

'Shut up, Danka.' The words were perfectly amicable, even affectionate. 'We all know you're a fully-fledged heroine, so don't begrudge Marek his chance. If he wants to take it, that is.'

Marek said nothing.

Stefan tinkered for a moment with the empty glass that stood on the table before him, running his finger round and round the wet rim until it sang in the silence. At last he raised his eyes again, suddenly switched into English. 'You can operate a radio?'

'You know I can.'

'We're in action against the Warsaw / Cracow railway at the end of the week. I need an extra operator. You game?'

'I'm not supposed –' Marek saw the quick gleam of triumph, and stopped. 'All right. As long as no one at the laboratory – or in London – finds out.'

'They won't.'

Danusia looked worriedly from one to the other, trying to follow what was being said. The others round the table had lost interest, and another conversation had started. Leon snored on.

'OK,' Marek said, quietly.

Stefan smiled his most wayward smile. 'Good. I'll be in touch. Now –' he stood, held out a hand to Danusia, switched again into Polish – 'I suggest you finish sleeping off your hangover. Danka? Coming for a walk?'

Her hesitation was momentary. Then without looking at Marek she took the proffered hand.

Marek watched, tight-lipped.

'If you change your mind,' Stefan said, again in English, 'you will let me know?'

And for the second time that day Marek used an expression his mother would have abhorred, and then wished he had not.

Chapter Seven

In the days that followed, Marek cursed himself time and again for having been so weak; for having allowed himself to be goaded into a reaction he knew to be almost lunatically stupid. In a couple of weeks the planned airlift was to take place. He, the precious rocket components and the vital research that had already been done were – at great risk to all concerned – to be collected and flown back to Italy, and thence to England. The V1s were already falling on London; it was desperately important that the Allies win the race to prevent the V2s from being used as a terror weapon against the civilian population of the British Isles. And while he was not fool enough to believe himself – or anyone else – to be indispensable he was well aware of the close to criminal irresponsibility involved in accepting Stefan's challenge. His orders had been precise; he was to aid and assist the Polish scientists and engineers, familiarise himself with their research and, until his mission was accomplished, above all keep out of trouble. The thought made him wince; God alone knew what would happen if London discovered that he had agreed to operate a radio on a Partisan sabotage raid.

Danusia was blunt. And angry. 'You mustn't go. Of course you mustn't. It's ridiculous! You've told me time and again – you aren't a soldier. Could Stefan do what you do? No! Does anyone think the worse of him for that? No! So why do you think anyone thinks badly of you because you fight in a different way? Marek, please!'

He shook his head, miserably stubborn. 'It's no good. I have to go. I said I would, and I will.'

'Oh, for God's sake, you're worse than he is! I at least thought that you were sensible!'

'And a coward?' He lifted his head to look at her.

She stopped her restless pacing, hesitated, took a quick step towards him. 'No! Oh, Marek no! I never thought that!' All anger was gone. She dropped to her knees beside him and took his hand in hers. 'How could I think that? You could be safely at home in England. You risk your life as much as any of us do. Don't you see, it's just –'

'What?'

She remained silent for a moment. Then she lifted his hand to her cheek. 'It's just that I'm afraid for you. It's bad enough to have to worry about Stefan, but at least I know he can take care of himself.' She stopped, biting her lip, knowing she had said the wrong thing.

He disengaged his hand from hers. Stood up. 'And I can't?'

She sat back on her heels, shrugging helplessly. 'I didn't mean that. You know I didn't.'

'Of course you did. Because it's true. At least I've always believed it to be true. Perhaps it's time I found out one way or another?' He walked to the open, boarded window, looked down into the shattered street. They were in Danusia's apartment. A fine summer rain drifted from clouded skies. He felt the warm wetness of it on his face. 'Will you be there?'

'On the raid? No. I probably won't even be at the camp. It's Olga's week. You'll have to travel on your own.'

He turned, smiling wryly. 'If the truth were told, you don't even trust me to do that, do you?'

She had come to her feet, tucking her hair behind her ear. 'Don't be silly. I'm concerned for you, that's all.'

He held her eyes with his. 'Are you? Really?'

'You know I am.' She came to him, touched his arm. 'You know I am,' she repeated quietly.

In the wet street a convoy of trucks roared by, obliterating any chance of conversation. They stood in an oddly intimate silence, eye to eye, until it passed. I love you. The words were in his head; desperately he wanted to say them. *I love you.* 'I'd better go,' he said into the dying growl of the engines. 'I've work to do.'

'Yes.' Her eyes were soft. She made no move.

He bent, awkwardly, to kiss her cheek in farewell. She moved her head slightly; their lips touched, feather-light. She stepped back quickly.

'Danka –' he began.

'Don't. Please don't. Not now. Not yet.'

He followed her to the door, and as she opened it kissed her again, very gently.

'Be careful,' she said. 'Marek, if you must do this ridiculous thing, at least, please, be careful. Listen to Stefan. He knows what he's doing.'

'I will.'

He left her standing at the door, watching him as he ran down the stairs to the street. For the moment his fears were forgotten. He was trembling; shaking with excitement and delight. She had kissed him. And then – not now, she had said, not yet. Not now. Not yet. That, surely, did not mean 'not ever'? Could it be – could it? – that Stefan's hold on her was weakening?

Danusia returned his last wave, then stepped back and

closed the door. Wearily for a moment she leaned on it, her eyes closed. Fool! she said to herself savagely. Fool! Isn't life complicated enough without making things worse? Yet still she could feel the gentle touch of his lips, see the open yearning in his eyes. Stefan had never looked at her like that. Not even right at the beginning, not even when they made love. Not even when she kissed him goodbye knowing, as they all knew, that each time might be the last. Stefan – brave, self-reliant, confident Stefan – never fell over his tongue when he talked to her nor looked at her with open worship in his face as did Marek. Marek, despite his declared cowardice, would die for her, she knew it. Stefan, on the other hand, if circumstances and his own peculiarly personal code of honour demanded it, would kill her; she knew that too. Yet he loved her; surely – surely! – he did love her?

'Damn Stefan!' she said aloud, rubbing at her wet eyes with her knuckles like a child. 'Damn him!' Tiredly she reached for her jacket. It was time to visit the Pawiak again.

Marek was in bed and half asleep, many hours after curfew that same night when a soft, insistent tapping on his door startled him awake. He sat up, heart pounding. There was a moment's quiet, then the tapping came again, more urgently. 'Marek! Marek? Please – oh please – open the door – Marek!' Danusia's voice, quiet, desperate and tearful.

Marek leapt from the bed, scrambled into his trousers, buttoning them up with one hand as he groped in the darkness for lamp and match. 'Wait. I'm coming.' The match flared. With an unsteady hand he set it to the wick. A moment later he was at the door. Danusia stood in the darkness outside, leaning against the wall, head tilted back, eyes closed, tears running down her face. Her clothes were dishevelled and dirty, and there was a smear of dust on her cheek. As the door opened she turned her head to look at him in the flickering lamplight. Marek thought he had never seen such misery in a face. 'Danka, for heaven's sake! What is it?'

She stepped forward into his arms, laid her head upon his shoulder and sobbed like a broken child. He held her for a moment, stroking her hair. 'Darling, what's the matter? Whatever are you doing here at this time of night? What's happened?'

The sobs died a little. She took a couple of deep breaths; he felt the effort she made to control herself. At last she lifted her head, and the lamplight fell directly on her ravaged face; and in that moment Marek knew beyond doubt that what he felt for this woman was no passing infatuation. She was in his blood and in his heart and there was absolutely nothing he could do about it. 'Sit down,' he said gently. 'Tell me what's wrong.'

She sat on the bed, head bowed, shoulders tense. 'Czesia's dead,' she said, quietly, and then again with a sudden, shocking agony, '*Czesia's dead!*'

For a fraction of a second Marek stared at her blankly. Then he remembered. 'Your sister?'

'Yes.' She was shaking again, trying to control the tears that threatened once more to overwhelm her.

Marek dropped to his knees beside her and took her hands in his. 'What happened? My darling, what happened?'

She took a long, slow breath, looked him levelly in the eyes. 'She died in the Pawiak,' she said. 'And it's my fault.'

He watched her uncomprehendingly.

She won her struggle for control, though her breath still caught in her throat as she spoke. 'She's never been strong. Not since –' she hesitated – 'not since we came to Warsaw.' She withdrew her hands from his and clasped them in her lap, sat for a moment, head bowed, hair veiling her face.

Marek stood up and went to the battered cupboard, took out a bottle and two glasses. She watched him as he poured the vodka and took the glass he offered her. She turned it in her hands. 'I'm sorry,' she said.

'Don't be silly.'

'You don't understand. You don't know what I've done.'

He came to sit beside her, guided the glass to her lips. 'Then tell me. And anything I can do to help I'll do. Anything.'

She lifted a tired hand to his face. 'Dear Marek.'

He smiled very faintly. 'That makes a change from "Poor Marek". Now tell me – exactly – what's happened?'

It took a long moment for her to marshal thought and word. When she finally spoke she did not, could not, look at him. 'There was something I didn't tell you before. About what happened to me and Czesia. My parents were killed, as I told you, and we were raped. Several times.'

He flinched at that but said nothing.

'A few weeks later we escaped and came to Warsaw.' She was playing with the material of her skirt, twisting and untwisting it. With an almost defiant movement she turned her head to look at him. 'What I didn't tell you was that Czesia was pregnant. By one of the animals that raped us.'

He closed his eyes for a second. 'Jesus Christ.'

'She was beside herself. She almost went mad. She threatened to kill herself.' The girl was quite still now, eyes distant. 'When we got to the city, it was in total chaos. We lived in a cellar. I begged, and I stole. I kept us alive. Czesia –' she spread her hands helplessly – 'Czesia simply lay there, willing herself to die.'

Marek took her hand again, and this time she did not draw away. Her voice was a whisper in the quiet room.

'I found someone – an old woman – who –' she cleared her throat – 'who knew how to deal with such things. Who explained how –' She threw back her head, eyes closed, sat silent for a moment. Then, 'I aborted her,' she said. 'With a knitting needle.'

'God Almighty!' Marek put down his glass and reached for her, crushing her to him, his face buried in her silky hair. Her body shook within his arms.

At last she pulled away, sat up, pushing her hair back from her eyes. 'I didn't make a very good job of it, I'm afraid. At least she didn't die, but she never really recovered. She was always so delicate – so frail. I tried to take care of her. I did! And then – on the day I brought you to Warsaw – she was arrested.'

'What for?'

She shook her head wearily. 'That's the irony. For nothing. She's never been involved with the Underground. She was working in a café – the Germans suspected that it was being used as a cover for clandestine operations and raided it. They arrested everyone – you know how they operate – and Czesia was taken to the Pawiak. And once you're there, innocent or guilty, you're there until such time as they choose to do something about you. I told you what happened to me. It can take months – years! – before they get round to interrogating you.'

'It was she you had been visiting the day I saw you?'

'Yes.'

'But surely no one could blame you for visiting your own sister?'

'Oh yes, they could.' She nibbled her lip, lifted her head to look at him. 'There are strict rules about such things. And with very good cause.'

Something in her eyes warned him that the story was not finished. He waited.

'Czesia became very sick in prison,' she said at last. 'I

bribed a wardress to have her put in the prison hospital. I told you her health was very poor. She needed food, care, medicines. Such things don't come cheap in the Pawiak. The woman was greedy. For more than money.'

'What do you mean?'

'She wanted information. Czesia was feverish a lot of the time. She rambled. Often she thought she was talking to me – she didn't know what she was saying.'

'The wardress discovered you were working for the Underground?'

'Yes.'

'Then why didn't she have you arrested?'

'She tried. Today. You see – it was all for nothing! Czesia died anyway. This morning, in the hospital. The Gestapo came late this afternoon. They raided the house. By sheer chance I had gone out to buy a paper. I hid in the ruined house next door. They arrested everyone.

'But why wait until now? Why didn't she turn you in immediately?'

'I told you. I was a source of money and of information. And she was greedy. She sold the information I gave her to the Germans. Once Czesia was dead she had no more hold over me, so she sold me too.'

'What sort of information?' Marek asked. And then again, when she did not answer, 'Danka? What sort of information?'

'Most of it was useless. I promise you it was! Nothing – nothing! – about Stefan. Half-truths, or out-of-date information that could be verified but that could harm no one. At least –'

'What?' He was gentle.

She buried her face in her hands. 'I made a mistake. A terrible mistake.'

He had already added two and two together. 'The *Chronicle*?'

'Yes.' She whispered the word. 'I gave an address. They were supposed to have left it the week before, but plans had been changed at the last minute, and I didn't know.'

'They were all arrested.'

'Yes.'

There was a long silence.

'You know what will happen to me if anyone finds out?' Danusia asked at last.

'Yes.'

'There's only one punishment for betrayal.' Trembling visibly, she lifted the glass to her lips and tossed back the contents in a single gulp.

He took the glass from her, pulled her to him. 'No one will find out anything from me, my darling. I promise you that. You did what you did and you had your reasons for doing it. How can I blame you for that?'

'Stefan will kill me if he ever finds out.'

'He won't. Believe me.'

'He's done it before.' She spoke as if she had not heard the words. 'A friend of his, a man who had fought beside him. He was captured by the Germans and tortured. They broke him; he agreed to collaborate, and because of him a Partisan group in the Tatras was wiped out. He was tried by a Home Army court in his absence and sentenced to death. Stefan carried out the sentence – in broad daylight, in the Aleja Szucha, outside the Gestapo headquarters.'

'I tell you he'll never know.' His arms were still around her. He tightened them a little, feeling her relax against him. 'I told you I'll do anything, anything that's necessary, to keep you safe.'

She lay against him for a long moment. 'Come on,' he said at last, 'you're dog tired. Get into bed. I'll sleep on the floor.'

Her head came up. 'No.' And then, into the silence that

followed the word, 'Why do you think I came to you? I've other friends, other hiding-places.'

The thought had occurred to him. 'I don't know,' he said simply. 'I'm just glad that you did.'

She had stopped crying, though her eyes were dark-ringed in the shadowy light, and her face was still gaunt with grief. 'You love me,' she said.

'Yes.' The word was calm.

The small lamp guttered a little, the flame dying and then flaring.

'Then show me. Please – show me.' Her voice was hoarse with the tears that she had finally defeated. 'I don't want to be alone. Not tonight.'

'You aren't alone. I'm here. I'll sleep on the floor.'

'No,' she said again.

'Danka, you're upset, you're tired.'

'I'm frightened. Yes, I'm all of those things.' She had stood up, kicked off her shoes. Her fingers were at the buttons of her dress. Her eyes steady upon his, she undid them, one by one and then allowed the dress to slide from her shoulders to the floor; stood before him naked but for a pair of knickers, her hands at her sides, the deliberate display of her body challenging yet paradoxically at the same time submissive.

He could barely breathe.

She did not move.

Very, very slowly his eyes explored her nakedness. The long, narrow-waisted body was exactly as he had imagined it, the full breasts with their dark, enticing nipples silk-smooth and heavy. He reached with both hands to slip the knickers over her hips, then let them drop to the floor. She stepped forward. He laid his face against the smooth warmth of her belly; felt her fingers gentle in his hair, holding him to her. 'I love you.'

'Then love me,' she said, simply. 'Now.' She drew him

to his feet, put her arms about his neck and kissed him, her body close against his. He could taste the salt of her tears on her face. 'I'll turn out the lamp.' She stretched a hand.

He caught her wrist, held it lightly but very firmly. 'No,' he said. 'You won't.'

He laid her upon the bed and he loved her, with almost painful tenderness, his hands and his body gentle until the end. Afterwards he lay propped on one elbow watching her as she slipped into troubled slumber, brushing away the tears that had begun once more to seep from beneath her closed lids. He watched so for hours, as gradually the restless tears stopped and she slept peacefully at last. For his part he had no desire to sleep; if he could have stopped the clock for ever at that moment he would have done it. For now, for this brief, enchanted, unexpected night, Danka was his. She had given her body willingly and warmly, had shown with unaffected pleasure the delight his body had given her. And if she had not once during their lovemaking actually told him that she loved him, his own feelings were so strong that for the moment at least simply having her there beside him, arms flung wide, cheek turned to the pillow, her naked skin, pale in the lamplight, smooth and cool to the touch of his hand, was enough. She must love him a little? Surely she must. And even if she did not, he truly believed he did not care. Not at this moment.

At last he turned the lamp out and settled down to try to rest; yet still he could not. As dawn began her stealthy assault on the darkness, he reached once more for the woman beside him and tried with stubborn self-deceit to tell himself that it did not matter when, as she turned, sighing, into his arms, the name she spoke was not his own.

*

Danusia left the next day while he was at the laboratory; with her cover blown in Warsaw she could be of little use in the city, and in any case would be in constant danger of arrest. The sensible option, having taken the precaution of concocting a story that would satisfy Stefan, was for her to go into the forest at least for a while. In vain he asked her not to leave for another couple of days; she said she would not put him at risk by staying in his room; that was the only – and to be fair reasonable – explanation she would give for her haste and he had to accept it. Yet he hoped, a little, that she might be there still when he returned that afternoon, and was helplessly disappointed when she was not.

That night was bleak. He lay alone and lonely on his bed, his hands behind his head, staring into the darkness, fretting for her safety, fretting to hear her voice, fretting for the touch of her body. One night. Might that, after all, be the end of it? She had gone to Stefan, to the man she had told him she loved. To the man whose name she had murmured as she had stirred from sleep. To the man who, no matter what his feelings for her, would undoubtedly kill her if he ever found out what she had done in her hopeless attempt to save her sister. Not that it was likely that anyone would disbelieve Danusia's account of what had happened; it was so firmly grounded in the truth that the chance of any suspicion falling upon her was minimal. Czesia had been arrested. In prison she had fallen ill; everyone knew how frail her health was, everyone knew the conditions in the Pawiak, no one would doubt it. In delirium before she died she had innocently betrayed her sister's connections with the Underground. The house had been raided. The lies were of omission, and the truth – of the arrest, the illness and the death – easily, if it should ever prove necessary, verified. No one knew the truth but Marek and Danusia. Desperate, and unable for all her strength to cope alone, she had confided in him. In him, and in no one else; that was the extent of her trust. Surely there must be hope in that?

He lay in the darkness, sleepless, and wished, with some strength, that he hadn't eaten all the chocolate she'd brought him. Perhaps after all he should take up what had always seemed to him the extremely peculiar habit of smoking? It seemed to work for everyone else. At the very least it gave one something to do.

A mite oddly, the thought of the hold that Danusia's confession had given him over her did not occur until the early hours of a bright and promising summer's morning. He tried to dismiss the notion almost from the instant it entered his head but it would not be dismissed. It crawled, festering, about his brain as he lay and watched the city-filtered light creep into the corners of the room.

He remembered their lovemaking. Remembered her open, lovely smile, her laughter. He rolled on to his stomach, his hands clasped despairingly over his head.

Never. He could never do that to her.

She was with Stefan. With bloody Stefan.

Somewhere in the house a quarrel had started; voices were raised, a dog yelped.

As the world woke about him, Marek struggled with the notion of coercion, of total and self-centred possession.

And, with the decision made, he could not truly decide whether he had won or lost.

Chapter Eight

'You don't have to come, you know,' Stefan said in English. He was sitting at a table methodically and painstakingly cleaning his gun; Donna lay at his feet, her chin on her paws, her wide, melancholy eyes fixed on her master's face. 'In fact to be honest I'd rather you didn't.'

'I beg your pardon?' Marek had been standing at the window of the hut watching the comings and goings in the clearing outside. He turned now, his face startled.

Stefan lifted his head. 'I said you don't have to come,' he repeated peaceably. 'We really don't need another operator, and if you don't know the terrain you're likely to be more a liability than an asset. Best you should stay here in camp, I think.'

Marek was staring at him in growing anger. 'What? But you said –!'

'I know what I said.' Stefan went back to polishing the long, already darkly gleaming barrel of his rifle. 'I'm just telling you I've changed my mind.'

Marek was at the table in two long, furious strides, leaning across it, resting upon his hands, glowering into his half-brother's calm face. 'Oh no you don't! Not this

time!' The dog lifted her head and made a small growling sound in her throat. Marek, temper for once routing
prudence, ignored her. 'So what's the game now? Let's
make a fool of Marek? You've done it often enough
before! By Christ you have! But not this time – *brother*!'
He invested the word with all the fury and contempt he
could muster. He flung away from the table and back to
the window, shaking with rage. 'Not this time!' he said
again.

'Pack it in, Donna.' Stefan did not raise his voice. His
eyes on Marek, he propped the gun carefully against the
wall beside him, leaned back in his chair. 'I'm sorry,' he
said.

'If you think you're going to make it look as if I've
chickened out at the last minute – what?'

'I said I'm sorry. I had no right to goad you into this. I
was drunk. It was pure mischief. Habit, if you like.'

Marek had turned and was staring at him in astonishment. Stefan tilted his chair back and rested one booted
foot on the table. 'Don't look so bloody surprised. Even I
say sorry sometimes, you know.'

'Never to me.'

Stefan considered that, nodded. 'You're probably right.'

'I damn' well know I am.' Marek was determined to
sustain his outrage.

'There's a first time for everything.'

Marek eyed him suspiciously. 'Danka's had something
to do with this, hasn't she?'

Stefan looked truly surprised. 'Danka? Of course not.
Why should she?'

'She doesn't think I should go.'

'Sensible girl. Neither do I.'

'But you said –'

'I *know* what I said.' With sudden and characteristic
impatience Stefan slammed the chair legs back on to the

floor and stood up. 'For Christ's sake I'm trying to unsay it! That's all.'

'Why? You think I'm not man enough? You think I'm a coward? You think I'll fuck up and land you all in it?'

Unexpectedly the other man laughed in genuine amusement. 'The truth?'

Marek would not be so easily disarmed. 'The truth,' he said, obstinately unsmiling.

'"No" to the first two and "yes" to the third.'

'Sod off! You said you needed another radio operator and you've got one whether you like it or not.'

'We don't have a spare radio.'

There was a long, precarious moment of silence. 'I don't believe you,' Marek said flatly.

'It's true. The bloody things are like gold-dust, and we never recovered the one that was dropped the night you arrived. We have only one.'

Marek dropped into a chair. 'I could kill you,' he said conversationally. 'As slowly and painfully as possible and preferably in front of an audience.'

Stefan grinned. 'We all have our fantasies.'

'I'm glad you think it's funny.' Marek threw up exasperated hands. 'Why didn't you tell me? Why did you let me come?'

'I didn't intend to. I intended to get a message to you through Danka. I meant to let you stew a bit, that's all.'

'Why? *Why?* What have I ever done to you that you should constantly go out of your way to persecute me?'

'Is that what I do?'

'Yes. It's what you've always done. And I'm asking you – why?'

Stefan could not resist. 'Because I'm a bastard?' he suggested trying to coax some gleam of amusement from Marek at the self-deprecating dual meaning.

Marek threw his head back and closed his eyes for a

moment. 'That's – not – my – fault,' he said at last, slow emphasis on every word. 'It's never been my fault.'

'Of course it hasn't. The same as it's never been your fault that you were the clever one. The pampered one. The well-spoken one. The posh one.' Stefan could not resist the jibe. His eyes flickered to his brother's face. Marek said nothing. Stefan shrugged a little. 'The legitimate one,' he went on. 'The one who could have anything he wanted.'

'Is that what you think?'

'Yes.' The word was simple and, surprisingly, spoken with no rancour. Stefan reached into his breast pocket for his cigarettes.

This time Marek did laugh, but there was little amusement in the sound. 'And how do you think I saw you?'

Stefan paused with the cigarette half-way to his lips, considering. 'As the family embarrassment who bullied you mercilessly, I should think?'

'There's something in that.' Marek watched as he lit the cigarette. 'But it isn't all the story.'

'Oh?'

'I envied you.'

His half-brother narrowed pale eyes against the smoke. 'You envied me,' he repeated. '*You* envied *me*?'

'Yes.'

'In God's name why?'

'You were the strong one. You cared for no one. No one ever bullied you. No one ever tried. You could run faster, jump higher, fight better than anyone. Christ, you could shoot better than most grown men when you were ten years old! No one controlled you; you did as you liked. You were never afraid.'

Stefan was watching him, his face utterly expressionless. 'Wasn't I?'

'You know you weren't. While I fretted and depended

on people, and tried to please everyone, and jumped at my own shadow, you just went your own way. You were fearless. No one could break you and you knew it. You terrified me.'

Stefan laughed a little, very quietly; a little bitterly. 'I was brought up in a much harder school than you were.' He was looking down at the dog, his hand light upon her head.

The room was quiet. It struck Marek, suddenly and strongly, that this was the first real conversation he had ever had with this brother-cousin of his; the first, that is, that was not grounded in dislike, distrust or sheer cruel mockery. Despite himself, his anger had ebbed. 'I said before –' he walked to the only other chair in the room and dropped into it – 'that wasn't my fault.'

'I know. I've always known.'

'Then why –?'

The other man's head came up fiercely. 'Because I couldn't punish the one whose fault it was, you fool! Can't you see? I could only, whenever possible, punish his son. His legitimate son.'

There was a long and pensive silence. 'You're very like him,' Marek said at last. 'Much more than I am. Did you know that?'

'Yes.'

'He knew it too. You probably won't believe it but he used to hold you up to me as an example of what a real boy – a real man – should be.'

Stefan's eyes narrowed again, faintly puzzled, faintly suspicious, wholly on guard.

'He had a private nickname for me, did you know?'

Stefan shook his head.

'If you laugh, I'll flatten you. Even Father never used it in front of anyone but Mother.'

The other man raised derogatorily expressive eyebrows but said nothing.

'He called me Pansy.'

Stefan, taken by surprise, ducked his head, pulled at Donna's ears, his long mouth clamped against the amusement Marek had warned him against. It was however Marek himself who broke first, his smile reluctant but genuine. 'Oh, all right, laugh if you must.'

His half-brother's answering grin was wide. Stefan stretched out a brown wrist, glanced at his watch. 'Tell you what, I've an hour or so before we leave, and the actual operation isn't until dawn. Time for a small one? And I'll swap confidence for confidence. I'll tell you what our mutual Papa used to call me. He obviously had a talent for nicknames.'

Marek hesitated, his expression wary.

Stefan shook his head. 'Not an under-the-table session, I promise. You may not believe it, but I do know when to drink and when not to. Just a tot.' He paused for a moment, his face inscrutable. 'For old times' sake?' he added.

'OK. Why not?'

Stefan stood and picked a half-empty bottle of vodka from a rough wooden shelf, together with two small obviously unwashed glasses, which he wiped perfunctorily on his shirt before pouring the drink. Marek accepted his in silence. 'So – what did Father used to call you?'

Stefan eyed the room through the glass he held for a long moment. 'Hob,' he said.

Marek looked at him blankly.

The pale eyes flickered to him, the expression sardonic. 'The only thing I ever asked a teacher to do for me was to look up that word.'

'And?'

'She gave me two meanings. It's short for hobgoblin – what she took great pleasure in explaining as a wicked and ill-tempered sprite – and –'

Marek waited.

'– and it also means a slow-witted country bumpkin.' He lifted the glass, regarded Marek with a mildly acrimonious eye. 'Clever, eh? And more than apt for a kid that spent more time playing truant on the marshes with a gun or poaching for the pot than he ever did in a schoolroom, I don't deny it. So come on, little brother – a toast. To Father, to bright, frightened Pansy, and to stupid, fearless Hob.' He tossed back the drink, smiled an intransigently mocking smile.

Marek studied him. 'Are you?' he asked, gently.

'What? Stupid? Or fearless?'

'Don't be daft! We both know you aren't stupid.'

'Then I can't be fearless either, can I? Only the stupid are entirely fearless. Courage isn't lack of fear, Marek; it's the overcoming of fear. You asked me earlier if I thought you were a coward. I answered honestly. You aren't, whatever you think. You've proved it simply by being here, by being ready to come with us.' He reached for the bottle, splashed a small amount into the glass, offered it questioningly to Marek, who shook his head. 'Show me a totally fearless man and I'll show you a fool; a fool who should never be trusted with other men's lives.'

'So you are afraid sometimes.'

'Of course I am.' Stefan's eyes lifted to his. 'And – can't you see? – it gets worse rather than better. No matter which way you look at it, the odds are shortening.'

'What do you mean?'

Stefan stood, glass in hand, and wandered to the window. Unbidden, Donna followed, huge, lanky and raw-boned, to drop to her haunches at his heel. 'I've been too lucky for too long.'

Beyond the window someone called and was answered by a light, musical voice. Marek lifted his head, his heartbeat quickening. Danka's voice. He joined Stefan at the

Teresa Crane

window. Danka had been waylaid half-way across the clearing and was standing talking to a young man in the high boots and eclectic uniform of a seasoned Partisan – his field grey German jodhpurs dashingly set off by an Allied airman's flying jacket and scarf. It was a cool and windy day. Danka was in her forest-camp outfit of a man's shirt and belted trousers, a scarf tied about her hair to stop it blowing about her face.

Both men stood watching her for a long moment. Then, 'Too lucky for too long,' Stefan repeated.

Marek glanced at him.

Stefan did not take his eyes from Danusia. Almost he might have been talking to himself. 'I came to Poland more than four years ago. I've fought in the north, in the east, and now here, in the south. I've lost count of the number of actions I've been in. Lost count of the close shaves, the near misses. Lost count of the men and women who've not been as fortunate as I have. Good friends some of them.' He dropped his cigarette butt to the floor and ground it out with his heel. 'Luck's a dangerous lady to rely on. She can be a lover or she can be a vindictive whore. She can be as steadfast or as capricious as any other bloody woman. And she can be jealous as hell.' His eyes had found Danka again; Marek wanted to ignore or to misinterpret the look in them but for the life of him could not. 'If she decides to run out on you there's not a lot you can do about it. Except to make sure you're the only one who's in the shit.'

Danka lifted a hand in farewell, and turned. Even at this distance she looked pale and a little strained. Marek's heart ached for her. 'Danka's taken her sister's death very badly,' he said.

'Yes. She has.' Brusquely Stefan tossed back the last of the vodka and turned. 'So that's settled, you stay here. And that, whether you like it or not –' he had lifted a finger as Marek opened his mouth to speak – 'is your Commanding Officer speaking, not your pain-in-the-arse half-brother. You don't have a choice. You can be a hero some other time. We'll get you back to Warsaw and your bloody rockets tomorrow. In one piece. OK?'

'OK.' His initial anger had been vanquished by such a strange and muddled mix of emotions that even Marek himself would have been hard put to express them. Relief, certainly, there could be no denying that. But, too, there was an odd regret; that this tentative and unexpected change in Stefan's attitude towards him would not be further strengthened by shared action, shared danger. But then again, the old insecure inner voice whispered, neither could it be destroyed by physically unco-ordinated incompetence. The bridge that had been woven between them in these past minutes was fragile as a spider's thread. Best not to threaten it by a breath, let alone a possible gale. He did not try – did not want to try – to analyse why this should be so important to him.

'I'm leaving a skeleton force. Alex is in charge in my absence. There's a possibility you'll be called on for guard duty.' Stefan was at his desk, clearing a space, folding a map.

The door opened. 'Hello, you two.' Danka looked from one to the other. 'Everything all right?'

'Everything's fine.' Stefan hardly glanced at her. She looked at Marek. He smiled and nodded. Pale and drawn as she was, he thought he had never seen anything or anyone so beautiful.

'So you're staying behind with us.' Her voice was soft, her tired smile warm.

'Yes. Seems I'm considered a liability.' He caught the quick lift of Stefan's head and tempered that. 'Seems there's no radio anyway, so a second operator might be a bit surplus to requirements. I'm assigned guard duty.'

She laughed. 'With your eyes?' The light words were for Marek, but her eyes were upon the apparently absorbed Stefan.

Stefan picked up his handgun, sighted it, spun the chamber, reached for a box of ammunition.

'You're leaving now?' Danka asked.

'Soon.'

There was a dense moment of quiet.

'I'll –' Marek firmly quelled his desperate desire not to leave them alone together – 'that is, I suppose I'd better find Alex and see if there's some way I can be useful.'

'I doubt it.' Stefan slanted a bright and graceless glance that for a moment held something so close to the mocking camaraderie that he usually directed at friends that Marek could only assume that he must have imagined it.

'I'll see you later.' Danka was still watching Stefan.

'Yes.' Awkwardly Marek side-stepped, half-offering a hand, which Stefan either did not see or ignored. 'Good luck.' As he said it, remembering their earlier conversation, he could have bitten off his tongue.

'Thanks.'

There was no alternative but to leave. Marek stepped out into the wind. Behind him he sensed Danka's movement towards Stefan, heard her say, 'Stefan, be careful – please, please, be careful.'

The trees tossed about the clearing, the wind in their leaves an incessant, almost hypnotic, background noise. A group of perhaps a dozen young men had gathered, precious guns – in such short supply in this beleaguered and occupied land – either propped close to hand or slung on their shoulders. They lounged against the side of a battered lorry or sat on the tailgate or on the dusty ground, smoking and talking. Waiting. They greeted Marek as he passed. Even after Stefan's talk of fear and danger he felt another small and, he knew, perverse twinge of regret that this adventure, after all, was not to be his. There was an air of comradeship, of brotherhood about these men that he envied, and that never had been his.

Brotherhood. A word that until today had meant little or nothing to him. Yet now? Was it possible that he and Stefan were moving at last towards at least some kind of natural relationship? And if they were, could such a fragile bond survive the discovery that they both loved the same woman? For that was the truth, and Marek could see no point in denying it. He wondered if Stefan knew how openly the love and the pain had shown on his face as he had watched Danusia from the window just now. Wondered what he would do if he knew of that night in Warsaw, the night of Czesia's death; the night Danusia had admitted her betrayal of the *Courier* cell. Not for the first time that thought brought the dark stirrings of something within himself that he would rather not face. Never one to lie to himself, he knew that to use what she had, in her exhausted anguish, so precipitately confessed to him to bind her to him would make him no better than her tormentor at the Pawiak. There was a deservedly ugly name for such behaviour, yet it was undeniable that in the small, dark hours of the night the possibility still haunted him. He loved her. He wanted her. He needed her. Wasn't all supposed to be fair in love and in war? Did Stefan agonise so when he saw something he wanted? Or did he use every method and means to his hand to achieve his end?

Stefan will kill me if he ever finds out.

Why had she come to him, Marek, that night?

You love me, she had said. And, *Yes*, he had replied. Yet it had been Stefan's name she had spoken in her sleep. The worst thought of all was that she had come to him that night only because she knew he had seen her coming from the prison. Had she simply been afraid that he might inadvertently let slip something to someone who might add two and two together and come up with the simplest and most damning of answers? He could not bear the thought.

The wind gusted again. A door banged.

He remembered her open smile, the warmth in her eyes, and could not, would not, believe her so perfidious.

And if she were, still he would love her.

Danusia half-closed her eyes against the glimmer of the shaded lantern. She was tired – worse than tired, she was worn out; with grief, with guilt and with nerve-racking emotional strain. Slumped in her chair, her cheek resting upon the heel of her hand, she felt her eyelids drooping again, was aware of Marek watching her across the table as he sorted through the greasy, dog-eared playing cards that had been dealt him. The wind had risen again, tossing the trees in the darkness, gusting through the open door of the hut.

'They'll support us in the end, you wait and see. They'll have to. And anyway, they hate the Boche as much as we do.'

'The sodding Russians? Don't make me laugh! Support us? They'll watch us bloody die like flies and then they'll walk in and take over, neat as a pin. Trust the Bolsheviks? In a pig's eye! I'd as soon trust a boa-constrictor. Look what happened at Katyn. Twist.'

A card was turned. The speaker eyed it gloomily. 'And again.'

'Do we know what happened at Katyn?' A weary-looking young man with a day's growth of beard looked around the circle of faces. 'Do we?'

'We do. The Allies do. It's just that no one will admit it. Not now. Not ever. You know what they call Poland – the Christ of nations; crucified between two thieves. If one doesn't get us then the other one will, and no one else will do a bloody thing about it. Sod it. Bust.' The other man threw his cards down in disgust. Eyed Marek with no friendly gaze. 'What will the British do to support us against their precious time-serving eastern allies? How far will they go to protect Polish sovereignty against the Bear?' He held up a hand, palm out, before Marek could open his mouth. 'Don't tell me. It'd be hard luck to die laughing after what I've been through these past few years.'

Marek smiled his gentle, imperturbable smile. 'I couldn't answer you anyway. My contact with the great, the good and Mr Churchill is minimal. Well, non-existent actually. But if you want my opinion –?'

There was a small, interested silence. All eyes were turned to him. Danusia, with a surge of affection, saw the faint lift of colour in his face as he found himself the centre of attention. He was fiddling with his cards, narrowing his eyes, tilting his head. For goodness' sake, why wasn't he wearing his glasses? She shifted in her chair, trying to straighten her back to defeat the aching exhaustion that threatened to overwhelm her.

'I suspect that Britain may find herself between the devil and the –' He stopped. A figure had appeared in the doorway; a young man, hesitant, frowning.

Alex stood, hand reaching for his rifle. 'Jerzy? What is it?'

The young man shook his head. 'I'm – not sure. It's just –' he shrugged, obviously embarrassed – 'a feeling,' he finished lamely. 'The dogs are restless. It's probably the wind.'

Cards were tossed on the table, chairs pushed back.

'No reports from the lookouts?' Alex asked crisply.

The wind-tousled head shook again. 'No.'

Alex walked to the door, stood, head lifted, looking out.

Danusia, for all her tiredness suddenly and instantly alert, watched him. Someone doused the lamp. The wind gusted and then for an instant died.

They all heard it. The quiet snicker of a horse.

'Get out!' Alex was already moving. '*Get out!*'

There was a flurry of movement in the darkness. Danusia was aware of Marek, still sitting, bemused and uncertain. She dodged around the table, barking her shin painfully upon a fallen chair. 'Marek! Come on!' She reached for his hand, pulled him to his feet. Out in the windy darkness someone shouted. There was a single shot.

'This way. No!' Marek had automatically made for the open door. She hauled him back. '*This way!*'

As she threw open the window at the back of the room the wind blasted through, slamming the door and lifting a scattering of abandoned cards into the air. She flung a leg over the windowledge. As she did so, a powerful searchlight swept the clearing in front of the hut, sweeping the trees, casting dancing devils' shadows that were black as pitch. The forest was tantalisingly near; headlights and flashlights glimmered like Will o' the Wisps.

'*Hände hoch! Sie sind umstellt! Flucht ist unmöglich!*'

Marek scrambled over the windowledge behind her. She grabbed his hand, dragging him down into the darkness beside her. 'Down!' she hissed in his ear. '*Down!*'

And as she spoke all hell broke loose around them.

C *h a p t e r* N *i n e*

In the pandemonium that followed the initial attack Danusia and Marek crouched in the shadows, listening and watching, their hearts in their mouths. It seemed that the camp had been overwhelmed in moments; what had happened to the guards Alex had posted was anyone's guess. The German patrols rolled in from the forest, an unstoppable wave of searchlights and machine-gun fire. In the corner of the clearing where the field kitchen was situated a desperate but obviously hopeless defence was being put up; the defenders, caught totally by surprise, were going down like ripe corn beneath a scythe. A grenade was tossed into a hut, and the small building disintegrated in a blast of fire.

'We have to take a chance.' Danka's mouth was close to Marek's ear, yet still she had to raise her voice. 'Try for the forest. Don't run. Keep down.'

'But –'

'We can't help them!' Her voice was fierce. 'There's nothing we can do. We aren't even armed, for God's sake! And there are Stefan and the others to think of. Come on!' She dropped on to her stomach and began to pull her way forward by her elbows. The hut behind which they were sheltering was not a stone's throw from the admittedly doubtful haven of the trees, and the ground between was protected and shadowed further by another hut, standing at right angles; yet to Marek the expanse looked as wide and as mercilessly exposed as the Sahara desert. Another hut blew. Someone screamed. Orders were shouted. Automatic gunfire shattered eardrums. Shaking with terror he crawled after Danusia, the skin of his unprotected back creeping, certain that one of the roving, hostile searchlights would pin them in its beam, or that a bullet would rip into bone and flesh.

At least to start with, luck was with them. After what seemed to Marek half a lifetime they reached the shelter of the tangled undergrowth in safety, lay sweating and panting, listening to the confused sound of carnage behind them. Every so often a light swept the trees above, silent and deadly; in the reflection Danusia's face was very pale and, like his own, slick with perspiration. Then, quite suddenly, the shooting stopped. In the comparative quiet the engines of motor-cycles revved, men shouted, a single pistol-shot sounded.

Marek felt Danusia's hand on his arm. 'Come on.'

Still crawling, they moved further into the trees. A twig snapped beneath Marek's hand and he froze, his heart in his mouth. From somewhere a little way to their left a German voice spoke sharply, and another replied. From the clearing there came another couple of shots, and then an ominous quiet. The forest was lit by the smoky red light of the burning huts, and the air was acrid. Along the wide track that wound through the trees lorries rumbled, their headlights rocking and dancing in the darkness as the trucks bumped over the rutted surface. A small squadron of horsemen rode with them. Marek's hands and knees were sore; he stopped for a moment, rocking back on his heels, rubbing his hands together.

'Just a little further, then we can walk.' Danusia's voice, whispering, close to his ear. 'We'll make sure we're clear, then we'll turn south.'

'South? Why south? Wouldn't it be safer to head towards Cracow?'

'Of course it would be. But we can't get to Cracow in time to warn Stefan. And if we don't warn him, he and the others will come back tomorrow and walk straight into a Gestapo trap.'

The forest around them was quiet, the activity all, apparently, in the clearing. Marek forced himself to relax, to breathe easily and naturally. 'So how does it help Stefan if we go south?'

'There's another radio,' she said, 'hidden in a cave. I think I can find it.'

There was a long moment of quiet. 'A radio,' Marek said, his voice expressionless.

'Yes. The one that was dropped the same night you arrived. We recovered it a couple of days later.'

'You recovered –?'

'*Ssh!*' The small sound was urgent. Marek stopped speaking and strained his ears.

Nothing.

He waited a moment, then stirred his cramped legs and straightened his aching back. 'It's OK. There's no one.'

'*Halte! Wer ist da?*' A powerful flashlight flickered in the trees some sixty yards or so to the right. Marek heard Danusia's sharply drawn breath, felt the movement beside him as she gathered her legs beneath her. The flashlight probed the darkness, swinging towards them. Another voice called, and was answered, this time from the left and slightly behind them. Another flashlight, again moving towards them. In the faint bloody light of the fires he could see that there were two, perhaps three, uniformed soldiers converging on their hiding-place.

'It's no good. We'll have to run for it,' Danusia whispered. 'Follow me if you can. Ready? *Now!*' And she was off like a gazelle, running low, ducking and weaving in the lurid shadows, bearing to the right as she ran. Marek followed, legs pumping, arms flailing as he tried to keep his balance on the uneven, trackless ground. Brambles tore at and clung to his trouser legs, roots tripped him, the lairs and burrows of the forest's animals lay in wait for an unwary foot. A shot rang out and then another. The bullets whined viciously through the leaves and branches above his head. There were shouts, and orders, and footsteps pounded behind them as their pursuers crashed through the woodland. There was another ragged burst of gunfire. Something thumped viciously into a tree trunk inches from his head. His lungs were bursting, his breathing ragged and painful. He could feel, actually physically feel, again and again as he ran, the impact of a bullet between his shoulder blades. Ahead of him Danusia still ducked and wove, stumbled, recovered herself, ran fleetly on. For his own part he felt that every bone and sinew was already strained to exhaustion, yet still it seemed that he was moving in agonised slow motion; it was every nightmare become real. He cannoned into a tree, banging his shoulder painfully, by a miracle managed to stop himself from falling, drove himself forward again. His breath rasped painfully and still his main emotion was sheer terror, absolute certainty that his back was a target as wide as a barn door. As another volley of small-arms fire rattled behind him and whispered in the branches, he cringed and flinched, unable to believe he had not been hit. This was it, then. A bullet between the shoulderblades as he ran; no way to escape it. So why try? Why not give in here and now, simply stop, take what was coming – get it over. Yet still his legs pumped and his heart hammered, beyond his control, beyond sense, beyond pain.

Faintly in the darkness ahead he saw Danusia veer more sharply to the right, and a moment later understood why as he stumbled out of the clawing undergrowth and on to a narrow, moonlit, curving path. He followed her, willing his aching legs to carry him.

With a shock he tasted the salt of blood in his mouth.

He had been hit then.

He had to stop. He had to.

Still he ran.

Moments later Danusia slowed, dropped back, reached a hand to catch his arm. 'Stop. Listen!' She could barely speak.

The moment he stopped his trembling legs gave way. He dropped to his hands and knees, head hanging, trying to control his gasping lungs. Again he tasted blood, and spat.

'They've – given up – I think.' Danusia too was on her knees, shoulders heaving.

Gulping for air and through the roaring in his ears he could hardly hear her. He fought for and very gradually managed to obtain control of his breathing. He listened. Certainly he could hear no more shots. He sat back on his heels, wiped his mouth with the back of his hand, and in the pale light of the moon saw the faint, dark smear of blood; yet, oddly, he could feel no wound, no pain in his back, no sign of blood anywhere but in his mouth. He fought against a choking need to cough, and then under-stood; the blood he was spitting was from his overstrained lungs. He was not wounded. He had sur-vived. For as his pounding heart quietened it seemed that Danusia was right. Their pursuers had lost them in the darkness and given up. The sound of their voices and their movement through the forest was faint and getting fainter. They were going back to the camp.

He turned his head to look at the girl beside him. 'Are you all right?'

'I – yes.' Her head was hanging, he could not see her face, curtained by her hair. She hunched her shoulders, her left hand clasped to her right upper arm.

'Danka? What is it?' He put a hand to her, touched her arm. And before he could register the fact that the wet, warm stickiness that his fingers had encountered could be nothing but fresh blood, she had fainted.

He caught her as she fell, lowered her gently to the ground. It was only moments before she stirred and moaned a little. Then her eyes flew open. 'It's all right,' he whispered. 'It's all right. I'm here.'

Still the glow of fire lit the sky behind them; smoke drifted across the silvered face of the moon. The sound of engines and of voices rang distantly through the trees. But here it was quiet, peaceful almost.

'We can't stay here.' Danusia struggled to sit up. In the moonlight Marek could see now the darkness of blood upon her shirt-sleeve.

'Wait.' He shrugged out of his jacket, pulled his own shirt over his head. His hands were shaking, as much from exhaustion as from the tension that strung his nerves taut. Clumsily, using his teeth, he tore the shirt into strips and, hampered by the darkness, bandaged the wound as best as he could. 'At least it seems to have stopped bleeding.' He helped her to her feet. 'Can you walk?'

In the light of the moon he saw the faint, pale flash of her smile. 'Is there an alternative?'

'Where's the nearest sympathetic doctor?'

'There's one in a village about four miles west of here.'

'Can you make it?'

'No.'

He looked at her, startled.

'We aren't going west,' she said. 'We're going south. We're going to warn Stefan.'

'But, Danka!'

'We're going to warn Stefan,' she said again stubbornly. 'Then we'll think about doctors.'

'Wouldn't there be a radio in the village where the doctor is?'

'There might be. And then again there might not. I won't take the chance. If we're where I think we are, we can follow this path for a couple of miles or so and we'll come to the main road that runs east-west through the forest. There's a track that goes south for another two, maybe three miles, to a hill farm. The radio's hidden there. If I can't make it, you'll have to go on alone. Be careful crossing the road, it's patrolled. The track to the farm's about half a mile along the road to the east. Have you got that?'

'I'm not leaving you,' he said.

She shrugged in the darkness, and winced. 'Let's hope you don't have to. Come on. We have until dawn.'

It took them over an hour to cover the couple of miles to the road. The path was ill defined and uneven. Several times Marek heard the sharp intake of Danusia's breath as she stumbled and jarred her wound; several times he tried to force her to stop, to rest a while, but she would have none of it.

'I'm all right. If I stop, I'll never get started again. We have to find the farm. We have to get to that radio before dawn.'

'Stefan told me the radio was lost.'

'It wasn't. I told you we found it a couple of days later.'

'Then why –?'

'He didn't want you to go on the raid. He knew he shouldn't have goaded you into it – What was that?'

Somewhere, far ahead, the faintest of lights had flickered, a will-o'-the wisp in the darkness.

They stopped. 'Listen,' Danusia whispered.

A familiar sound, distant but unmistakable. The roar of engines.

'The road,' Danusia said. 'It must be. What would you say – half a mile?'

'Something like that.'

'Christ, I wish I knew what the time was! I wish we had a bloody torch!' There was a sudden tense edge of frustration in the words.

They stumbled on. Ahead of them the road was dark and quiet now.

Danusia's teeth had begun to throb with pain; they were clamped so tightly against the agony of her arm that the very roots ached. The wound had begun to bleed again. Every step jarred through to the bone; a misstep – and in the tree-shadowed darkness there were many of them – was torture. She would have given half of her remaining days to curl up in a quiet corner and let the blackness that lapped at the edges of consciousness overwhelm her. Simply to stop moving would be a blessing in itself.

They approached the road cautiously. Another convoy, slow-moving and ponderous, with its inevitable noisy escort of armed motor-cycles herding the lorries like dogs herding sheep, rumbled over the cracked surface of the highway. Danusia and Marek lay in the undergrowth in the shadow of the trees. The column seemed endless. Danusia felt her eyelids drooping, forced herself fiercely awake. She had to get Marek to the hidden transmitter before Stefan's group split up after the raid. She had to. They must be warned.

The few miles to the hill farm where the radio had been hidden stretched like a painful infinity before her. She laid her head upon her arms for a moment, closed her eyes again.

'Danka? Danka – darling.' Marek's voice, urgent, almost panic-stricken.

She hauled herself out of pain-filled darkness. Lifted her head, flinched as fire shot through her injured arm. 'It's all right. I'm here.'

'I thought –' He stopped. 'The road's clear. Should we cross now?' She could hear the creditable effort he put into sounding calm.

'In a moment. Make sure they're gone. Then we'll cross. Separately.'

They scuttled across the road like beetles in the darkness of a cellar.

'The other track's not far. Best not to stay on the road. It's patrolled regularly.' Wearily Danusia struck off into the woodlands again, keeping the moonlit road to her right. 'It's not so far now.'

From then on it was simply a case of endurance. They found the track that led south into the mountains, turned away from the road that once more was alive with headlights and the sound of engines. 'They're moving out,' Danusia said. 'It's true then. The Russians must be coming.'

'But – isn't that good?' Marek ventured. 'They're our allies after all.'

Danusia did not reply.

They trudged on in silence. Danusia estimated that two hours, perhaps a little longer, had passed since the attack on the camp. Hampered as they were by the darkness and her wound, it must be at least another hour and a half to the farm. Then Marek would have to go up the hillside to the cave, set up the radio –

Gritting her teeth, she tried to push herself to walk faster.

*

The moon had gone from the sky when the track led at last into a wide clearing in which, very faintly, the dark, looming bulk of a small house and a barn could be made out. Danusia stopped for a moment, closing her eyes in sheer relief. A dog barked, and a chain rattled. Marek started forward. Danusia held out a hand, detaining him. 'Wait! A good patriotic Polish bullet can kill as quickly as a German one. Jozik doesn't take kindly to strangers.'

They stood in the darkness, straining ears and eyes. The dog barked again, fiercely, and again the chain that restrained it rattled. A door opened, there was a snapped command, and the animal fell quiet, growling in its throat. Then, 'Who's there?' A man's voice, rough and strongly accented.

'Friends.' Danusia's hand still held Marek's arm firmly. 'We have news of your cousin in Cracow.'

There was a moment's silence. 'The name of this cousin?' the voice asked then, suspiciously.

'Her name is Marisia,' Danusia said. 'Jozik, it's me, Danka.'

'Who's with you?'

'A friend. We need to use the radio.'

'Wait. Don't move.' There was movement in the darkness, and a moment later the dim light of a shaded lantern. It moved slowly towards them, borne high by a massive man who carried a long shotgun that was pointed uncomfortably steadily at Marek. Marek stood quite still as the light was brought close to his face, saw the surprise in the suddenly narrowed eyes that squinted in a lined and weather-beaten face.

'Please, Jozik,' Danusia spoke quietly, 'we don't have much time. The camp was raided. Stefan and some of the men are away. If we don't warn them, they could walk straight back into the arms of the Germans. Marek needs to be shown where the radio is.' Her voice faltered a little.

Marek, ignoring the shotgun, turned to her and stretched out a hand to steady her. 'She's hurt,' he said. 'For God's sake, man, are you going to stand there for ever?'

The man Jozik grunted and turned towards the house. 'Come.'

The room into which he took them was primitive, with a stone floor and roughly hewn wooden walls. There was a brick stove in one corner, a bench along one wall, a small table by which stood two stools. As Jozik hung his lamp upon a nail driven into the wall, Marek saw on a shelf beside it the treasures of the household; a framed photograph of a young man in uniform, a small black box with a brass key and a brightly painted wooden egg displayed on a little rickety stand.

'The radio,' Danusia said, 'Will you take him to it?'

'Someone should look at your arm.'

'The radio is more important. My arm can wait.'

'If you want to lose it, yes.' The man was laconic. He strode to a door, rapped upon it. 'Come, Mother. Danka's here. She's hurt. I'm going out.' He turned to Marek, jerked his head. 'We'll fetch a lamp from the barn.'

Marek glanced anxiously at Danusia. She was very pale and her wounded arm hung useless at her side. 'It's all right,' she said. 'The old lady will look after me. Go. Hurry!'

Marek turned to find Jozik looking him up and down in faint and almost malicious amusement. 'You're going to have trouble with those shoes,' he said.

He did. The climb was neither steep nor particularly difficult, but the path was extremely narrow and the footing uncertain to say the least. Jozik, carrying a lantern, strode ahead as if he were walking a pavement; Marek scrambled behind as best as he could. The only concession Jozik made was to offer a strong hand when they came to a spot where the path slanted perilously across a scree slope, an obviously fresh slip of small stones and rock that slid from beneath their feet and rattled into the darkness below as they inched their way across.

Marek squinted a little worriedly at the sky, that he fancied was lightening a little. 'Is it much further?'

'No.' His monosyllabic companion turned and tramped on. A few minutes later he stopped at a spot where a bush grew out of the rock. Holding the lantern high, he drew it aside to reveal a small dark hole. 'In there,' he said, and handed the light to Marek. 'I'll watch.' And without waiting for a reply, he hunkered down, elbows on knees, his back to the rock wall.

The radio was of a type very familiar to Marek. There were a few moments of anxiety when Stefan's operator at first did not respond to the call-sign that Danusia had given him, but once contact had been made, the simple message that he and Danusia had agreed upon was relayed quickly.

As he carefully packed the precious equipment away and replaced the box on a ledge at the back of the cave, Marek spared a wry thought for Stefan's companions once the news was given to him. They would probably hear the resulting explosion from here. He pushed past the sheltering bush to where Jozik still squatted, peaceably smoking a foul-smelling cigarette. By now there could be no doubt about it, the sky held a definite hint of a rosy summer dawn. The dark forest that spread beneath them looked mysterious and strangely alluring in the lifting light; Marek was reminded of the enchantment and the terror of the fairy tales of childhood.

Jozik hauled himself to his feet. His boots were scuffed and holed, tied around his thick calves with string. His breeches too were filthy and worn and his leather jerkin sweat-stained and battered. 'OK?' he asked.

'OK.' Marek was aware of a sudden almost euphoric lift of relief. They had done it. Whatever happened now, Stefan and his men would not walk unprepared into a Gestapo trap. And he, Marek, had been instrumental in warning them. Surely even Stefan would have to admit that he'd been of some use this time? All that remained now was to get Danusia to a friendly doctor as soon as possible. He hoped she hadn't lost too much blood – hoped the wound had been well cleaned – if an infection set in – Unwarily absorbed, he stepped on to the scree slope behind Jozik.

'Careful!'

The brusque warning came too late. The paper-thin soles of Marek's city shoes, rubbed even slicker by the scramble up the path, skidded on the stones as if on ice. Helpless, he felt his feet go from under him; there was no way in the world he could stop himself or regain his balance. In a small avalanche of stones and rock he slipped and fell, knocking the breath from his body, tumbling over and over down the steep slope.

He heard his companion's shout, heard his own shocked cry before his head struck a rock and consciousness deserted him in a splintering flash of pain.

By the time Jozik reached him he had come to rest jammed up against a rock, arms outflung, a contusion the size of a small saucer on his forehead and the bones of his shattered right leg sticking razor-sharp and bloody through his torn trousers.

'Jesus Christ,' the big man said, almost reverently. 'Sweet Jesus Christ!'

INTERLUDE

Danusia

Chapter Ten

'So what the hell happened?' Stefan ducked through the low doorway and stood surveying the still figure on the bed.

'He slipped on the mountain. On the scree slope. Jozik says he's lucky to be alive.' Danusia laid a hand upon the sleeping Marek's forehead. 'At least there's no fever. The doctor gave him something to make him sleep. But everything's in such short supply –' she shrugged, nibbling her lip – 'he's going to have a tough time of it these next few days.'

'There's no question he can be moved?'

She shook her head. 'Have you seen his leg? No. There's nothing for it; he'll have to stay here.'

Stefan ran an irritated hand through his hair. 'What a bloody mess! Warsaw's going to love this!'

'It isn't Marek's fault.' Her voice was quietly defensive. 'Remember, if it hadn't been for him, you and the others might not be here now.'

'I know. I know.' Stefan moved to the end of the bed, leaned with his hands on the iron bedstead, cocked a mild eyebrow. 'I only wish the silly bastard could for just once in his life learn to tell his left foot from his right.'

Danusia laughed quietly. 'Poor Marek.'

The man on the bed stirred a little, muttering.

Stefan reached for a cigarette. 'So tell me what happened at the camp.'

'I don't know what happened. All I know is that the Germans came at us out of the forest like a ton of bricks –'

'You had guards posted?'

'Of course. But still we had no warning. God only knows what happened. One minute all was quiet, the next there they were. Felix and some of the others tried to fight them off but it was hopeless. It was obvious from the start that they were overwhelmingly outnumbered. They didn't stand a chance.'

'Did anyone else get away?' He lit two cigarettes, offered her one.

'Not that I know of. But it was dark, and there was a lot of confusion. I couldn't be sure. All I could think of was to get Marek to the transmitter to warn you –' She caught her breath sharply as she turned to take the proffered cigarette with her left hand.

'What is it?'

'Nothing.'

He eyed her for a moment, then came round the bed to where she stood and took her right hand in his. She flinched a little. Very carefully he unbuttoned the sleeve of her shirt and rolled it up to reveal the neat bandage above her elbow. 'Nothing?' he enquired gently.

'A scratch, that's all.'

'A bullet?'

'Yes. But I was lucky. It hasn't broken the bone.'

'You should have it in a sling.'

'I know.' She lifted her eyes to his. 'But I hoped you wouldn't notice. I didn't want you to know.'

'Why not?'

'I didn't want to worry you.' There was a long moment of silence broken only by Marek's heavy breathing. 'It – would worry you?' she asked then, an aching uncertainty in the words despite all her efforts.

He took a slow breath, lifted a hand to her face. 'Oh yes,' he said, 'it worries me. It worries me that you might have been killed, or captured. It worries me that you're hurt. It worries me that you're here. It worries me that I can't keep you safe –'

She stood quite still, her breath held.

He let his hand drop, turned away. 'And it bloody worries me how the hell we're going to get this silly bastard down south to catch that plane.'

'We're not.' The words were crisp. 'There's no question of it. It was the first thing I asked the doctor. He says there's no way he'll be fit to travel for a month or more. He'll have to stay here. It's as safe as anywhere. We'll just have to tell the Committee to go ahead without him. Perhaps there'll be another airlift later.'

'Or perhaps there won't.' Stefan was grim. 'Things are happening fast. The Russians are advancing – the Germans are beginning to panic.'

'The pick-up's scheduled for some time in the next two or three weeks. Marek won't be ready to travel by then, that's for sure; even if he could, the chances of getting caught are far too high. With an injury like this he'd be questioned at every corner. He'd never get away with it. He can write a report with a broken leg. I'll see it gets delivered to Warsaw. Then we'll just have to sit it out here until he's well enough to be moved. We can only plan day to day for the moment.'

Stefan turned back to her, lifted his hands to her shoulders. 'I have to report to Warsaw. You know that.'

'Yes.'

'It's possible they'll keep us there. There's a lot of talk – a lot of rumour.'

'Warsaw will fight?'

'I hope so. I believe so.'

'Not for a little while, I hope.' She lifted her head to look directly into his eyes. 'I've waited for as long as you have for this. I want to be with you.'

Uncharacteristically gentle, he drew her to him and rested his cheek for a second upon her hair. 'We'll see,' he said. 'Just be careful. And look after that bloody idiot. Try not to let him break the other leg.'

She smiled. 'I'll try.' She lifted her mouth for his kiss, clung to him for a moment before he stepped away with a lifted hand and a swift grin of farewell. She watched him to the door, heard his quick command to Bella who waited for him in the other room.

'Danka?' Marek mumbled behind her. 'Danka?'

She bent over him, smoothing his hair from his forehead. 'I'm here.'

A voice called outside the window; Stefan answered. An engine growled into noisy life. Danusia straightened, listening. There was another exchange of voices, the truck ground into gear. She heard it jolt, protesting, over the rough track that led from the farm, and within minutes all was quiet.

A cow lowed, mournful, into the echoing mountain silence.

Stefan had gone. Again.

Danusia cradled her sore arm for a moment in her left hand, her eyes distant, ears straining for the last sound of the engine.

Bloody war.

Bloody men.

She smiled a little at her own sudden tired, almost involuntary vehemence; sobered as she felt again the odd and all but intolerable intensity of those last few moments with Stefan.

Does he love me? If so, why has he never told me? Surely it can't be so very hard to say those simple words? When we're alone – when he loves my body – I never doubt him then. Am I such a fool?

She closed her eyes for a moment, squeezing them shut.

'Danka?' Marek's eyes were open, pain-filled and confused.

'I'm here,' she said again soothingly. 'It's all right. I'm here.'

It was a month before she saw Stefan again, a tranquil and – at least after the first few painful days – remarkably beguiling month spent sitting with Marek, or helping Jozik and his mother about the farm, or walking alone on the hillsides and in the forest. Her arm healed quickly, and Marek's delight in her company and fierce determination to get back on his feet as quickly as possible made him the easiest of patients. They spent the long, idle hours together in discussion and often in laughter; there was little enough distraction in this primitive backwater – no books, little contact with the outside world. Later she discovered that while she nursed Marek back to health and her own wound healed in the comparative peace of the countryside, in the world beyond the sheltering forest, in a bloodied and battered Europe, the war was at last moving towards its bitter climax. While weary Londoners learned to live with the seventy V1s – so-called 'doodlebugs' – that rained on them each day and once more took to sleeping in shelters and in underground stations, the Western Allies broke out from the beleaguered beachheads of Normandy and began their advance towards Berlin. From the east the Russians rolled inexorably across Polish soil towards the Vistula.

In the aftermath of a bungled attempt to assassinate Adolf Hitler, the man who was arguably Germany's greatest and most brilliant soldier, Erwin Rommel, was forced to commit suicide. For the first time the Nazi war machine was showing signs of breakdown. As June moved into July and the summer wore on, tensions in Warsaw grew; the Polish High Command was torn. Just a few months before, in March, the Commander of the Home Army, General Komorowski, known to all by his pseudonym of General 'Bor', had set his face firmly against the idea of an uprising in the city, considering the risk to the civilian population and the possibility of grave damage to the historic capital too great. Now, however, with the situation changing almost daily, that decision was being questioned. With every advance of the Red Army it became more and more obvious that once the fighting had ceased and the occupying forces had retreated, the Soviets had no intention whatever of collaborating with the Polish Army under the Polish Commander-in-Chief in London, as had been hoped. On the contrary, Polish units who had been encouraged – indeed positively ordered – by their superiors to contact the advancing Russians were routinely either disarmed and arrested or incorporated willy-nilly into what was looking dangerously like yet another invading force. It was becoming more and more urgent that the Poles themselves should take the initiative, should show the Western powers that, as Poland had been capable of determined and unyielding resistance throughout the Occupation, now she was ready to fight openly for her freedom and independence. Warsaw, the city that had experienced and survived the worst of the invaders' savage repression, was a potent symbol of Polish pride and patriotism; where better to make a stand? At best it would mean that the advancing Russians would be faced with an already liberated free Polish capital city whose sovereignty surely could not be questioned; and at worst if the Russians should arrive before the Germans had been vanquished, they surely, in honour, could do nothing but aid the insurgents against the common enemy? Arms and ammunition were in terribly short supply, whereas the Russians had both. They had men and materials. They had air power. It could not be long before they were within striking distance of Warsaw. The arguments for insurrection became more powerful by the day.

Danusia, however, for the first time in five years, found herself almost completely isolated from outside news. There was no wireless at the farm and little contact with the world at large, apart from Jozik's weekly visit to the local village market. The grizzled and taciturn man and his ancient mother had little time for anything or anyone beyond the boundaries of the land from which they, in the footsteps of three generations, scratched a living. The transmitter hidden on the rocky height behind the house was a purely personal favour to Stefan, as was the silent but ready acceptance of two guests who could, in truth, be nothing but a nuisance and just as easily could prove to be a positive danger.

What Stefan had done to deserve such privilege Danusia had never known, but it had always been beyond doubt that here he was considered a second son; Marek's likeness to him and the obvious family connection was, she realised, undoubtedly a factor in the present situation. The room which had been given to Marek was Jozik's own; Jozik slept, rolled in a blanket, on the floor of the tiny living-room. For Danusia a pallet had been contrived in his mother's room, a mixed blessing this, since, though the old woman slept like a log from the moment her head touched the pillow until first light of dawn and thus thankfully demanded nothing of companionship or conversation, she snored and grunted, non-stop, from the moment her eyes closed until the moment they opened, like a herd of pigs being driven to market.

'I've had to make a pair of earplugs,' Danusia told a sympathetic but laughing Marek. 'It's impossible! How can it be that someone who makes no noise at all during the day – I mean for heaven's sake, if your life depended on it I doubt you could get a word out of her! – make enough noise to wake the dead all night?'

'Poor Danka,' Marek said teasingly, and flinched a little as he moved his splinted leg.

'Here. Let me –' She was beside him in a moment, both hands around the swathed limb. 'Is that better?'

'Yes. Thank you.'

'The doctor says you're doing marvellously well. Healing quickly. It must be a family trait.'

He smiled.

'You'll be as good as new soon, you'll see.' She stood at the window looking out into the clearing. 'How very peaceful it is. Almost like –' She stopped.

'What?'

She shrugged a little. 'I was going to say "almost like home". I told you – I was brought up in the country.'

He watched her with sympathetic eyes. A fine mist of warm summer rain drenched the dripping woodlands and the smell of it drifted through the open window. 'I'm a city boy myself.'

She turned from the window, smiling again. 'We'll have you back in your smelly city in no time, you'll see.' She came to the end of the bed. 'I'm really sorry you're going to miss your flight. You might have been back in England by the end of the month.'

'It can't be helped.' He smiled his own diffident and oddly attractive smile. 'And there are consolations.'

'Our cut-throat games of cards?'

'Of course. What else?'

'Fancy a game now? I've got the bit between my teeth, you know; after last night you owe me three matchsticks. That's thirty thousand zlotys. I hope you aren't a welsher?'

He laughed, watched as she took the ancient pack of cards from the shelf. 'Any news from Warsaw?'

'Not since I sent off your report.' The document had been handed to a courier a week or so earlier. She pulled a chair close to the bed and smoothed the cover to make a playing surface. Marek wriggled himself upright, his still splinted leg stiff and awkward. 'Here – let me –' Danusia leaned forward and put her arm about his shoulders. For a moment he lifted his hand to hers and held it there, his face very close to hers. Trapped, she dropped a quick, light kiss on his cheek and then pulled away to fuss with the bedclothes.

'Danka –' he began.

Very gently she laid a finger upon his lips.

Equally gently, he bit it.

She pulled her hand away and shook the finger at him, mockingly severe. 'Behave yourself!'

He pulled a rueful face, shifted his leg. 'Can I do anything else? But I can dream, can't I? There's no law against that. Besides – isn't it normal for the injured hero to fall in love with his nurse?' The words were light.

She stilled for a second, then riffled the cards in practised fingers. 'Perhaps, for the moment,' she said carefully, 'it's best if no one falls in love with anyone.'

He held her eyes, his own still wry. 'Isn't it a little late for that?'

She chose deliberately to misunderstand him. 'I hope not.'

'Don't you know?'

She thought about that. In the past few weeks the bond

of friendship that had already bound her to this man had inevitably deepened. His mild good humour in the face of considerable pain had won her admiration, his gentle attentions could never be regarded as disagreeable; on the contrary, as each day passed she found her affection for him growing. They both knew that she had used his attraction to her to her own ends, and that in doing so had handed him a weapon of considerable potency; yet he never by word or implication referred to the fact. And, perhaps paradoxically, this intrigued her the more. Most men, she was certain, would have taken full advantage of the power his knowledge of her gave him. A word to Stefan – a word to anyone – and her life would be in the deadliest of danger. Yet still his approach to her was nothing but gentle, nothing but utterly and courteously considerate. He made no demands, and despite what had gone before obviously had no intention of doing so. In a way – and she knew well that in this she was being perverse – it piqued her a little. Sometimes she wondered if it were not simply another kind of game, but at times like these, with his eyes so open and honest upon her, she knew that to be less than fair. He loved her; or at least he thought he did.

And she –?

She had grown very fond of him. Perhaps too fond in the circumstances. For there was Stefan. Difficult, ruthless, dedicated Stefan. Always there was Stefan –

'Well?' Marek asked.

'No,' she said, 'I don't know. And that's the truth.'

They sat in a silence broken only by the steady drip of the rain from the branches beyond the window. Then Marek leaned forward and took the cards from her. 'My deal, I think?'

Stefan arrived unexpectedly on the first day that Marek, with the help of a stick and with Danusia's support, ventured outdoors. It was a warm and sultry day and he and Danusia were sitting on a crude bench set by the kitchen door when the familiar long-legged figure strode from the forest, Bella trotting beside him.

'Stefan!' Danusia was on her feet in a moment and running to him. Marek watched, his face expressionless as she flung her arms about his half-brother and kissed him. They stood for a moment talking, too far from him for him to hear what was said, then turned and strolled towards him.

'Well –' Stefan threw himself down on the bench, stretched his legs in front of him – 'how's it going?'

'OK.' Marek lifted the stick. 'As you see, I'm getting about better every day. The leg's a damned sight more comfortable with the smaller splint. I'll be good as new soon. What news? How did the airlift go?'

'They made it – on a wing and a prayer, but they made it. Apparently the countryside was crawling with Boches. In fact a couple of German fighters landed right on the bloody airstrip, and took off just a couple of hours before the flight was due. Then the damned Dakota bogged down after it landed. They almost had to give up and set fire to it.'

'Christ! What happened?'

'They've had a lot of rain down south. The ground was just too wet. The bastard just sank into the soft ground. Three times they tried to take off. Three times they unloaded the passengers and the cargo. Bloody thing wouldn't move.' Stefan shook his head amusedly. 'Whole operation was supposed to take eight or nine minutes at the most, but an hour and a half they were there. An hour and a half! Christ, I'll bet the air was blue!'

'But they got off in the end?'

'Yes, they did. And managed to get home in one piece. We heard on the BBC. Your precious report and the bag of bits are in the right hands. We've heard from other sources too. It's counted as a bit unfortunate in London that you aren't.'

'I can imagine.'

Stefan shrugged. 'Can't be helped. Hey, Jozik! How are you?'

The big man had emerged from the barn, smiling widely. Marek watched the enthusiastic back-slapping and comradely hugs in some mystification. In his experience Jozik was anything but a demonstrative man, yet here he was welcoming Stefan like a long-lost brother. Bella too received a rough but affectionate greeting. Then, 'Mother!' Jozik called over his shoulder. 'See who's here! Set another place!' He turned back to Stefan, punched him playfully on the shoulder, a blow that might well have floored a smaller man. 'You stay! At least for tonight you stay! I have a bottle saved.' Another huge slap on the back, and this time even the laughing Stefan staggered a little. 'Tonight we open it!'

The bottle proved to be three, and the contents home-brewed vodka of blistering strength. After a great bowl of rabbit stew had been scraped clean, Danusia helped the old woman to clear the dishes away, kissed her goodnight and then came back to her chair, resting her elbows on the table, nursing her glass and watching the three men. The talk so far had been of the war, of the possibilities of peace, of the danger that lurked, as it always had, to the East and the subject now under discussion was, in Jozik's words, the 'sodding certainty' of the betrayal of the Polish cause by her Western Allies once Hitler and his Third Reich had been crushed.

'Oh, come on! Surely not?' Marek shifted in his chair, easing his leg. 'The British people wouldn't allow that.'

'The British people won't give a bugger.' Solemnly Jozik poured another glass, brim-full, and handed the bottle, the third to be passed around and already half-empty, to Stefan. 'You can't blame them. They've had enough. They won't stand up to the Reds. No one will.' The last words were drunkenly scornful.

'Churchill might.' Thoughtfully Stefan took the bottle, eyed it, swilled the contents. 'What's in this stuff? Dynamite and pig shit?'

'Something like. Scares you, does it, pernickety bastard?'

Stefan grinned, poured a glass, handed the bottle on to Marek.

Marek for a moment did not notice. He was frowning a little. Danusia smiled. She knew that look.

'Hold on a minute.' The words were as close to truculence as Marek ever came. 'We –' suddenly self-conscious, his colour high, he hesitated for a moment – 'the British, that is – they care about freedom. Oh, for God's sake, they've proved it over the past few years, haven't they?' He took the bottle that Stefan was waving beneath his nose, looked at it in some slight puzzlement, as if he could not quite divine its purpose.

'And when they get their freedom? When the danger to their homes and their children and their cities is past? Who could blame them? Do you think they will want to fight a former ally – a powerful former ally – for the sake of poor benighted Poland – so far away, so unimportant?' Jozik emptied his glass at a swallow. 'Think again, my friend. Think again.'

'So –' Stefan held his glass to the lamplight and looked into it! 'So – there is only one thing for it.' He lifted the glass as if in a toast, and looked, bright- eyed, from one to another around the table. 'We free ourselves.'

'Warsaw,' said Danusia.

Stefan turned to her, his face alight. 'Warsaw. An uprising. A victory for Poland. One last effort. As I said – we free ourselves.'

Jozik's huge fist hit the rickety table with such force that Danusia barely suppressed a shriek, of surprise if not fright. 'Warsaw! Here's to Warsaw and her fighters! May they all be as valiant as our Stefan! If they are, I pity our enemies! Marek, my one-legged friend – pass the bottle!'

Marek tilted the bottle unsteadily, filled his own glass and handed the vodka over to Jozik. 'I still think –'

There was a moment of silence. All eyes turned to him. 'What?' Stefan asked, interestedly.

Marek blinked, considering. Danusia could almost pinpoint the second when he lost his train of thought. 'I still think – you're right,' he said. 'Dynamite and pig shit. Sorry.' The last word was vaguely aimed in Danusia's direction.

She laughed. 'It's OK. I've heard worse, believe me.' She looked again from one to the other. Jozik was, quite simply, completely and happily drunk. Marek, serious as a judge and blinking like an owl, was not far behind him. And Stefan? Stefan's bright, subversive eyes were clear as ever. Catching her looking at him he smiled, and her treacherous heart turned over.

'Stefan, lad – drink up!' Jozik leaned to him, flung a bear-like paw across his shoulder, regarded Danusia with intent black eyes. 'A hero, this boy. That's what. A hero.'

'Oh?'

'Saved my life, didn't you, lad? Saved my bloody life.'

Stefan attempted to disengage himself from the other man's comradely embrace, and failed. He shrugged a little, picked up his glass.

'Six of 'em. Bang! Bang! Bang! Didn't know what hit 'em. Six of 'em.'

'Four,' said Stefan.

'Six. Swear it was six.'

'Four.' Stefan lifted his glass. 'And it was a long time ago.'

'What – exactly – happened?' Marek asked in inebriated interest.

Stefan shook his head, opened his mouth, and was forestalled by Jozik.

'Down on the road it was. Three, p'raps four, years ago. I was coming back from market when a Boche patrol stopped me. I gave 'em some lip and the next thing I knew I was face down on the road with a gun to my head – well, you know what the swine are like. I could feel that sodding bullet going through my skull, I can tell you that. Then, like I said – bang! They went down like ninepins, stone dead, all six of 'em.'

'Four,' said Stefan.

'I'll tell you I never saw such marksmanship! One bullet apiece and that was that. And me in the middle of it all without a scratch! I thought it was an ambush. Thought there must be at least three guns. Then out of the trees strolls this bastard, bold as brass and all alone. 'Cept for Bella, of course.'

'What were you doing there?' Danusia asked Stefan.

'I was on my way to Cracow. Heard the patrol coming and got off the road. It was just luck.'

'Good for me and bad for them,' Jozik said, and roared with laughter. 'We buried them in the forest. I know the place. Oh, yes, I know the place. I spit each time I pass it.' He heaved a gusty sigh, looked from face to face and then toppled forward, laid his head on the table and began to snore loudly.

'He's gone to sleep,' Marek said seriously.

'Four men,' Danusia said, very quietly.

Stefan lifted his head, his eyes narrowing. 'Four Germans.'

'Four sons. Four lovers. Four brothers. In an unmarked grave that Jozik spits on as he passes.'

'They'd have killed him.'

'I know.'

'I've killed many more since.'

'I know that too.'

'I think,' Marek said, 'I'd better go outside.'

Stefan pushed his chair back and offered his hand. 'Up you come.'

Danusia watched them out of the door. Jozik snored on. Outside, an owl called hauntingly.

She was still sitting, her drink untouched, when Stefan ushered a pale and chastened-looking Marek back into the room. 'Time for bed, I think.'

'I can manage. If you'll just give me my stick, I can manage.' Marek stood swaying unsteadily.

Stefan shrugged, handed him the stick. 'For Christ's sake don't fall over and break the other leg.'

'I shan't.' Very much on his dignity, Marek made his slow and painstaking way to the door of his room. 'Goodnight.'

Danusia smiled. 'Goodnight.'

Jozik stirred, spluttered, snored once, extraordinarily loudly, then fell silent.

'Time for us all to turn in, I think.' Stefan, beside her, picked up her glass and tossed it back in one swallow. Then he tilted her chin, forcing her to look into his face. 'I'm sleeping in the barn.'

'Yes. I know.'

'It isn't far. Just across the yard.'

She said nothing.

He dropped his hand and stepped back. 'It's up to you.'

She stood up and went to him, kissing him long and gently. He did not move. 'Goodnight, Stefan,' she said, and left him.

The old woman was soundly and noisily asleep. Danusia undressed and slipped between the rough blankets. She heard the outer door close, heard Stefan's footsteps.

She lay for a very long time staring into the stifling darkness.

It was two in the morning and the house was quiet as the grave when she knew that the battle was lost. She reached in the darkness for her shirt and trousers, pulled them on and opened the door. In the small living-room the lamp still burned and Jozik still lay, dead to the world, his head on the table.

She passed him and pushed open the outside door. The velvet night was warm, no breath of air stirred the trees. The bulk of the small barn loomed in starlight.

A shadow in the shadowed night, Danusia slipped across the yard and into the dusty warmth where Stefan waited.

PART TWO

Stefan

Chapter Eleven

The morning was hot and almost unbearably sultry. On this, the first day of August, Warsaw sweltered, her streets airless, her vegetation – even the sturdy weeds that had made the rubble their own – parched and yellow.

Stefan, sweating in his overcoat, sat on the tram that was taking him to Wola, a suburb to the west of the city, watching through the window the activity in the streets, that for the time of day were unexpectedly and noticeably crowded. Everywhere there were young men and women, for the most part dressed as Stefan was, despite the weather, in high boots and shabby jackets or coats, some carrying bags or knapsacks, moving with unusual purpose about the drab and dusty city.

A little disturbingly, in the east an ominous silence had fallen. For days now the rumble and crump of artillery had boomed through the city as the Soviet Army had fought a pitched battle with the Germans for control of the suburb of Praga and the eastern bank of the Vistula. Now, quite suddenly – now, when a Russian break-through would mean so much – all was quiet.

The tram clanked past an apartment building whose

walls were plastered with the placards that had been posted everywhere by the Nazis a couple of days before, calling for one hundred thousand citizens of Warsaw to report for duty to dig fortifications around the threatened city.

No one had done so. The citizens of Warsaw had their own ideas about defending what was theirs.

Stefan lit a cigarette, careful as he tucked the crumpled packet back into his inside pocket not to reveal what nestled hidden beneath the heavy serge of his coat, though he was as sure as he could be that the middle-aged woman who sat beside him had already guessed at his errand, and at what he was carrying. She caught his eye, and smiled, and in her face was the same spark, the same hidden excitement that was apparent on those eager young faces in the streets. For days now Warsaw had been seething, a powder-keg ready to explode; and now, at last, the fuse was lit. There could be no going back.

They passed a heavily fortified German administrative building protected by barbed wire and a blockhouse, the windows of the first couple of stories blocked by sandbags. A machine-gun post had been set up in front of the well-guarded door.

How much did the Occupying Forces know? How much did they guess? Why, when until a few days ago they had been evacuating the city in what could only be described as panic, had they suddenly changed their minds and declared their intention of defending it?

How long was this damned tram going to take to get him to his unit's mustering point in Wola? Surely the journey had never been so long?

He looked at his watch. Nearly midday. The order to mobilise had reached him only an hour before; the all-important decision that the time at last was ripe to take up arms had been taken too late the night before for the orders to be dispatched before the curfew hour of eight o'clock; the consequent confusion and excitement was almost palpable as all over the city Home Army personnel tried to join their units ready for the action that was due to begin at five that afternoon.

And that brought another question – to Stefan perhaps the most worrying of all. Why the change of timing? So far as he was aware, all the insurgents' original battle plans, all of their training, had been geared to a surprise night attack, not to open rebellion on a hot Tuesday afternoon in broad daylight.

The tram rocked across an intersection. A tank lumbered menacingly across the open space, swivelled, settled like a primeval monster waiting for prey, the long barrel of its gun moving slowly, as if scenting the air for blood.

The Germans almost certainly knew or guessed that something was afoot, that the explosion was near. In a city of over a million inhabitants such a secret could not possibly be kept for long.

And then again, who knew? Perhaps the odd and apparently perilous haste in which the long-awaited orders had been issued would prove after all to give the insurgents an advantage. Perhaps Stefan's own misgivings – that there must surely be many would-be combatants who would not make it to their units in time, that it would certainly be almost impossible to organise the distribution of the well-hidden arms caches that had been so painstakingly built up over the past months, that to begin the fighting at five in the afternoon with the streets full of ordinary Varsovians returning home from a day's work would be bound to increase civilian casualties – would prove unfounded?

Perhaps.

The tram stopped. There was a surge of movement

among the passengers as Stefan, together with several other young men and women, stood up. The woman beside him touched his arm. 'Good luck, son,' she said quietly. 'May God bless you all.'

He stepped down on to the road. A little further along the street an armoured train clanked over the rails that encircled Warsaw, a train of steel, a grim, slow-moving and impersonal agent of destruction, its huge guns trained steadily upon the stirring city.

Stefan, pausing to watch it, found his hand reaching unconsciously for a rough, warm head, the quick touch of a wet tongue. With a brusque movement he shoved his hand in his pocket, felt the precious bullets stowed there. Bella, stoic but reproachful, had been left back in the Old Town with Danusia and Marek.

Looking around, sensing the all but unbearable tension and expectation that gripped the city and was awakening, however hard he tried to deny it, in his own blood, he found himself wondering, remarkably dispassionately, if he would ever see any of them again.

'What's going on out there?' Marek stood at the window of Danusia's room, looking out, as he had done once before in what now seemed another life, over the tiles and spires of the Old Town. 'How's it going?'

'Hard to tell.' Danusia had just come in, having spent the morning carrying messages and mobilisation orders about the city. 'The Germans are cracking down everywhere. I had a hell of a job getting round this morning. There must be some who didn't make it.'

'You think the Germans know?'

Danusia shrugged expressively. She looked tired and drawn but her eyes shone, and her colour was high. Marek thought she had never looked so beautiful.

She joined him at the window. Bella paced behind her,

shoved a mournful nose into her hand. 'It's starting,' Danusia said. 'At last it's – What was that?'

Marek leaned out of the window, listening. 'Gunfire. From the north.'

She looked at her watch. 'It's too early. It's only two o'clock.'

'Well, something's happening. Listen.'

They stood for a moment in silence. 'Zoliborz, I think,' said Danusia. 'They've jumped the gun. Someone was bound to, I suppose.' She walked to a chest and opened a drawer, pulled out two red and white armbands. Smiling, she came back to the window, handed one to Marek. 'Your uniform,' she said. And then, all laughter gone, she turned back to the view of the city that sweltered beyond the glassless window. 'By this time tomorrow – God willing – Warsaw will be Polish again.'

It was an understandable but misplaced hope; Stefan's more realistic fears were better founded. The precipitate way in which the Rising – so long anticipated, so long hoped-for – had finally been set in motion caused confusion and ill fortune from the start. Desperately-needed arms caches had to be abandoned when those few who knew of their whereabouts could not reach their units, or in some cases because the arms themselves were hidden in a part of the city too quickly controlled by the Germans. With nerves strung almost to breaking point and the explosive excitement brought on by the promise of action at last, it was inevitable that in some places fighting broke out too soon; in Zoliborz, to the north of the Old Town, the overhasty and overzealous insurgents opened fire on a car full of German police at two in the afternoon; in the three hours of heavy fighting that followed, the Poles suffered terrible losses, and their one advantage, that of surprise, was gone. By late afternoon, although they were still not entirely certain that the sporadic outbreaks of fighting in the city were to be the trigger for a major uprising, the Occupying Forces were on full alert. Well-armed, steel-helmeted men in field grey streamed into the city, occupying buildings and strong points. Tanks and mobile armoured guns took up strategic positions on the streets and bridges. Civilians caught in the pockets of fighting huddled in doorways and cellars, cut off from homes and families. Communications were difficult; in some cases impossible. Many Polish units found themselves fighting valiant but desperate individual actions instead of the co-ordinated attacks that had been planned, and their casualties were often heavy. Lack of arms and equipment had to be compensated for by personal valour, and a fierce, unflawed belief in their cause. Five brutal years of Occupation had forged a fighting spirit in Warsaw that would take on a tank with a home-made petrol bomb, a machine-gun nest with a pistol and bare hands. But courage – harshly, some might say foolhardiness – was never going to be enough. One by one the insurgent attacks against the main German positions were beaten off; the Vistula bridges remained in German hands, as did the airport, the radio station, the army and police headquarters, though their lines of communication were cut and the insurgents had managed to seize at least some valuable supplies of arms and ammunition. And still, in those parts of the city where the insurgents held, optimism and something close to joy swept the population.

Polish flags, carefully and secretly stored throughout the Occupation, or as carefully and secretly sewn against just such a day, appeared as if by magic, some in windows, some flying in the smoky wind high on the roofs of buildings occupied by the Poles, including the Prudential building, the highest in the city. One word was on everyone's lips, and that word was 'freedom'. They were

outgunned and outnumbered, they were poorly nour-
ished, poorly equipped – indeed there were many more
insurgents without arms than with – and flames licked
and roared already in large areas of their city. Yet at last
they were free. The barricaded streets were theirs. Women
and children gave flowers, cigarettes and sweets to the
insurgent soldiers as, in shabby civilian clothes or working overalls, their only uniform their forage caps and the
red and white armbands that at last they could wear
openly, they made their way to the front lines that wound
their way through the city. Willing hands helped to build
the barricades; paving stones, fences, rubble from ruined
buildings, large and small pieces of furniture – civilians
and insurgents worked side by side to block roads and
squares from attack by German tanks and troops. First
Aid posts were set up in houses and in shops. By the zero
hour of five o'clock, the fuse had burned through and the
powder-keg of the city had finally exploded; fifty-four
square miles of streets and squares, parks, buildings and
suburbs had been turned into an urban battlefield.

Marek saw little of that first day of the battle for the Old
Town. Knowing himself, with his poor eyesight and still
troublesome leg, to be nothing but a liability on the fighting front, he had volunteered to join one of the
Underground hospitals. So for those first hectic hours he
was kept busy tending to the less serious of the wounded
that were brought to the cellar dressing station, first in a
trickle then, as the fighting became worse, in a flood. It
was from them he heard the garbled and personalised
version of what was going on in the streets above.

The Germans were falling back, said one.

No, said another, they were advancing.

Zoliborz was lost, those defenders still alive having fled
to the forests.

Zoliborz was still fighting.

Old Town was cut off.

No; Old Town was still linked with the City Centre. This informant knew personally of a messenger girl reporting in from there.

The Russians were coming; they were to cross the river that very afternoon with arms and ammunition for the insurgents.

The Russian advance had been crushed; no help would be forthcoming there – if there had ever been any intention of such anyway.

This brought debate. Hadn't they all heard the Soviet radio appeal two days before that had spoken so stirringly of 'direct, active struggle in the streets of Warsaw, in its houses, factories and stores'? That had praised and encouraged the 'sons of Warsaw' and their determination to drive the 'Hitlerite vermin' from the sovereign land of Poland?

As he cleaned, disinfected and bandaged and handed out cigarettes, and as the building above them shook under artillery fire, Marek gave up trying to distinguish truth from wishful thinking. On a personal note he was simply aware that he had no idea where Danusia was, or whether Stefan had managed to reach Wola and join his unit before the fighting had started. When a smiling woman civilian came to relieve him for an hour, he made his way into the deserted building upstairs and stood in shock and awe looking out through the shattered window over fighting Warsaw.

An ill-smelling pall of smoke and dust hung above the city, the underside lurid with the glow of flames that licked and curled about the burning buildings. Sheaves of sparks eddied and flew in the swirling wind caused by the fires. A barricade had been hastily constructed at the end of the street; beyond it a German tank burned fiercely. A file of youngsters – little more than boys, Marek saw –

passed by on the other side of the street. Of perhaps a dozen, only the leader carried a carbine. The rest were armed with bottles filled with petrol. Marek had already heard of the directive to capture arms from the Germans even if it meant doing so initially by fighting with sticks and clubs. Incongruously, one of the youngsters had topped his shabby civilian outfit and armband with a German soldier's distinctive steel helmet.

Another explosion shook the building; the bombardment was intensifying. Behind the windows of a house further down the street flame flickered and smoke curled about the already blackened walls.

Marek stood for what seemed to be a very long time, appalled and fascinated by the sights and sounds of war. The whine of the shells, the deafening explosions, the staccato rattle of automatic fire and the sharp crack of individual shots. The shouts and occasional screams. The sound of running feet. The hell of high explosive and fire that ravaged a city of treasures. A city of culture and of music. A city that had cast the die and must now shake off the chains of Occupation, or perish.

Marek shifted, easing the pain of his leg; he had been standing in one place for too long. He shook his head, bemused. The peace, the quiet and the laughter of the almost idyllic sojourn in the country with Danusia, that had ended less than a week ago with their return to Warsaw, seemed a million miles, a million years, removed from this threatening, frightening chaos.

Danusia. Where was she? He looked again into the perilous beauty of fire and destruction beyond the window.

She might be dead already. Many were. He knew that for a fact.

His hands, his clothes – for all he knew his face – were caked with the blood of others. Once again he found himself praying to the God he did not believe in: keep

Danusia safe. Please. Do anything You like with me, but keep Danusia safe.

Further up the road a wall collapsed, the whole of the front of a building simply sliding into the street in a huge, billowing cloud of dust and sifting rubble.

As the dust settled, Marek heard something else, an odd sound, somehow, and yet the most natural in the world. It had begun to rain. He stood for a moment, listening, before he turned and went back down to the doubtful safety of the cellar.

No one could have projected the unprecedented savagery of those first few days of fighting. Within hours of the outbreak of the Uprising, Himmler, the Führer's right-hand man, had called in Berlin for the total destruction of the city and its inhabitants, insurgents and civilians alike. No prisoners were to be taken, no man, woman or child was to be left alive. Warsaw was to be reduced to ashes, a barbarous example to the rest of Europe. Warsaw had defied the Third Reich. Warsaw was to be made to suffer terribly for it.

In Warsaw, people had other ideas.

During that first day and night's fighting, over two thousand Home Army soldiers had been killed or injured; many more thousands were forced to flee the city and take refuge in the forests. Because of the pattern of the fighting at first the units of the Home Army had enormous problems of communication, and many of them fought individual and independent actions without having any idea of what was going on in the rest of the city. The problem was that the districts the insurgents held were cut off one from the other by the fiercely resisting German troops in a chequerboard effect that often brought to Marek's mind the thought of a bizarre game; a game of death and destruction. The past five years, however, had taught the Poles nothing if not ingenuity. Within a couple of days, improvised tunnels had been blasted through the cellars and basements of the city, creating signposted and patrolled underground routes from district to district. Since, after seventeen desperate hours of fighting, the Home Army had succeeded in taking the main electricity station, it was even possible to light them. Where it could be done, tunnels were dug beneath roads held by German tanks and artillery, or – more dangerously – crossing points were set up for those whose business took them about the city; carrying messages, arms, supplies. In her capacity as a messenger, Danusia was one of the first to use these routes, and one of the first places to which she was sent was Wola, where General Bor-Komorowski's GHQ was situated and where Stefan was fighting.

'Did you see him?' Marek asked when she came to find him at the hospital. It was late evening, and the fighting had died down. Despite the rain that still fell, the skies above the city were lit angrily by the glow of the inferno beneath.

'Yes. Briefly. He's all right. He's seen some heavy fighting – he was in the unit that took the Post Office building.'

'He isn't hurt?'

'No.'

'What's the situation? Does anyone know?'

She shrugged tiredly. 'So far as I can make out, we're holding the City Centre, Wola, a couple of districts along the Vistula – and here, of course. There's new fighting in Zoliborz. And we're holding Mokotow. The Nazis do seem to have been taken by surprise. They've called for reinforcements. There's talk of aid coming to us from the West – drops of arms and ammunition. And there's still hope the Russians will help us with supplies, if not with men. A few more days, Marek, and it could be over. Our people are fighting magnificently. They can't lose. They can't! God wouldn't let it happen!'

Marek said nothing.

'I'm off duty for a couple of hours.' Danusia looked around. 'Is there anything I can do here?'

'Don't be silly.' He took her arm gently, and turned her towards the door. 'Go and get some rest. You're dog tired.'

She grinned at him suddenly. 'That reminds me. Guess who was the first person that Stefan enquired after?'

'No contest. Bella.'

'Right first time.' She yawned, rubbed her eyes with dirty hands. 'P'raps I will go home for a while. I'm back out again at midnight.'

'Be careful.'

'I will.' She pushed her hair behind her ear. 'It's good to know that Stefan's safe, isn't it?'

'Yes. It is.' But better to know that you are, even if only for a couple of hours. He did not voice the thought aloud, and could not even face the one that followed it. Not for the first time he turned his mind from the knowledge that his half-brother was in the thick of the fighting, that Stefan being Stefan would not seek safety. That Stefan might die. And if he did –

Someone called. He snapped out of his reverie. 'Sorry. Coming.'

The danger in which Stefan and his comrades stood was indeed deadlier than any of them knew, though this did not become apparent until two or three days later. As the Occupying Forces rallied and were reinforced and still no outside help reached the Home Army fighters, plans were laid literally to smash a way through the insurgent-held centre of the city to reopen German lines of communication and to divide the City Centre from the Old Town. The drive was to be from the west to the east, from the working-class suburb of Wola with its narrow streets and cramped tenements to the Vistula. And Himmler's edict, his sentence upon the city and its inhabitants, had not been forgotten. No prisoners were to be taken, no quarter given to fighters and civilians alike. No building was to be left standing, no sanctuary left, no hiding-place. Wola was to be wiped out.

The troops that were to implement this barbarous policy were well chosen; the brigade known to all as Dirlewanger's criminals – thieves, murderers, rapists, thugs, who had been released from prison on condition that they fight to the death for the Fatherland, and a brigade of renegade Cossacks commanded by SS Brigadeführer Kaminski, a notoriously hard-drinking deserter from the Red Army.

The attack was begun by the Luftwaffe shortly after dawn on August 5th, wave after wave of bombers thundering at rooftop height to drop their loads of high explosive and incendiary bombs upon the crowded, mostly wooden, houses that were packed with civilians and refugees. In no time the district was an inferno. Men, women and children fled in panic towards the centre of the city, driven like sheep before the advance of the German brigades, slaughtered like animals if they were caught. Thousands died, trapped by fire or by the rampaging troops. Hospitals were burned, the wounded murdered by fire, by bullet or by a casual blow with a rifle-butt. Where the insurgents dug in and tried to halt the advance, civilians were driven in front of German tanks as human shields. Women were raped, children murdered. Cellars crowded with terrified people had flame-throwers turned upon them or grenades tossed down the stairs. In the days and nights of terror that followed that first attack, between forty and fifty thousand people lost their lives and the district of Wola was all but

wiped out. The new commander of the city, General von
dem Bach, to his credit, tried to stop the rampage by
countermanding Himmler's infamous order, but it was
too late. The Cossacks were drunk, the bloodlust of
Dirlewanger's Brigade was aroused beyond control, and
the orgy of slaughter went on.

In the comparative safety of the Old Town Danusia and
Marek listened in growing horror to the tales that were
emerging from the battleground of Wola. They heard
nothing of Stefan apart from a report from a bedraggled,
badly wounded Home Army soldier that he had been
seen still alive on the second day of the fighting. After
that, the battle had become a desperate street-by-street,
house-by-house affair and communications had broken
down almost entirely.

They could do nothing but wait, listening to the distant
clamour, watching the blood-red sky to the west.

Danusia came off duty late on Tuesday night and made
her way back to the apartment house with a heavy heart.
Most of the occupants spent the best part of their time
and all of their nights in the cellar for fear of bombardment. Danusia hated the cellar; it was hot, overcrowded
and, no matter what attempts were made to keep it clean,
smelled horribly. The thought of sleeping down there was
to her infinitely more awful than the thought of a stray
shell. She climbed the stairs slowly and opened the door
of her room. A candle flickered on the table. She stood for
one heart-stopping moment before throwing herself upon
the grim figure who sat, exhausted, on a patched and
grimy chair, his head bowed, his face buried in Bella's
rough fur.

'Stefan! Oh, Stefan! We thought you were dead!
There've been such terrible stories! Stefan, Stefan, Stefan!'
Tears ran down her cheeks and she clung to him fiercely.

He did not move except to turn his head slightly, to rest

it in the curve of her shoulder. He was filthy dirty, smelled rankly of smoke and cordite and was very thin. But it was when he lifted his head at last and turned to look at her that she caught her breath at the change in him; for the change was in his eyes, sunk deep and burning in his haggard face.

'Stefan – what's wrong? Are you hurt? Are you sick?'

He smiled a small, bitter smile, shook his head.

'Wola?' she asked after a moment. 'What's happened? Has Wola fallen?'

He stretched out a hand to the dog's head again. 'There is no Wola,' he said at last. 'Wola has been destroyed. Razed to the ground. Savaged by beasts.' His voice was hoarse, almost unrecognisable. He lifted his head and looked at her again, and again she winced at the expression in his eyes. 'We need help against these filthy bastards, Danusia. We need weapons, we need support from our allies. If it doesn't come – if we should fail –' he stopped for a moment, cleared his throat, wiped spittle that was black with smoke from his lips – 'then God help Warsaw and Christ preserve her people.'

Chapter Twelve

Stefan slept, fully clothed except for his boots, for the best part of twenty-four hours, almost without stirring, and without knowing that as he slept the Germans won the ferocious battle to open their lines of communication across the city to the Kierbedz Bridge. In doing so they also succeeded in cutting off the insurgent-held Old Town from the City Centre to the south, that was also in Polish hands, and Zoliborz to the north. With Wola lost, the Home Army Headquarters had now been established in the Old Town; encircled by the enemy, the various Polish-held districts were isolated one from the other; each was left to fight its own battle alone and unsupported. And each did, to great effect. The initial euphoria may have died, the unrealistic conviction of an early victory may have faded, but the heart was still there as well as the staunch courage, and the will to be a people once more, to throw off the yoke of the oppressor. Too many people had suffered too terribly. There was no alternative but to fight, if necessary to the death.

Stefan woke, finally, to the sound of gun- and artillery-fire; a sound that had echoed eerily in his nightmares. His head throbbed and he was ravenously hungry. He swung his feet to the floor and buried his head in his hands. There was a quiet movement beside him and a strong, cold nose nuzzled him. He put an arm about the shaggy black neck and rested his unshaven cheek on the dog's head. The two sat like that for a very long time, still as statues. At last Stefan raised a weary head. 'Bella,' he said, his voice still hoarse from the smoke of Wola, 'this stinking world doesn't deserve to survive, you know that? What have we done to ourselves? What dog would treat his kind the way man treats his own?' As so often, he spoke to the dog in English.

Bella leaned against him. Never heavily built, she too had lost weight; he could feel the bone and sinew of her through the warm fur.

He straightened his aching back, rubbed her ears roughly. 'No quarter, they said, and no quarter they gave.' The words were quiet, and bitter. 'Women. Children. Tiny babies. The sick and the wounded. Nuns and priests. Doctors and nurses. They tortured them, they slaughtered them and then, dead or alive, they burned them. Well, now it's my turn. One bullet, one German. Until it's over for us all, Bell, I'll take at least what revenge I can for those poor benighted souls. By Christ I will.'

He stood, wincing, and padded to where a cracked mirror hung at a wild angle on the wall, peered into it, studied the haggard, dirty, unshaven face with a certain mild astonishment. 'God Almighty!' he said in a conversational tone to the dog, 'you could scare children with that on Hallowe'en!' He turned, smiled for the first time in days as the dog watched him, tongue lolling, huge dark eyes trusting on his. He dropped to one knee, beckoned her to him. 'You don't care, do you, old girl? You don't give a damn what I look like, or where I've been, or what I've seen, or been doing, or what I'll do in the future.

You're just glad I'm back. Well, so am I. I don't know how the hell I made it, but I did. And now I'll show those bastards that they didn't get us all.' He reached for his boots, pulled them on, picked up his rifle. 'Come on, my lovely. Food first, if we can find any, then we start.'

A couple of hours later, with a bowl of hot soup inside him and in defiance of a German air attack that rocked the city to its foundations, he succeeded in finding the remnants of his unit encamped, with its one most senior surviving officer, in a school near the Market Square. There were pitifully few of them and they were to be attached to one of the Home Army units already operating in the Old Town.

Stefan had other ideas; and within the hour, having received more than willing permission to put his personal request to a contact in Home Army HQ, Captain Stefan Anderson had been seconded to the special duties to which he was particularly suited, as a sniper.

This was work that he was predictably good at. From the doubtful shelter of the gaunt and shattered buildings that constituted the meandering front lines of this bizarre battlefield, his deadly accuracy as a marksman came into its own. Whether backing the defenders of a barricade that had come under attack – two or three German officers coolly picked off could turn the tide of a dangerous assault – or nesting alone in a building near a German-held thoroughfare, he rarely missed his chosen target. One bullet, one German; his motto, and his success in implementing it, became a byword. Nor, as the days wore on and the battle for control of the Old Town grew more intense, was his rifle the only weapon the enemy had to fear; the slender, razor-sharp knife he wore always at his belt was a weapon of silence and moreover provided the added advantage of saving ammunition.

The Poles were not the only ones to use snipers to pin

down and demoralise the enemy – indeed because of the fact that the Home Army had no regular uniform apart from the familiar red and white armbands, and because those that acquired uniforms frequently did so from dead or captured Germans, it was relatively easy for enemy marksmen to infiltrate the lines and take up a position in the ruins within the embattled enclave of the Old Town itself, picking off a target and then disappearing into the crowds, an anonymous soldier in a city that was full of them. Civilians queuing for water or for supplies, the Boy Scouts who scrambled through the shattered streets delivering messages and letters, volunteers building and repairing barricades, all were considered legitimate targets. As Stefan well knew, a lone sniper, with nerve and a good supply of ammunition, could pin down an entire unit and inflict disproportionately high casualties, especially if the attack came from an unexpected direction; it was here that he used his hunting skills to most advantage. He became known for his ability to stalk and flush out these sometimes recklessly courageous German or Ukrainian marksmen, and rarely did his quarry survive. In his own way, and on his own terms, Stefan was waging a deadly one-man campaign to avenge the dead of Wola. Danusia had no problems with that; her worry was that she suspected he was in danger of coming to enjoy it.

The three of them – Danusia having been bombed out of the building in which she had been initially billeted – had taken up unofficial residence in a cellar beneath a burned-out building near the centre of the Old Town. Their different duties and involvement in the fighting meant that they saw little of one another, but here at least they had a meeting place, a central point of contact, and Bella guarded it well for them. In the week that followed the fall and destruction of Wola, the enemy turned his full fury upon the Old Town in an attempt to destroy Polish resistance once and for all. Wave after furious wave of infantry attack, preceded by air attack and artillery bombardment, battered the hard-pressed and ill-equipped insurgents day after day, but street by street and building by building – sometimes floor by floor and room by room – they stubbornly held out, and sometimes even counter-attacked successfully. Despite the difficulties and dangers and the obstinate withholding of help by the Russians, some Allied planes got through and managed to drop supplies; and though inevitably much of those supplies fell to the enemy, at least some of them reached the hands for whom they were intended, and the effect on morale was remarkable.

Casualties were high. Four days after Stefan's return, Marek volunteered as a medic to help recover the wounded, insurgent and civilian, from the streets.

'Marek, you really shouldn't,' Danusia said, worriedly 'Your leg –'

'Oh, blast my leg! There are a lot of people far worse off than me doing far more, and you know it.' The usually even-tempered Marek was red-eyed and snappish. In that he was not alone. The almost ceaseless air raids, the lack of sleep or of adequate rations, the constant and imminent threat of death or injury were taking their toll on most people's nerves. Even at night, when for a very few short hours the fighting died down, many found themselves unable to rest.

'I only meant –'

'I know.' He came to her quickly, put an arm about her shoulders. 'I know. I'm sorry. But I feel I need to do more than I'm doing. I'm a man and I'm strong. It's no good wasting a gun on me, we both know that. This way at least I'm out there doing something positive.'

She nodded tiredly. 'Yes. I do see. It's just – these people work under fire – and they aren't even armed.' She lifted her head to look at him. 'Oh, Marek, do please be careful? It's bad enough worrying about Stefan –'

'Stefan? Who's worrying about Stefan?' The voice, quiet and amused, came from the open doorway. A familiar figure, long gun slung from his shoulder, leaned in the shadows against the doorjamb. Bella ambled to him, licked a greeting.

'No one,' Danusia said. 'Everyone knows that Stefan can look after himself.'

'True enough.' He came into the room, stood looking around speculatively. He carried a bulky canvas bag, and now as he stepped into the lamplight Danusia saw he was carrying not one gun but two. His eye lighted upon the low pallet bed in the corner. Swiftly he bent, and first the strange weapon and then the canvas bag were slipped quickly beneath it. 'There. That will have to do.' He straightened.

'What's in the bag?' Marek asked.

'Gold dust.' Stefan laughed at their suddenly startled expressions. 'Ammunition,' he explained amiably.

'Where did that come from?' Everyone knew that ammunition was even more strictly rationed than food. It was the lifeblood of the Rising and kept it alive.

'I – found it.'

'Found it? What do you mean, "found it"?'

'What I say.' Stefan threw himself into a rickety chair and reached to pull his boots off. 'I found it. In an attic in Brzozowa Street. The gentleman to whom it belonged – well, let's say he doesn't need it any more.'

'You have a gun,' said Danusia. 'Aren't you supposed to hand captured weapons in?'

'Oh, I don't think so, do you?' Stefan spoke easily. 'Fair's fair. I had to climb up five flights of stairs to get it. And there weren't many left. Stairs, I mean. Bella, what

are you like – what use are you?' he added in English.
'You'd think at least you'd learn to help me off with my
boots, you silly sod.'

'And what was at the top of the stairs when you got
there?' Danusia asked.

'A sniper's nest. Neat and sweet as you like. An enemy
sniper's nest. All feathered and fine. They do look after
their own. Which reminds me –' he reached into a pocket
and pulled out a bottle, two-thirds full – 'good German
Schnapps.' He eyed Danusia amusedly. 'You think I
should turn that in too?'

'You killed him?'

'I killed him.'

'Good. I hate those bloody people.' She looked around.
'We haven't got any glasses.'

Stefan pulled the cork from the bottle with his teeth,
took a swig, handed it to her. 'Who needs glasses?' he
asked peaceably, as the ground suddenly shook and a
blast of hot air gusted into the cellar. 'Here they come
again, the bastards.'

Marek turned. 'I'd better go.'

His brother's hand caught his wrist as he passed. 'Wait.'

'But –'

'Wait. You'll be of use to no one blown to bits. Wait.
There'll be work enough for us all later.'

The words, from Marek's point of view, were horribly
prophetic.

Later that day the Germans attacked a barricade with
three tanks; coming under fire, the two larger tanks withdrew, while the third, under covering fire from the
German infantry, was abandoned. Euphoric at their victory, the insurgents dismantled part of the barricade and
drove their prize through it. A huge and excited crowd
gathered about it. Just over half an hour later the booby-
trapped vehicle exploded, killing hundreds and maiming

many more. Marek did not get back to the cellar that was home that night.

'Stefan?'

Stefan took his eyes from the hand of cards he was playing and lifted his head.

'The German rifle.' Danusia hesitated. 'Please? May I have it?'

'No.' The word came out on the instant and with no thought.

'Stefan, *please!*'

'No. I'm sorry, but no.'

'Why not? You don't need it.'

'I might.'

'*Stefan!*'

'No.'

Danusia threw down her cards and turned from him. In the darkness of the summer night a spasmodic burst of machine-gun fire echoed and died. A glimmer beyond the open door of the cellar showed that the fires caused by the incendiary raid of the afternoon still burned. There was a long silence.

'Why do you want it?' Stefan asked.

She flung back to him, enraged. 'Why? *Why?* You know why! I want to fight! Women are fighting – you know they are!'

'Of course. And well. But you have duties of your own.'

'A messenger girl! Penned in because there's no way through to the other sectors. Stefan, I've had enough! I want to fight! If I had a gun, any unit would welcome me – you know it! I can shoot – you do know that, don't you?'

'You're a country girl,' Stefan said, and lifted the bottle of schnapps to his lips. 'Come of the landed gentry.' His face was expressionless. 'Of course you can shoot.'

'Then –?'

'No.'

'I could take it,' she said.

'Don't try.' His words were gentle. 'It's mine.'

'But you already have a gun!' She stood watching him, eyes blazing with anger. 'I'll report you.'

He shrugged.

She tried once more. 'Stefan. Please?'

He shook his head.

She knew the look too well. Shaking with fury, she turned her back on him. 'You're a stubborn bastard, you know that?'

He did not bother to reply. Quiet had fallen over the still-burning city outside. Water was too short to be wasted upon the fires; ancient timber roared and glowed and shivered to ash. Swirling columns of sparks rose into the pall of smoke that hung constantly over the city.

Stefan let the silence lengthen. Then he stood and came to her, turned her to face him. 'Come on, now, don't be silly.'

'Don't patronise me, Stefan.' The words were very quiet, the anger in them pent and chill.

He stood looking down at her for a long time. Then, 'It looks as if Marek isn't coming back,' he said softly, lifting a hand to cup her face and bending to kiss her.

She stood like stone, rigid and still, her mouth hard under his.

He straightened, sketched a small, sardonic salute. 'I see. I'm dismissed, am I?'

She said nothing.

He shrugged, turned to pull his boots back on. 'May as well go and see if anyone else fancies my company, then.'

She watched him, grim-faced, refusing to speak, refusing to ask him to stay.

He stood, reached for his gun, ruffled the dog's ears. 'Take care of her for me, Bell.'

At the door he stopped and turned. 'I won't be so crass as to remind you that at the moment time is probably the most precious commodity we have,' he said quietly.

'The soldier going to war? We may all be dead tomorrow?' In her anger and exhaustion the cold words were out before she could prevent them.

His mouth tightened. 'So be it. But, Danka,' he pointed to where the German gun was concealed, 'don't touch it. You hear? German ammunition doesn't fit my gun. It fits that. I can always capture more; and I can make better use of it than most.'

'One bullet, one German,' she said. 'Are you determined to fight this bloody war on your own?'

He nodded. 'Something like that.' And he was gone into the smoky night.

It was a full minute before she moved. Then she turned and dropped on to the pallet bed, head bowed, tears sliding in silence down her dirty cheeks. 'Damn him!' she said. 'Oh, damn him!'

On the few occasions that their paths crossed in the next few days – and they were, Danka suspected deliberately on Stefan's part, very few – the atmosphere between them was strained. As the Germans brought more and more reinforcements into Warsaw the attacks on the Old Town intensified, and by now the desperate resistance the Poles were still putting up was beginning to worry the Nazi leaders. On the whole, insurgent tactics when attacked head on were simple but effective. German assault troops, often even when they were backed up by tanks, would be allowed to advance almost to a barricade with no resistance; then at the last moment the machine-guns would open up, Piat mortars, petrol bottles and hand grenades would be used against tanks and personnel carriers, snipers posted high in nearby buildings would pick off the officers. As German intelligence was remarkably poor, they had only a very general idea of how many insurgents they were actually facing in the various Polish enclaves; if there were consistent reports that the Poles were short of arms and ammunition, the intensity of the fighting did not appear to bear them out.

A week after the fall of Wola, Allied planes again got through and managed to drop supplies, but at huge cost to the brave crews who flew the missions. Of seventy-nine aircraft, only twenty won through to the gallant, burning city. Fifteen aircraft and more than one hundred crew were lost. Many of those who returned were badly wounded. The supplies were welcome, and boosted morale, but no one who watched helplessly from below as the friendly planes were pinned in German searchlights and raked with anti-aircraft fire, no one who saw aircraft after aircraft wiped from the skies in a sheet of flame, believed that such carnage could continue. And still the Russians, so close that their guns could be heard, refused to help.

Marek set down his end of the stretcher on which lay a badly wounded man, straightened, and staggered. He was dead on his feet; he had eaten little and slept not at all in the past twenty-four hours.

'Get some rest, man.' The weary doctor who had come to his side laid a hand on his arm. 'You're no good to man nor beast as you are. It's a little quieter. See if you can get your head down for a couple of hours.'

'But –'

'It's an order,' the man said gently, his haggard face stark in the lamplight. The man on the stretcher seemed to have stopped breathing.

Wearily Marek nodded.

He stumbled through the subterranean system of

cellars and passages that led towards the centre of the town. The route was busy, and had been disrupted by the complete destruction of a building that had collapsed, blocking the way. Already a well-worn and signposted path led round the obstruction. Many of the cellars were full of people and of what pathetic belongings they had managed to rescue from their wrecked homes: a bundle here, a mattress there, the odd chair, a holy statue with a candle burning before it, a photograph pinned upon the wall. In the corner of one such underground room a young couple made love, ignoring entirely the ceaseless shuffle of feet through the dust and rubble scarcely half a dozen yards from them.

There was, Marek noticed not for the first time, little communication now between the fighters who made their way through these passages and the civilians who huddled helplessly in them for shelter. The euphoria of those first few days was gone; now more and more people had begun to question. What had happened to the fine plans for an early victory? What was to become of the civilian population if the Rising failed? There were too many stories, too many rumours, of what had happened after the fall of Wola for anyone to be sanguine at the thought. Some of these people had been trapped here since the precipitate start of the Rising, cut off from their homes and families by the fighting, not knowing if their loved ones were alive or dead. Food was scarce; most of the horses in the Old Town had already been eaten, and they had started on the dogs and cats. Children, and in particular babies, were beginning to die of starvation. Little wonder, then, that the relationship between fighters and civilians was becoming strained.

Tired as he was when he came to the point where a short scramble overground would take him to the cellar he shared with the other two, Marek quickened his pace;

the concern that had been nagging at the back of his mind for twenty-four hours pushing him on. Danusia had gone out two days earlier and he had not seen her since. Surely she must have come back by now? If she were not at the cellar, there might at least be some indication that she had come home and left again. Some indication that she was alive.

Flinching from the thought, he stumbled through the rubble, ducked his head into the passage that led down into the cellar and saw the glimmer of light around the door. He flung it open in relief. 'Danka!' He stopped.

Stefan paused in the act of lighting a cigarette. Shook his head. 'Sorry, no. It's me.'

Marek glanced around the room. The only thing that had changed since he had left was that Bella was gnawing on the carcass of what could only be a dead rat. There was no sign that Danusia had been back. 'Where the hell is she?'

'Has she been gone for long?'

Marek rubbed his face tiredly. 'A couple of days. At least. She's never been missing for so long before.'

Stefan shrugged a little, lit his cigarette. 'She could be anywhere. There's to be an attempt to break through to Zoliborz tonight, to join up with our forces there. There's a lot of activity. She's probably busy.' He lifted his head as an explosion shook the room and flakes of plaster dropped from the ceiling. 'That was close.'

Marek paced restlessly. 'I don't know what to do – I don't know whether to go and look for her.'

'Oh, don't be daft! Look for her? In this lot?'

'The hospitals – the field stations –'

'Marek, for Christ's sake calm down. There's nothing you can do. She'll come back or she won't, it's as simple as that –'

Marek stared at him. 'You cold-hearted bastard!'

Stefan looked at him long and steadily. Then, unexpectedly he put his hand in his pocket and tossed something on the table. 'Present for you.'

It was a pair of wire-rimmed glasses. Marek picked them up. Tried them on. 'I say – hell, that's better!'

'Sure? I can always steal another pair,' Stefan said, straightfaced.

'No, really. Thanks.' The last word was awkward.

'Thought you might as well at least see who's shooting at you.' Stefan pushed himself away from the table. 'I have to go. Do me a favour?'

'What's that?'

'Make sure you shut the door when you leave. Don't let Bella out on her own. I don't want her ending up in someone's stewpot.'

'Of course.'

Stefan slipped his gun on to his shoulder, raised a hand and was gone, leaving the puzzled and exasperated Marek to wonder whether his half-brother really was more concerned about his dog than about the missing Danusia.

Chapter Thirteen

Marek had no idea how long he had been asleep when Bella's bark woke him. He sat up, muzzy-headed. The dog was by the door, her flag of a tail wagging excitedly. A moment later the door opened.

'Danka!' He was on his feet in a moment and had thrown his arms about her, almost sweeping her from her feet. 'Where have you been? God, I've been so worried.' He stopped, sniffed, stepped back from her in surprise.

She pulled a face, smiling tiredly. 'Horrible, isn't it? And that's after they spared me some water to wash.' She tossed the bundle she was carrying on to the table.

'Where have you been?' he asked again.

She lifted her head. 'I've been to the City Centre.'

It took a moment for the words to sink in. He stared at her. 'You can't have been!'

She said nothing.

'There's no way through. It's been cut off for two weeks or more.'

'There's a way now. It isn't pleasant, but it is a way.'

'How? Where?'

'Through the sewers. They've opened up a route to Zoliborz, too. Some of our men went through last night. General Pelczynski is hoping to take the Germans by surprise and consolidate the two districts. From what I hear, no one seems to believe he has much of a chance, but there you are. God, I'm tired.'

He dragged a chair forward. 'Sit down. Christ, I'm pleased to see you! I thought –' He stopped.

She smiled and laid her head wearily against his shoulder. 'Dear Marek.' She stood for a moment, quite still, resting against him. Gently he put an arm about her shoulders and drew her to him.

She laughed a little. 'I smell atrocious!'

His arm tightened about her. He closed his eyes. 'I love you.'

'Marek –' She tried to pull away from him.

He held her to him. 'Don't say anything. You don't have to say anything. I just want you to know. When I thought – when I thought something had happened to you – I so wished I had told you. I kept thinking I might never see you again. I love you. I'm not asking for anything, not demanding anything. I just want you to know. We both know it's unlikely we'll get out of this alive. I didn't want to die without telling you. That's all.'

'Don't!' She flung back her head fiercely. 'Don't talk like that! We have to believe we'll survive! We have to believe we'll win! Or it's all for nothing!'

He said nothing.

'The Russians will come; sooner or later, they'll come. Or the Allies will break through to Berlin – something will happen, Marek, something will happen to help us! I know it! Please, my love, don't give up hope now.'

He put her from him, stood looking down at her, a quizzical look on his thin face. 'What did you call me?' he asked softly.

Her lashes veiled her eyes and she would not look at him.

An ominous quiet had fallen outside, of the kind that quite often preceded a fresh attack. Through the open door the sky was eerily lit with white flares that hung above the shattered ruins of the town like fierce goblin lanterns.

He tilted her face towards him. 'What did you call me?' he asked again.

Her eyes met his, but still she said nothing.

'You do care for me?' he asked at last. 'At least a little?'

'You know I do. Oh, Marek, you know I do!' In a moment she was in his arms again, this time clinging to him as if she would never let him go.

He drew a long, quiet breath before saying in quite a different tone, 'And that's not just because I've put aside half a loaf of bread and some cheese for you?'

'Oh, good Lord! *Cheese?*'

'To say nothing of half a bottle of good red wine.'

'I don't believe it!'

He grinned. 'Stefan isn't the only forager in this outfit.'

'Cheese!' she said again. 'I haven't tasted cheese in weeks! My mouth's watering at the thought.' She pulled herself up and lifted a finger. 'You do know I'll kill you if you're joking?'

He laughed. 'I'm not joking. An old lady gave it to me yesterday. The cheese and the wine, that is. The bread's normal rations. It seems that a boy I dug out of a cellar the other day is her grandson.' He went to a box in the corner.

Danusia watched him. 'You're limping badly,' she said suddenly.

He shrugged, came back to the table. 'A little.'

'Your leg's hurting again?'

'Eat your cheese.' He had laid bread and a small piece of cheese in front of her.

She sat and looked at it. Picked it up. Licked it. 'Mmmm!'

He watched her, smiling. Bella had come to join them, her head on Danusia's knee, her great eyes longingly on the cheese.

Marek pushed aside the bundle that Danusia had laid on the table and set the wine bottle down.

'Oh, I forgot –' Danusia reached for the bundle, untied the string, shook out a heavy camouflage shirt – 'here. There's one each. Get rid of the SS insignia, though, or we'll all get ourselves shot!'

'Where did they come from?'

'Our boys captured a store full of them. Everyone's wearing them.' She nibbled a tiny corner from the cheese. 'God, this is good.'

He took a sip from the wine bottle and handed it to her. They both turned their heads to the door as the unnatural quiet was broken by the sudden crackle of machine-gun fire and the crash of grenades. Within seconds the roar of artillery had joined the cacophony as shells rained death once more on the beleaguered city. Marek stood up. 'Something's happening. I'd better go.'

She held out a hand. He took it, allowed her to draw him down to her. Very gently she slipped a hand behind his head and guided his lips to hers. As the world outside disintegrated once more into a hell of high explosive and crumbling buildings she kissed him, her mouth very soft beneath his. At last she drew back. 'Be careful,' she said.

'I will.'

She smiled. 'Thank you for the cheese.'

'My pleasure. Enjoy it.' He kissed her again, very lightly, and straightened, picking up his jacket. Almost at the door he remembered something, turned back to the table and picked up the glasses Stefan had given him. He perched them on his nose, grinned at her. 'As Stefan pointed out, I might as well see who's shooting at me.' He lingered for a moment longer to watch her smile before he ducked through the doorway and out once more into the lurid dust- and smoke-filled darkness that was the Warsaw night.

The attempted break-through to Zoliborz was a failure; in the blazing hot summer days that followed, the German General von dem Bach methodically set about reducing the Polish-held enclaves one by one, and his first target was the insurgent-held Old Town. Conditions here were already a nightmare; streets and courtyards were so filled with rubble it was almost impossible to move about, food and ammunition were running out, the hospitals had had no anaesthetics for days. In the intense summer heat the place swarmed with flies and the smell of death was terrible on the air. The time had long passed when armies of ready volunteers were available to dig the dead and the wounded from beneath shell- and bomb-shattered buildings. No one knew how many had died.

At eight in the morning on 19 August, almost three weeks after the start of the Rising, a massive German attack was launched. Ten battalions of infantry and several platoons of flame-throwers were supported by dive-bombing Stukas, Tiger tanks, fifty so-called 'Goliaths' – remote-controlled vehicles filled with high explosive – howitzers, mortars, the fire-power of the fearsome armoured train to the north and a gunboat on the Vistula to the east. The effect was devastating. Marek, who found himself trapped by the battle near the Royal Palace where the most bitter, close-fought and long-drawn out of the fighting was taking place, could not believe it possible that brick still stood upon brick nor stone upon stone. Death thundered and rained over the city. Fires burned out of control. The dead and the wounded were everywhere. And still every barricade, every building, every inch of every unrecognisable street was defended, sometimes literally, to the last drop of Polish blood.

A makeshift first aid post had been set up in the cellar of what had once been a chemist's shop. Two doctors and four nuns tended the endless stream of wounded, with precious little more than skill and faith, even the most basic of supplies having run out. Marek, himself blooded – and luckily only that – by a splinter of shrapnel that had grazed his upper arm painfully, had teamed up with a boy of about fifteen called Michal and volunteered to help bring in the wounded. Michal was a cheerful lad, veteran of five years of Occupation and alive to tell of it. To Marek's amusement he was inordinately proud of the fact that his newly acquired partner was an Englishman parachuted in by the RAF.

'That's what I'm going to do,' he announced, lips clamped on the stub of a cigarette, eyes half-closed against the smoke of it, 'when I can get out of here. Join the RAF.' He leaned out of the doorway in which they were sheltering and made a basic and obscene gesture to the sky, where the wheeling and unhindered Stukas strafed and bombed the city through a pall of smoke. 'I'll get one of those buggers one day, see if I don't.' He, like Marek himself, wore one of the looted SS shirts, and a German forage cap was set at a rakish angle on his lank and dirty straw-coloured hair. 'Look out!' He turned and slammed Marek back against the door behind them. A second later a shell exploded further down the street and the front of a building slid in an avalanche of choking dust into the road.

A small group of armed men ran past, dodging from doorway to doorway. One stopped on seeing the red cross on Marek's armband. 'There's a woman and a kid back there –' he gestured back in the direction from which they had come – 'they need help.' He ran on.

Marek and Michal worked their way carefully down the road. Reaching what had once been a tree-lined square but was now simply an open, ruined space paved with rubble, they saw the woman; she lay sprawled, unmoving, in a pool of blood. Beside her a small, half-clothed child, thin and dirty but demonstrably alive, screamed hysterically above the sounds of battle.

'The woman's dead,' said Marek.

'The kid isn't.' Michal started forward.

Marek grabbed him. 'Wait!'

Michal shook off the restraining hand. 'We can't leave the poor little bastard there.' He ran, crouched low, dodging and weaving, to where the woman and child lay. Without stopping, he snatched the screaming child from the ground and ran on towards the shelter of a ruined building on the other side of the street. He almost made it. Above the rattle of machine-gun fire in the next street Marek heard the single crack of a rifle shot. Michal stumbled and sprawled, still clutching the child. He lay for a moment among the dust and the rubble, unmoving, then slowly and painfully he began to crawl.

The sniper's second bullet shattered his skull.

The child, dazed and bloody, had stopped screaming. It sat, perhaps a dozen yards from safety, beside the dead boy.

A plane howled overhead, very low, the black crosses on the undersides of its wings seeming almost close enough to touch. Marek ducked as its guns strafed the street, then, bent double, made a limping dash for the other side of the road, expecting at any moment the bullet that would maim or kill him.

It did not come. The marksman had, it seemed, been distracted by the plane.

Marek began to work his way through the ruins towards where the child still sat. In a matter of moments he was at the spot closest to it, crouched in the shelter of an unsupported, leaning wall. Above him an empty fireplace set into a wallpapered wall was all that was left of the house that had once stood here.

Michal was dead, his young face shattered, flies buzzing already around the stickiness of his blood.

The child, a boy of perhaps eighteen months, whimpered softly. Marek dropped on to his hands and knees and began to crawl towards it.

Two shots came in quick succession. A bullet screamed over Marek's head. He flinched, and kept crawling. In a couple of moments he was by the child's side, pulling him down close to him, using Michal's body as a shield. He lay still for a moment, waiting for another bullet. None came.

Clutching the now screaming child under one arm he began awkwardly to haul himself back into the shelter of the wall. Just as he reached it, a group of young men and women wearing the distinctive red and white armbands of the insurgents ran into the street, scattering into doorways. A girl dropped beside Marek, panting. Her face was sweat-streaked and filthy dirty and her trouser leg was bloody. In her hand she held a home-made petrol bomb. 'Tank!' she said, and flicked a lighter; and as the flame licked and caught at the short fuse the monster appeared, rumbling and heaving through the rubble, its long gun blazing. Marek crouched over the screaming child. He sensed a movement beside him, and the girl had gone, running not away from but towards the oncoming tank. Marek lifted his head. A flying leap took the girl on to the tank; he saw the blaze of the bomb in her hand. The explosion rocked the wall behind which he sheltered. The crippled tank slewed and tipped on its side, engulfed in a sheet of flame.

Marek picked up the child and, despite the pain in his leg, ran for both of their lives.

The fighting lasted until darkness fell, and with the darkness came a strange and eerie quiet. For the first time the guns and the mortars fell silent, and the heavy, fire-reddened sky was empty. So savage had been the defence of the Poles, so fanatically determined their resistance, that the two front lines had become inextricably enmeshed; for the moment the Germans dared not use their firepower for fear of causing casualties to their own men. Insurgents might occupy one house, while the width of a single wall away, German troops held its neighbour. In some cases, bizarrely, friend and foe actually occupied different floors of the same building. Dog tired, yet still aware that they had proved once more that they were far from broken, the men and women of the Home Army shared what frugal rations were left and rested as best they could.

Marek found himself in a church. There was no glass in the windows, no statues adorned the fire-scarred niches, the altars were bare and the pews long ago used for fuel, but a church it was. The sounds of movement and quiet talk echoed, whispering, to the lofty, damaged roof. He sat on the floor in a corner, his back against the wall, in his hand a small chunk of hard black bread he was almost too tired to eat. He closed his eyes. Images flashed across the darkness of his lids. Screams echoed in his head.

A strong, cold, wet nose nuzzled his ear.

He opened his eyes.

'Mind if I join you?' Stefan loomed above him, a familiar figure, his long gun slung across his shoulder.

Marek rubbed Bella's ears. 'Of course not.'

Stefan hunkered down, produced a cigarette, lit it. Like everyone else he had thinned to the bone, and his face was haggard and dirty. Candlelight flickered behind his mane of fair hair that had grown shaggy and unkempt. 'I asked at the first aid post. They said I'd probably find you here. Drink?' A flask appeared from nowhere. He held it out.

'Thanks.' Marek had long ago given up wondering where Stefan's apparently unlimited supplies of liquor came from. He tilted his head and the spirit ran like liquid fire down his throat. He coughed, took another swig before he handed the flask back. 'Have you seen Danka?'

'A couple of hours ago.' Stefan's voice held a strange little bite of amusement. 'Women! Have you ever known one who didn't get her own way in the end?'

Marek looked at him. 'She's all right?'

'She's fine.' Stefan blew smoke to the ceiling. 'She's fighting,' he added. 'She's joined my unit.'

'*What?*'

Stefan grinned in sudden and genuine amusement. 'She took the German gun and walked in bold as brass.' He shrugged. 'Just as well she did, really. The cellar took a direct hit a couple of hours later. Silly little sod. She must have known I'd have given it to her in the end.'

'Danka's *fighting*?' Marek was aghast.

'You worry too much. She can look after herself. And, anyway, she's a damned sight safer with a gun in her hand than without one.' Stefan propped himself up against the wall beside him, reached into his pocket for an ill-smelling gobbet of meat for the dog. 'Rat,' he said, conversationally, at Marek's look. 'I shot one for her yesterday.'

'I'm surprised someone hasn't tried to take her from you.'

Stefan's smile lacked humour. 'Oh, someone has,' he said mildly. 'I – persuaded him – that she wouldn't make good eating. He saw my point. What happened to the kid?'

Marek blinked. 'What kid?'

'The one you ran off with this afternoon.'

'How do you know about that?'

'I saw you. That blasted sniper had been playing merry hell all afternoon around that district. They sent for me to get him.'

Marek remembered, suddenly and clearly; two shots, and only one bullet, then nothing. 'And you did.'

'Yes.'

'So –' Marek shook his head, half-laughing, self-mocking – 'I could just have picked the child up and walked away?'

Stefan shrugged. 'You weren't to know that. What happened to it?'

'I don't know. I got him back to the post and a woman took him. She'd lost her own child, I think.'

'It was a boy, then?'

'Yes.'

Stefan was toying with his knife, running his finger along its keen edge. Marek, watching him, was suddenly overcome by a dizzying and almost irresistible wave of fatigue. For a moment he allowed his eyes to drift shut.

'There's a proverb, isn't there?' Stefan asked quietly, wiping the knife on his shirt-sleeve. 'Something about the three things a man should do in his life?'

Marek, with a huge effort of will, forced his eyes open. 'Have a son, build a house, plant a tree.'

His half-brother laughed softly, spread his hands to indicate their surroundings. 'Not a lot of point in doing any of that at the moment, would you say?' He lifted his head, suddenly and sharply. 'What the hell's that?'

He was not the only one to have heard it. The shuffling

and muttering and whispering in the church died. All movement stopped, every head turned, listening.

Somewhere very close someone was playing a piano. The instrument was ill-tuned and lacking in tone, but the touch of the player was masterly, and the music he played was Chopin's. The measured notes of the haunting and gentle Nocturne in E fell into the quiet of the warm night like raindrops on the leaves of summer. Men and women, filthy, exhausted and hungry, stopped what they were doing and listened with their breath held. Not for five long years had it been possible openly to play or to listen to the music of their national composer; to hear it here and in such circumstances was an experience of heart-stopping poignancy. When the last note of the piece faded to silence there was a murmur of appreciation, but before anyone could speak the unknown pianist had swung into a light and lilting waltz, the Waltz in C. From somewhere in the distance came the crack of small-arms fire. The sky above the burning city was like that above an open furnace. Over the sound of the quieter passages came the sound of the armoured train with its punishing payload of heavy artillery being shunted into position. And still the pianist played; polonaises and mazurkas, études and waltzes, evoking every mood, every precious memory. For almost an hour within this tangled enclave that was Warsaw's front line, friend and foe alike were spellbound within the magic web of music. When the rippling, storming notes of the stirring Étude in C – the so-called 'Revolutionary' étude – crashed in the darkness, more than one of those tough and seasoned street-fighters was in tears; Marek himself found that his face was wet. He glanced at Stefan. His brother had his arms about Bella, his face hidden in her fur, his shoulders hunched about his ears, his big hands clenched so that the knuckles stood white. As the last, crashing, climactic chord of the piece died and a sudden, final quiet fell there was no applause; the still silence itself was the only adequate tribute that could be paid, a silence broken only by the soft weeping of a woman.

Marek put a hand on Stefan's shoulder. Stefan lifted his head; the face he turned to his half-brother was dry-eyed and fierce. 'Save your tears, Marek,' he said, shaking the hand from his shoulder, his voice as harsh as it had ever been. 'There's worse to come. Much worse.'

The next morning the assault on the Old Town resumed with renewed and even greater ferocity.

Chapter Fourteen

The battle for the Old Town – the battle for the heart of Warsaw – lasted for two more long and savagely exhausting weeks. Time and again the Germans threw everything they had into the attack, and time and again the fiercely tenacious insurgents held, though as each day passed, inch by inch they were being pressed and driven back, and they were taking desperately heavy losses. For every German who fell, another was there to take his place; a fallen insurgent was an irreplaceable loss. Arms and ammunition were short; Stefan's maxim of 'one bullet, one German' was now everyone's. And if the military situation was bad, the plight of the civilian population was worse; indeed it was almost unendurable. Conditions were barbarous. There was little food and hardly any water, and much of what there was was contaminated. There was no shelter to speak of – so many houses had been completely destroyed by the bombardment that what few cellars were left intact were intolerably overcrowded; in many cases there was no room to sit or to lie down. Under these merciless conditions and in the intense summer heat, children, babies

and old people died like flies. Small wonder then that as
the days and the weeks wore on, civilian support for the
Rising had all but evaporated, and that the young soldiers of the Home Army, once treated as heroes and
saviours, now found themselves faced with bitter hostility and lack of co-operation. Yet still, exhausted,
half-starved, desperately short of arms and ammunition,
they fought on. Towards the end of the month, however,
it became clear to the most stubbornly optimistic of souls
that no miracle was going to happen. The ancient and
lovely buildings of the medieval Old Town had been
reduced to a wasteland of rubble; the insurgents held
only half a square mile of territory. The Germans had
pinpointed the Home Army HQ and were pounding it
mercilessly; there was nowhere left to go. Several
attempts to break through the German lines and join up
with the Polish troops who still held Zoliborz and the
City Centre were defeated with heavy casualties. The situation was critical; on a hot night towards the end of
August the commander of the Old Town defences and
his staff escaped through the sewers to the City Centre,
leaving orders that what was left of the Old Town should
be defended for as long as possible. The move, not unnat-
urally, demoralised the already frightened civilian
population and did little to encourage the defenders of
what was left of what had once been the pride of
Warsaw.

Four days later Danusia and Stefan came to find Marek
to tell him that the Old Town was to be abandoned.
Fifteen hundred people – mostly fighters, though the
walking wounded and some chosen civilians were to be
included – were to be evacuated to the City Centre
through the sewers. Stefan's and Danusia's unit, since
most of them still possessed arms and ammunition, was
to be among the last to go. They had managed to get

Marek a pass to go with them. The badly wounded and most of the civilian population would have to be left behind; in effect a death sentence for them, since the Germans at this time were taking no prisoners. Danusia's dirty face was streaked with tears, but her voice was steady. 'We should try to stay together. Here –' she handed Marek a heavy pistol. 'There's no ammunition to go with it but at least it looks good.' Her smile was bitter. 'You could always throw it at someone.'

Marek tucked the thing into his belt, looked around in despair. 'I'm not sure I should go.' He gestured to the overcrowded cellar in which they were standing. Every inch of floor-space was taken up by the victims of the fighting with their filthy bandages and suppurating wounds. Men and women moaned, some cried, some were mercifully unconscious. There had been no medical supplies available for days. In the room next door someone screamed under the surgeon's saw.

'Don't be stupid; there's nothing more you can do here. The evacuation starts tonight, but we probably won't go through until some time towards dawn. The manhole's in Krasinski Square. Be there at midnight. By then we'll know more.' Stefan's face was grimmer than Marek had ever seen it, and he had a bloodied rag tied bandanna-style about his head. 'By Christ, I never thought the day would come when I'd find myself running away through a sewer like a filthy rat.'

'Stefan! Danka! Come!' A young man had appeared at the doorway. 'The Boches are attacking the square! Hurry! If they break through the barricades no one will get out!'

'Midnight,' Stefan said to Marek. 'Be there,' and he was gone.

Before following him, Danusia gripped Marek's hand urgently. 'Please come. It's our only chance. And Stefan's

right – there's no point in your staying. There's nothing
you can do. You'd simply die for nothing. Please – you
will come? Promise me?'

'I'll come.'

'I'll watch for you. Take care.'

'And you.' He watched her as she stepped over the pal-
lets with their pathetic and gruesome burdens and
disappeared through the door. Overhead the ceaseless
roar of bombs and artillery had increased. Not for the first
time he wondered if he would ever experience the blessing of silence again.

'Water – please – water –'

There was no water. Marek stood for a moment in a
rage of helplessness.

'Please!'

He dropped to his knees and took the extended hand,
watched as the shadow of death crept over a thin young
face, and cursed the God in whom he did not believe for
allowing such horrors to happen.

In the event the defence put up by the insurgents on that
first day of September was so furious that they fought the
German infantry to a standstill. There was no point now
in hoarding ammunition, so the last of the stores were
distributed and used to good effect; not one of the enemy
entered the square to threaten the precious manhole. Not
that the German Command had any idea of why the
fighting around Krasinski was so fierce; because they had
grown used to the fanatical courage with which the scare-
crow Polish army resisted any attack, there was nothing
so unusual here. So savage was the fighting and so heavy
the casualties that as evening fell the Germans were
forced to ask for a truce to clear the dead and wounded
from the approaches to the square. The Poles agreed; a
truce until dawn.

And in the uncanny silence that fell over the shattered city as the guns were silenced the barricades were quietly abandoned and the surviving defenders slipped through the ruins to Krasinski Square and the manhole.

No one was unaware of the dangers of the operation; never before had so many people been through the sewers together. At the best of times the journey was a filthy and terrible ordeal; the noxious sludge through which it was necessary to wade was sometimes waist deep, the air was so poisonously foul that candles would not stay alight and the smallest slip in the darkness could be fatal, for because of the danger to those behind there could be no stopping to assist someone who slipped into the foetid sewage. Everyone had heard the stories of men and women – toughened street-fighters of proven strength and courage – being driven to madness in these foul tunnels. And there were dangers other than the natural ones. It had not taken the Germans long to guess that the Home Army were using the sewage system as a means of communication; all manholes in German-held territory were opened and guarded; at the slightest sound, given the slightest indication that someone was moving through the tunnels beneath them, those manning these listening-posts would toss down grenades, or pour petrol into the tunnel and ignite it.

No one who stood in the orderly queue that had formed in the square awaiting their turn to climb down the long iron ladder could doubt the perils they were about to face. Watched by sullenly angry groups of civilians, one by one the units were swallowed up by the foul-smelling darkness. Subdued and quiet they shuffled forward, ragged and haggard, exhausted by weeks of fighting and days of starvation, knowing that four kilometres of horror stood between them and comparative safety. Four kilometres that could not be negotiated in less than four hours.

Marek stood with Stefan and Danusia and the rest of their unit, the pass Stefan had acquired for him safely in his pocket. This was no indisciplined mass exodus but a military operation run under tight control. No one without a pass would be allowed to leave. The likely fate of those who were forced – or chose – to stay did not bear thinking about. They stood now in silence. Bella, gaunt and thin as her master, sat at Stefan's feet, his hand as always resting upon her head. 'They surely won't let you take her with you, will they?' Marek had asked when first he had seen her. And 'Shut up, Marek!' Danusia had said fiercely. Since then, none of them had spoken.

Now, as the queue moved forward again, an older man with officer's insignia on his forage cap made his way down the line, checking passes. Beside Stefan he stopped. 'You can't take the dog, son.'

'I know.' Stefan's voice was nervelessly even. Beneath his fingers he could feel the bones of the dog's skull. Her eyes were sunken and dull, yet still she looked at him with the perfect trust of love. 'How long before we go?'

The man glanced at his watch. 'Five minutes. Perhaps ten.'

Stefan nodded. 'I'll see to it. Danka, hold this for me, would you?' he handed her his gun. 'I'll be back in a minute. Come on, Bell. Heel, old girl.'

The huge, half-starved dog hauled herself to her feet, stood unsteadily, watching him. He led her away from the shuffling queue into the darkness of the ruins that surrounded the once-beautiful square. The eerie quiet of the truce held; a smell of death and decay hung on the hot night air.

Stefan hunkered down beside the dog, buried his face for a moment in her unkempt, dirty fur. 'They won't get you, girl. Don't worry. They won't get you.' He found the sheath that hung at his belt. The dog's dry tongue licked his face, savouring the salt. A moment later, soundlessly, she slumped against him. He held her for a moment before gently lowering her to the ground. Then he straightened, wiping the knife on his shirt; stood for a long moment looking at the lifeless shadow at his feet.

On the way back to his place in the square he passed a group of civilians, three or four middle-aged men and a woman who carried a small lantern. They were standing in the shadows, watching resentfully the activity around the manhole. 'Here's one of them,' the woman said. 'Not so brave now, are we, sonny? The sewer's the place for you, if you ask me. We all know what deserts a sinking ship, don't we?' She lifted the lantern to light the face that Stefan turned towards her, and stopped.

'Come away, Ola,' one of the men said uneasily. 'Come away.'

When Stefan rejoined the other two none of them spoke. Danusia tried to slip a hand into his; knowing it to be blood-marked, he made a fist and pushed it deep into his pocket. Five minutes later they descended into hell.

The endless stooped and shuffling line, linked hand to hand, waded on in the darkness. As fires raged in the buildings above, the sewers were suffocatingly hot, adding to the desperate difficulty of breathing the poisoned air. The silence was broken by the lap of the sewage, the rasping of breath, the occasional whispered command or a frightened cry as someone lost their footing in the running filth through which they struggled. Danusia was between Stefan and Marek; the link of their hands the only comfort in the vile darkness. Unlike most others, she had been through the sewers before; she had thought she had known what to expect. But on those other occasions she had been part of a small group of perhaps four or five, led by a guide through tunnels lit at least in some places by electric light. This claustrophobic nightmare was different. The impression of being dragged forward, of being pressured from behind as hundreds upon hundreds of people moved inexorably on was terrifying; it was like being part of some monstrous, mindless animal – an animal that would shamble on over a fallen body without stop or thought. She had long ago lost all sense of time. She had no idea how long it was since they had taken their turn to climb down the metal ladder of the manhole, no idea of how far they had come or how much further they had to go. In common, she supposed, with most others she was reduced simply to concentrating on setting one foot in front of another and, above all things, on keeping her footing in the slime beneath the filthy water. Even as she thought it, something soft banged against her knee and she slipped and stumbled, stifling a cry. Both the men's hands tightened painfully on hers. She swallowed the rise of sickness. The body drifted away from her; she could have sworn she felt the touch of a cold hand. Someone behind her was crying very quietly.

Ahead, suddenly, there was a faint glow of light reflecting on the slime-coated walls of the tunnel; a whisper ran along the line, 'Stop.'

She felt Stefan's strong hand steadying her, sensed Marek bracing himself to protect her from behind. The line came to a halt and an uneasy silence fell. Again a single word was passed on a breath. 'Manhole.'

Danusia closed her eyes for a moment. Another hold-up. Another moment of terror and danger; the third since they had started out.

The line moved forward again, very slowly. Ahead, in twos and threes, people would be inching beneath the enemy-guarded manhole. One slip, one moment of panic and they would all be lost.

The light was coming closer.

She wanted to cough. She needed to cough. She would choke if she did not.

Another few steps. The water was deep here, reaching to her thighs. Her legs and back ached abominably.

The pale light was growing stronger, and at last there was a small drift of fresher air in the tunnel. As they came to a bend she saw why. They had reached a junction. The sewer widened and split ahead of them into two. Above, through the open manhole, could be seen a patch of pale sky, and the flicker of flame. Silently and stealthily, one by one, heads tilted warily back to watch the opening above them, the escapers were creeping around the patch of light and scuttling like rats into the mouth of the right-hand tunnel.

Stefan squeezed her hand, and let it go. She watched as he edged his way, plastered flat against the filthy wall, around the patch of light. She in turn gripped Marek's hand a little harder before she started forward alone.

Suddenly and shockingly there was a burst of raucous laughter above her head and a man's voice spoke in German, the words echoing hollowly.

She froze in the shadows.

Silhouetted against the lightening sky above she could see a man's back. A rifle was slung over his shoulder and a cigarette glowed between his fingers. He spoke once more, another voice answered, and again they laughed. The man stepped forward, out of sight.

Breath held, she began to move, steadying herself against the slippery wall.

The clasp of Stefan's hand as she slipped into the tunnel mouth had never been so welcome. Moments later Marek had joined them and they were once more part of the steadily moving column; but now, at least for a moment, the foetid darkness meant safety rather than danger, relief rather than fear. And surely – surely! – the ordeal must be nearly over? The light sky had meant dawn. They must have been walking for upwards of four or five hours.

The tunnel curved sharply to the right. The water was shallower, they could stand upright and walking was easier. Danusia flexed her shoulders. The German rifle strapped to her back was a dead weight.

Behind them there was a sudden shout, a shot, a scream, a confusion of voices.

'Down!' Stefan snapped, dropping to his knees and dragging her with him *'Get down!'*

The blast of the explosion threw her bruisingly against the side of the tunnel. A tide of sewage washed against them. People ahead, galvanised, were scrambling forward, slipping and sliding.

'Stay where you are,' Stefan said. 'You too, Marek. Get up against the wall.'

The sound of the second explosion drowned the last of his words. Although they were protected at least a little by the bend in the tunnel, still the blast took the breath from their lungs. People were pushing past them; and from the direction of the manhole a cacophony of screams and moans told their own graphic story.

They waited. Nothing else happened.

'Come on,' Stefan said. 'It can't be far now.'

It was not. Half an hour or so later they found themselves part of a queue again. People leaned wearily against the walls or on the shoulders of others, some talking quietly, others silent and subdued. One girl was sobbing uncontrollably. Ahead, willing hands were helping exhausted and filthy men and women up the long iron ladder to fresh air and freedom.

Stefan had pushed Danusia in front of him, so of the

three of them she was the first to be hauled out of the darkness into the brightness of a summer dawn. The young soldier who helped her out hugged her, patting her on the back before turning back to give Stefan a hand. A girl wearing the red and white armband of the Home Army stepped forward, smiling, with a jug of water, watched as Danusia drank greedily. Marek, pale and filthy as they all were and blinking bloodshot eyes behind his glasses, emerged from the manhole and scrambled into the square beside them. All around them people greeted each other, laughing and crying, or simply standing, dazed, in close embrace.

Stefan drank and drank again, handed the jug to Marek, reached into an inner pocket.

Danusia, eyes focusing at last, looked about her, drawing great breaths of the cool, smoky air. 'I'd almost forgotten,' she said quietly.

Marek came to stand beside her. 'Trees,' he said. 'Real trees, with leaves. And buildings – buildings with roofs, and windows – and look over there – it's a bloody shop! With a door, and shutters!'

'Hasn't anyone told them there's a war on?' Stefan asked mildly, extending to Danusia the flask he had pulled from his pocket.

Danusia took it, tilted her head to drink and promptly choked. Stefan relieved her of the flask, handed it on to Marek. The number of people coming out from the manhole had slowed to a trickle. Some of them were freshly bloodied, surviving victims of the hand-grenades that had been tossed down the last manhole.

'Well –' Stefan tucked the flask back into his shirt, hitched his rifle on to his shoulder in a characteristic gesture. For a moment it was as if a big, gaunt shadow sat at his feet. 'We made it!' He put an arm about Danusia's shoulder, extended a hand to Marek. 'Well done, brother.'

Marek stared at him.

'It's all right – you won't catch anything.' The words were mildly caustic. 'At least nothing worse than you're likely to have caught already.' Stefan indicated the man-hole with a movement of his head.

'Oh, don't be daft!' Marek grabbed the hand and shook it fiercely. 'It's just – I don't think we've ever shaken hands before?'

'I believe, as I recall saying before, there's a first time for everything,' Stefan observed amicably. 'Now –' he looked around – 'what do you say to finding ourselves a new home? Looks as if we're here for the duration.'

Within its limits the operation to evacuate the ruined shambles of the Old Town was a success; fifteen hundred seasoned fighters escaped that night through the sewers to join the thirty thousand defenders of the City Centre, but at terrible cost to those left behind. Tens of thousands of wounded and civilians were massacred as the Germans realised they had been tricked and poured across the abandoned barricades into the blitzed heart of Warsaw.

The Old Town was lost, and a bitter blow it was. But still the message was beamed to the world, in courage and defiance.

Help us, as you promised; Warsaw fights on.

Chapter Fifteen

'So much for our good friends the Russians!' Danusia said grimly, tossing a news sheet on to the table. 'At least they've finally come out into the open.'

Marek lifted his head. 'What now?'

'They've refused permission for Allied planes to use their airfields to make it easier to get supplies through to us.'

'On what grounds?'

Danusia pulled a face. 'Since when did the Soviets need "grounds" to do anything? They've just done it, that's all. They promise us help on the one hand and snatch it away with the other. Par for the course. Have you seen these?' She pulled a leaflet from her pocket and held it up.

Marek leaned and took it from her, looked at it. 'Yes.'

'They're unsettling the civilians. Some are trying to cross to the German lines. You can't blame them, I suppose.'

Stefan looked up from where he was cleaning his rifle. 'Shoot a few of them,' he said. 'That'd stop them.'

Danusia took the German leaflet back from Marek and tore it up. 'You sound like a Boche,' she said.

Stefan shrugged.

Danusia went to the window. 'Listen to that. They're hitting Powisle District again. Someone said the power station's been taken; the electricity's off for good if it has been. It'll be our turn next. They're just picking off the districts one by one.'

It was three days since they had crawled from the sewers, three days in which the Germans, encouraged by the collapse of resistance in the Old Town, had renewed their attacks on the other insurgent-held positions with increased vigour. Isolated pockets of resistance were being wiped out all over the city.

Attacks on the City Centre, the largest of the Polish-held areas, had so far been successfully beaten off, but yet again the old problems were emerging – lack of food and of water, of arms and ammunition and an increasingly sullen population that was being further unsettled by the leaflets with which the Luftwaffe daily bombarded the city exhorting them to abandon support for a Rising that could now only fail and to flee from a city that was doomed to destruction. So low was morale in some places that promises of safe conduct were taken at face value, despite ample evidence that such promises had never been honoured before.

Stefan clicked the last piece of the gun into place and stood up, slinging it on to his shoulder. 'Time to go.'

'Sod it,' Danusia said from the window. 'Here they come again. Air raid.'

Unmoved, Stefan strode to the door. 'It's still time to go.'

Ten minutes later they were making their way through streets that were heavy with dust and smoke and blocked with fresh mounds of rubble. Rafters stood from the ruins like splintered bones. Fires raged unchecked and bodies lay all but unheeded in the wreckage. A woman sat against a wall, rocking silently, a dead child in her arms. They picked their way around her. None of these sights was new, and the most sensitive of hearts became hardened in the end.

Four days later Marek was wounded.

Powisle had fallen, its power station destroyed – a disaster for the insurgents. Again, and despite promises, there had been mass shootings of prisoners and wounded. Attacks on the City Centre were now ferocious and constant. Access to the river had been cut off entirely. Stefan, Danusia and Marek had been attached to a unit defending a barricade along a once fashionable street to the east of the City Centre, Stefan as a sniper, Danusia as part of the fighting strength of the unit and Marek, together with a girl named Matynka, as a medic. It was midmorning on a blazing hot day; one attack had already been repulsed; on the German side of the barricade the wounded and dead in their field grey uniforms testified to the fierce resistance put up by the Poles. Grimly satisfied, the defenders watched as the attackers withdrew to a crossroads some fifty yards away, leaving the street clear, at least for the moment.

Beside Danusia a young boy of perhaps fourteen or fifteen, wearing ragged civilian clothes and armed only with a wooden club, scrambled to his feet.

She grabbed for him. 'Get down, Jurek!'

'No fear!' he said excitedly. 'There are guns out there!' and slipping from her grasp, he wriggled across the obstruction and made a loping dash into the street beyond. By the first of the German dead he stopped, clapped the fallen man's steel helmet on his own head, scooped up the heavy German rifle and slung it on to his back and then bent to unbuckle the dead man's ammunition belt.

Three feet from him one of the wounded men moved. Two shots rang out almost simultaneously. The German slumped; the boy Jurek screamed, the bullet from the man's pistol lodged in his spine. He screamed as he fell, and continued to scream as he lay there in the road; a piercing, childish scream of agony that rang above the sounds of battle.

'Come on.' Matynka was up and scrambling through the barricade in seconds. 'Quick! Before they come back.'

Marek was already on his feet. He limped after her. She reached the screaming boy and bent to him. The unexpected burst of machine-gun fire from the house opposite threw her completely off her feet and hurled her like a doll to the ground. Marek dropped flat. The gun ripped again. Jurek stopped screaming. The dusty ground around Marek erupted; he felt a stunning blow on his shoulder. He curled into a ball, waiting for the gunner to open up again. Then, above, in the frameless window of a ruined building he saw movement, a lifted arm, a small object flung with deadly accuracy towards the window from which the machine-gun had been fired. The explosion as the grenade struck brought the last of the already partly wrecked building down, and the machine-gun was silenced.

He tried to move, and could not. He lay quite still for a moment, summoning all his resources. It could only be minutes before the Germans attacked again. Lying here in their path he knew himself to be as good as dead –

He struggled to his knees, put a hand to the ground and collapsed as pain jolted through his shoulder like a thunderbolt.

The ground beneath him shook.

He lifted his head.

Around the corner rumbled two vehicles: a large tank, and a smaller one. They were linked by an electric cable;

a deadly umbilical chord. Gun blazing at the barricade, the larger tank stopped. The smaller one did not. Packed with high explosive and remotely controlled from the other vehicle it ploughed its way remorselessly on towards the insurgent barricade. Desperately Marek tried to drag himself out of its path. The thing rolled on inexorably, tracks churning choking clouds of dust from the rubble of the street.

He closed his eyes, listening to the roar of the monster, flinching already from the crushing weight of it.

Then rough hands were hauling him upright. He heard himself cry out as he was flung ungently across a broad shoulder. The Goliath hammered past them, almost hidden in its dust-cloud as he was taken at an agonisingly jolting run to the shelter of a doorway.

Before his rescuer had lowered him to the ground he had lost consciousness.

Behind the barricade the defenders watched the Goliath approach. 'Come on, Stefan,' someone muttered through clenched teeth. 'You're leaving it a bit late this time, mate.' The only defence against these unmanned monsters was to break the cable by which it was controlled; Stefan, with his marksman's eye and from his sniper's position above the street had perfected the art of using hand-grenades to do this. On two occasions in the past two days he had crippled just such a machine, once only using a single grenade.

The tank ground on.

'For Christ's sake!' someone exclaimed. 'Where the hell is he?'

The thing was almost on them. 'Run for it!'

It was too late. The street behind the death-packed Goliath was now aswarm with German infantry armed with flame-throwers, rifles and machine-guns as they waited for the explosion that would clear the barricade and decimate its defenders.

Danusia grabbed her gun and ran for her life. All around her people were running, slipping and stumbling in the rubble. She herself slipped, and, knowing herself about to fall, she flung herself flat, face down, her arms protecting her head. The blast shrieked over her and hammered painfully in her ears; the air was filled with dust and flying debris. Then came the familiar and terrible roar of the flame-throwers, the chatter of machine-gun fire, the shouts of the advancing infantry.

The position, defended so valiantly and at such cost, was lost; there was nothing for it but to abandon it and run.

Later that day, hungry, exhausted and almost out of her mind with grief and anxiety, Danusia made her way to the house where she, Stefan and Marek had been billeted. It was in a part of the town that had not yet come under direct attack – though that, she knew, could only be a matter of time – but the artillery shells and the bombing had taken their toll. Windows and doors had been blown out, and the civilian inhabitants had taken to the cellar. Usually a baby wailed, constantly and nerve-rackingly. Today there was a mordant silence as she passed the cellar door. Danusia tried not to draw the logical conclusion. She had faced too much of death today. Perhaps the child was asleep.

Marek and Stefan. Both missing. The one undoubtedly dead, the other stranded behind enemy lines, where to be caught was certain execution. They had all known their luck could not hold out for ever, but for the brothers to fall at the same time was something she had not prepared herself to face.

Wearily she dragged herself up the single flight of stairs, pushed open the door that hung askew on one hinge. Stood for a single, heart-stopping moment as if rooted to the spot. Then, 'Stefan!' she said softly. '*Stefan!*'

He sat slumped at the table, one hand guarding his eyes, the other curled around an almost empty bottle. At her entrance he had lifted his head, his eyes bright and burning in his thin face. He pushed the chair back and came slowly to his feet, supporting himself by the table. 'Jesus!' he said, 'Danka?' His voice was disbelieving. 'It's you?'

'Yes! Oh, yes!' She flew to him, flung her arms about his hard, gaunt body. 'Oh, Stefan, Stefan! You're alive! You're alive!'

His arms were locked about her, crushing the breath from her lungs. His body shook within her arms. For some moments he said nothing. When he finally put her from him she was shedding the tears she had until now obstinately resisted. He put a roughened, dirty hand to her face. 'Don't cry. Danka, don't cry.'

She leaned against him, weeping helplessly. 'I can't help it. I can't help it. I was so sure – so certain that you were dead. You and Marek. I couldn't bear the thought of losing you both.'

'You've lost neither of us,' he said, quietly. 'Not yet.'

She pulled from him, lifting her head, startled. 'What? What do you mean?'

'What I said. You've lost neither of us. Marek isn't dead either.'

'But – how can you know that? I saw him – the Goliath – he was right in its path – he was wounded – he couldn't possibly have survived.'

'He did. I got him to a first aid post in Jasna Street. He's got a couple of bullets in his shoulder. He had an uncomfortable few minutes while they dug them out, but for the time being anyway he's safe. I poured half a bottle of this down him –' he indicated the empty bottle on the table. 'Last time I saw him he was sleeping like a baby.' His arms tightened about her. 'Oh, Danka, Danka! I thought you were dead,' he said, after a moment. 'When that bloody thing went off –' He closed his eyes tightly and rested his face on her hair.

She shook her head. 'I was lucky. When I realised the Goliath was going to hit, I ran. A few of us got away.'

'How many?' The question was slow in coming and very quiet.

'I – don't know. Not many, that's for sure. I saw Jas, and Adam – Adam was wounded – most of the others –' Her voice trailed to nothing.

He dropped back into the chair, buried his face in his hands.

'Stefan – what's the matter? What happened? How –?'

He let his hands drop on to the table, lifted a face that was pared to the bone by fatigue and hunger, and something more, something that made Danusia catch her breath in pity. 'My fault,' he said. 'It was my fault.'

'What was?' She sat in the chair opposite, reached for his hand. It lay lax in her own. 'Stefan – please – tell me what's wrong? We're all alive – isn't that enough?'

'No. We aren't all alive. We three are alive – you through no doing of mine. If you had died, that would have been my fault too. I should have stopped that bloody Goliath.'

She gripped his hand urgently. 'Stefan, stop it! You can't take responsibility for everything that happens –'

'I can take responsibility for this. Danusia – don't you see? I didn't stop it because I wasn't there! I left my post. I – deserted – my – post.' He spoke very deliberately.

'I don't believe it. Not you.'

'I was watching when Marek and the girl went after that idiot of a boy. I saw Marek go down. I got the gunner; I thought the coast was clear. I knew I should leave him. I didn't even know if he was alive or dead. And either way I knew that my duty was to stay where I was.' He shook his head slowly. 'I couldn't. I don't know why, but I couldn't. I hardly remember getting down into the street. By the time I had, that bastard had come round the corner and was heading for him. He moved; I knew he was alive. I couldn't leave him. I couldn't.'

Danusia tightened her grip on his hand. 'I didn't see you. I don't think anyone did.'

'It was the dust. It was like a bloody blanket. I just grabbed him and ran. He passed out. I holed us up in a cellar; it turned out to be a remnant of one of the underground systems. Took us into Jasna. That's how I got him to the first aid post.'

'You saved his life.'

'At what cost? In saving him, how many did I condemn to die? Twenty? Thirty? More?'

'You might not have been able to stop the Goliath.'

Fierce eyes met hers. 'When have I ever not? Why did everyone leave it till the last minute to run? Because they knew I was there. Because they were waiting for me to break the cable.'

She said nothing.

'Because they trusted me,' he said, his voice harsh with self-disgust.

'Stefan, don't. Please don't. You mustn't blame yourself. You weren't to know they were going to send that thing against us.'

'I could have made a fairly educated guess. It's hardly the first time it's happened.'

She ignored his interruption. 'You saw your brother go down. It's the most natural thing in the world to do what you did.'

He shook his head.

'Stefan – he's your brother!' She hesitated for a moment, then added softly, 'And you love him. Don't you?'

He sat for a moment, his face impassive. Then he tilted

the bottle, drained the last drop of liquor into his mouth, set the bottle down very precisely on the table. An explosion shook the building; both of them ignored it. 'That was the second time I'd seen him do something like that,' he said. 'The first time it was a kid. I knew then – knew that he has a kind of courage that I don't. I couldn't do what he's been doing. It would scare me to death.'

She opened her mouth to speak, but he shook his head fiercely. 'Oh, I'm good with a knife and a gun, and I've never run away from a fight in my life, whatever the odds. I thought that was courage. Until I saw Marek crawling towards that damn kid, risking his life for an orphaned brat and without so much as a peashooter to defend himself with. That's courage. And this morning –' he heeled his hands into his tired eyes – 'I couldn't let him die. It's as simple as that. The choice was there and I made it. I betrayed every principle I've ever held and was responsible for the destruction of a fighting unit. I should be shot.'

'No! Stefan, I won't have this!' She caught his hands again, willing him to look at her. 'You're overwrought. Any man would have done the same thing. Any man with a heart, that is.'

For the first time he smiled, though the smile was bleak. 'You think I have a heart, then?'

'I know you have. You're the only one that doubts it.'

'You think Marek believes I have a heart?' The words held a glint of grim amusement.

She did not smile. 'Marek believes everyone has a heart,' she said softly. 'It's one of his most attractive qualities.'

He looked at her for a very long time. 'Marek and his attractive qualities,' he said at last, and the old, mocking note was back in his voice, though whether he mocked her, or Marek or himself Danusia could not tell.

'Marek is kind,' she said. 'And gentle. And yes, you're

right, he's brave, though I don't think he knows it. He's honest, and intelligent –'

'And he loves you.'

She held his gaze for a moment, then looked down at their linked hands.

'And you love him.'

There was a very long moment of silence between them. Then, 'We both love him,' Danusia said carefully, 'You know it.'

He smiled a little at the evasion, disengaged his hands from hers. 'Nevertheless,' he said, 'I should not have done what I did. I should have left him to die.'

'No!'

'Yes. I could have stopped that bastard. You know I could. You trusted me, all of you, and I betrayed that trust. I'll never forgive myself. I told you, and I mean it – I deserve to be shot.'

Great clouds of smoke were billowing from a nearby burning building, drifting chokingly through the window. From somewhere quite close came the crackle of small-arms fire. Danusia took a long breath. 'I have something to tell you,' she said.

The story did not take long to tell. He listened in silence. 'And – Marek knew about this?' he asked at last.

'Yes. He covered up for me. Stefan, you must see? It was a mistake. We all make mistakes. I honestly thought they'd left that address. And Czesia –' she stopped, spread her hands helplessly – 'Czesia was in danger. I had to try to save her.'

'Why do you tell me now?'

She came around the table and dropped to her knees beside him, her hands urgently on his, her head thrown back to look into his face. 'To show you that I understand. To show you that you aren't alone. To help you to forgive yourself.'

'And why didn't you tell me then?'

She kept her eyes steadily on his. 'Because I believed you would kill me.' She waited for a moment before asking, 'You would have killed me. Wouldn't you?'

'Yes.' The word was very quiet.

Before he could prevent her, she had reached to the sheath on his belt and drawn his knife, handling the sharp blade delicately, handing the knife to him hilt first. 'Then do it,' she said simply. 'If I deserved to die then, I deserve to die now. Isn't that true? I too betrayed a trust for the sake of someone I loved. If you truly believe I should die for it, then do it. Now.'

He held the knife steadily at her throat for a moment, then lifted his other hand to cup her chin and bent to kiss her. The knife clattered to the floor. His hard hand slid gently inside her filthy shirt, caressing her breasts. She could not for the life of her tell if the salt she tasted was from his tears or from her own. She lifted her arms about his neck and pulled him to her, opening her mouth beneath his.

In the thunder of the barrage neither of them heard the hesitant step upon the stairs, nor did either of them notice the tall, pale figure who leaned for a moment on the shattered doorjamb, nursing an arm that had been secured into a crude and dirty sling.

Marek closed his eyes for a second and drew a long, quiet breath, of thankfulness and of pain, before turning away and limping, with care, back down the stairs.

Chapter Sixteen

'Is this it, then?' Danusia's voice was so quiet that Marek could barely hear the words over the bedlam of sound that engulfed the burning city. She sat hunched next to him, her back against a bullet-scarred wall; she drew on her cigarette, passed it to Marek, who passed it on to the exhausted man beside him. 'Has it really all been for nothing?'

'It isn't finished yet.'

'It will be soon. It must be. We all know it. Czerniakow's gone. And Mokotow. Zoliborz has been all but wiped from the face of the earth. Now it's our turn.' She took off her greasy forage cap and ran tired hands through her hair. 'But damn it all, we came so close!' Her voice was suddenly ragged with frustration and unshed tears. 'If only the American drop had been better managed – all those supplies lost, wasted! If only the bloody Russians had crossed the river instead of stopping in Praga – if only – oh, if only, if only, if only! What's the good?'

He reached for her hand. 'Come on, now. Chin up.'

She smiled bleakly, and shook her head. 'I'll never forget seeing those American planes – never forget watching those damned parachutes floating down into the river or on to the wrong bits of the city.'

'It wasn't their fault. There was no way they could control exactly where the supplies fell. It was bad luck, that's all.'

'You can say that again,' said the man next to him, handing the cigarette, which had passed down the line and back, across Marek to Danusia. 'In spades.' They were a group of six or seven, all thin, all haggard with sleeplessness and hunger, the men unshaven. No one had eaten or slept for twenty-four hours and there had been precious little water. None of them was unscathed; scabbed and bloodied and bandaged they looked, Marek thought, like the bandits that the Germans always termed them. The fighting over the past week had been ferocious. They were exhausted and all but starving. Worse, they were depressed. The euphoria that had taken hold a few days before, when Russian fighters had suddenly appeared over Warsaw and driven the until now unopposed German bombers from the smoke-filled skies, had made the demoralising disappointment that had followed a thousand times more bitter.

The oncoming Soviet army had not, as had been hoped and expected, crossed the Vistula and taken Warsaw. They had chosen to sit on their hands on the eastern bank, despite the pleas of the desperate insurgents. Promise after promise had been made; promise after promise had been broken. A half-hearted attempt to drop supplies into the city had failed when Soviet planes had dropped containers without parachutes. Street by street, building by building, the city was being utterly destroyed and the anguished and exhausted Home Army fighters beaten inexorably back. Without help they could not hold out much longer, and only the most stubbornly determined tried to deny it.

Danusia looked at her watch. 'It's half an hour since they pulled back. Where the hell is Stefan?'

Marek shook his head. His right hand was tucked into the front of his shirt. A pistol he had taken from a dead fighter was stuck in his belt; the ammunition that had come with it was almost exhausted. If the building were attacked again – and it most certainly would be – he would, together with most of the others, finish up facing guns, bayonets and flame-throwers with nothing but his bare hands to defend himself. He took off his glasses, wiped them carefully, settled them back on his nose, looked at Danusia. She sat with her knees bent, her arms resting upon them, her head bowed, her lank hair – that had always been so smooth and shining – pushed back as always behind her ear. The bones of her face were stark, her body thin as an adolescent boy's. She was filthy dirty and had a nasty-looking gash on her forehead.

He loved her so much that it hurt.

He slipped his hand into his pocket, fingered the last of the bullets, counting.

Five.

Four for the Germans.

One to be saved. Just in case. He had heard too often of the fate of captured women.

Sensing his eyes on her, Danusia turned her head and smiled, tiredly. 'Where *is* Stefan?' she asked again.

'What's going on out there, Felix?' called the man who sat next to Marek.

A boy by the window shook his head. 'Nothing. They've pulled back.'

'Make the most of it,' someone else muttered, 'It won't be for long.'

'OK, you lot – we've orders to fall back while we can.' A tall young man in ragged civilian clothes and a German helmet had appeared in the doorway. 'There's a unit a little further down the street. We're to join them. Come on.'

They scrambled to their feet. 'Where the hell is he?' Danusia hissed to Marek.

'Playing the boy wonder somewhere, no doubt,' Marek said grimly. 'Come on – we'll have to go – he'll just have to take a chance on finding us.'

They followed the others out of the door and down a short flight of stairs that led into a courtyard. The house on the other side of it was burning. 'Run for it,' the young man in the helmet said, and, together with two or three of the others, dashed into the smoke.

Danusia was about to follow when she felt a hand on her arm. 'Wait,' said Stefan's voice quietly in her ear. 'Let them go.'

'Stefan! Where have you been?'

Stefan's smile was fierce, wolflike in his thin face. 'I met a friend,' he said. 'Now, come on. This way.'

He led them back into the house, down more steps to what had been a semi-basement kitchen. Outside, a machine-gun clattered and someone shouted. 'They're coming back,' said Marek.

'Danka, you first.' Stefan had crossed the room to where there was a window high in the wall but on ground level outside. The glass had long since been blasted from it and the grill had been removed and stood against the wall. 'When you get outside, go to the left. There's a gap in the wall that leads into a yard. Wait for me there. Up you go.' He had made a stirrup with his linked hands, bent for her to put her foot in it. 'Hurry. And be careful.'

Danka squirmed through the gap into a rubble-strewn alley. From the other side of the building came more shots, more shouts, but on this side, for now at least, the coast seemed to be clear. She scrambled to her feet and dashed to the left. As Stefan had said, there was a gap in a wall that had obviously once been a gateway, and beyond it a small cobbled yard. The houses on two sides of it had been demolished by the shells and the bombing, on the third side a house still stood, gaunt, and gutted by fire. She leaned, panting, against the wall. A moment later Marek joined her. He was very pale.

She put a hand to him. 'Are you all right?'

He nodded, unable for the moment to speak. He could feel his reopened wound throbbing, sickeningly, with his pulse.

'What's Stefan up to, do you think?'

Marek took a long breath, and when he spoke his voice was commendably steady. 'Only God and Stefan know that, as usual. I daresay one or other of them will let us know what's happening sooner or later.'

Soundless as a ghost, Stefan slipped into the yard and joined them in the shelter of the wall. 'Come on.'

'Wait.' Danusia caught his arm. 'Stefan, what are you doing? Where are we going?'

'We're getting out,' he said.

'Out?' she looked at him blankly.

'Out of the city. The Rising's finished. We all know it. They're negotiating surrender now – right now, as we talk. I'll not surrender. By Christ I won't! There are units in the forest ready to fight on. We're going to join them.'

'But – how?'

'There's a route. Through the sewers. There's a group about to leave. A mate of mine got in touch with me. We're going with them.'

They all ducked as a thunderous explosion shook the ruined house.

'But –'

'For Christ's sake will you stop jabbering and *come on*!'

He led them through the ruins, ducking and crawling through shattered buildings and the remains of tunnels and cellars. Around them the shells whined and howled. All over the city the last desperate battles were taking place, street by street and building by building. Once they turned a corner to be unexpectedly confronted by a small German patrol, three men who were, as startled as they were but who took a fatal second longer to recover than did the seasoned street-fighters they faced.

Stefan and Danusia fired together, at point-blank range. Marek's finger tightened on the trigger of his pistol. The boy who faced him could not have been more than eighteen, soft-cheeked and wide-eyed with terror. He had not even raised his gun. He put up his hands as if to ward off the bullet. Stefan's second shot dropped him where he stood. Swiftly he and Danusia stripped the bodies of their weapons and ammunition.

Blood was staining the sleeve of Marek's shirt.

A short while later Stefan stopped. 'Wait here a moment.' He turned and disappeared into the ruins. A couple of minutes later he was back, gesturing for them to follow him. He led them into a tunnel at the end of which a dim, flickering light glowed. In the cellar to which the tunnel led sat four men and a girl, all armed, all watching the newcomers with tired and slightly wary eyes. One of the men shook Stefan's hand. 'Welcome,' he said. 'Take a seat. We can't move until dark. All we have to hope is that the bloody Boches concentrate on the northern approaches for a bit longer. If they break through in the south we're in trouble.'

'Where's the entrance to the sewers?' Danusia asked. 'I thought they were all under Home Army control? They won't just let anyone down, will they?'

The man grinned, showing sharp, blackened teeth, and tapped the side of his nose with his forefinger. 'Trust me.'

'And trust that the sodding Jerries are well occupied,'

the other girl said. 'The last lot that tried to get out were gassed like rats.'

And on that comforting thought they settled down to wait.

It was the longest wait that Marek had ever endured. Even the flight from Brindisi had not been as bad as this. Every so often an explosion shook the cellar and dust and debris showered from the ceiling. No one spoke. Cigarettes were passed from mouth to mouth. Every now and again the leader of the group, whom Stefan called Staszek, checked the entrance to the passage. Once, as dusk was beginning to fall, they could hear a running battle taking place somewhere very close.

At last full darkness fell, a darkness, as always, lit by the furnace of the fires that devoured the city.

'Right.' Staszek stood, ground out a cigarette with his heel. 'Time to go.'

He led them south through streets that had been so badly damaged that it was almost impossible to identify what had once been a familiar townscape to all of them. They travelled openly, one ragged and limping armed unit among many; only when they approached a large ruined building whose wrecked walls stood like the stumps of broken teeth against the red night sky did Staszek draw them back into the remains of a doorway.

'Touch and go,' he said. 'That's not far away.'

A volley of shots had rung out, and a rip of machine-gun fire. They could hear the grinding of tank-tracks and the boom of a big gun.

'Hurry. This way.'

Marek, one hand clutching his shoulder, was behind the others as they made a dash for the ruined building. In the shadows he missed his footing and tripped, sprawling painfully. 'Here –' Stefan's hand hauled him upright – 'hold on to me.'

'My glasses –' Marek said.

'Sod your glasses. Come on!'

The manhole cover had been skilfully hidden beneath a pile of fallen timber. Eager hands dragged the burned beams free and hauled on the heavy grating. Whenever this route had been used before there had been people left behind to replace the grating and camouflage it again; this time they would have to take a chance. With the imminent fall of the city a certainty now, it was unlikely to be used again. All they had to hope was that the open manhole would not be discovered before they had gone far enough to be out of the danger of gas or burning kerosine.

'I'll go first. Janina, you follow –' Staszek swung his legs into the darkness, slid into the hole and disappeared.

The sound of fighting was coming closer. A figure flitted across the end of the street, turned to fire into the ruddy darkness and then disappeared into the smoke.

One by one they climbed on to the iron ladder, until Stefan, Danusia and Marek were the only ones left.

Stefan helped Danusia into the hole, then held out his hand to Marek.

'No,' Marek said. 'One-handed, I'll hold you up. I'm bound to be slow. My shoulder – it's not good. You go first. I'll follow.'

There was no time to argue. Stefan sat on the edge of the hole, twisted his body, found a foothold and began to descend.

Marek stood for a fraction of a second looking down after him. Clearly now he could hear the sound of a tank grinding along the road towards them. A tiny bobbing light at the bottom of the shaft showed where Staszek stood in the stinking mud of the near-ruined sewer. His voice echoed in the shaft, urging the others to speed.

Marek, knowing himself incapable of lifting the heavy grating back into place, began painfully and with the strength of desperation to haul the lengths of timber across the hole. His hands were slick with his own blood. He heard Stefan's shout, saw the white blur of his face as he looked up; heard Danusia shriek his name. 'Marek! *No!*'

Stefan had started back up the ladder. Marek heaved on a beam. It turned, toppled and rolled across the manhole.

The crackle of small-arms fire was in his ears. A small group of fighters had appeared at the top of the street, firing behind them as they ran.

One more effort, and the manhole was covered.

'Marek! *Marek!*' His brother's voice was agonised.

The tank rolled round the corner, gun blazing. Behind it, to Marek's blurred vision demon figures in the flickering, fiery light, came the German infantry, advancing in good order, firing as they came.

He stepped away from the manhole, out of the shadows into the open street. The little group of insurgents streamed past him. He staggered, a wave of darkness lifting in his swimming head. His shoulder and arm were sodden with blood. The tank was almost upon him, a huge, blurred metal leviathan with a flaming mouth.

Death, after all then, did not ride a pale horse –

Marek lost consciousness a second before the monster struck him.

It ground on without halt or stay into the burning city.

$E\,p\,i\,l\,o\,g\,u\,e$

East Anglia, September 1955

In the chill of an early September morning the dark tide flowed fast and cold, lapping against the mud banks, swirling in the creeks. Dawn was a blood-red line on the sea-horizon.

Two figures stood in the darkness, one some twenty or thirty yards behind the other, eyes and ears as alert and as keen as those of the dogs that sat patiently by their sides.

In the burgeoning light of the approaching dawn, Stefan Anderson glanced at the slight, still figure of his son whose own concentration was entirely centred upon the wide, clear sky. The boy stood easily, his scruffy tweed cap – a cast-off of his father's – pulled low over his eyes, his booted feet planted firmly in the cold, squelching mud, gun broken across his arm.

Wings whispered distantly on the air.

Two guns clicked quietly. The dogs cocked their heads.

The flight came in from the north, towards the boy, as Stefan had judged it might. He watched as the boy's gun came up, steady and sure.

Wait, Mark. Not yet. Wait.

The flight curled in the rosy sky and swept towards them. Mark's finger curled gently upon the trigger.

The bird dropped like a stone, the kill clean. Stefan swung his own gun through, sighting along the barrel, the birds sweet and clear above him, but he did not fire. Not without a twinge of regret he lowered the gun, snapped it open, removed the cartridges. The birds swooped and settled on the water. Stefan put up a warning hand to the patient dog by his side and waded to where the boy stood. 'Go on then. It's your bird. You've got to let her try.'

The boy nibbled his lip a little, bent to the younger dog and slipped the rope noose from her neck. 'Fly. Steady, girl.'

The dog trembled, watching him.

'Get on.'

She was off and into the water in a flash. Stefan narrowed his eyes, watching her. She came up on to a small island, cast about busily and entirely without direction. 'Use the whistle.'

Mark put the whistle to his lips. At the signal, the dog's head came up. Mark swung his right arm wide, pointing. The dog hesitated.

'Again,' Stefan said.

This time she understood. A moment or so later she was back in the water, swimming valiantly through the tug of the tide towards them, the kill in her mouth.

Stefan felt the boy's tension drain from him, saw the pride in the bright, thin face as the excited, dripping dog delivered her prize.

Mark bent to the dog, accepted the bird, and for a moment his hand was gentle on her head. Then, manfully, he straightened. 'Dry yourself off, then, you silly little tart.'

The dog shook herself exuberantly, sat panting delightedly at his feet.

Mark turned to his father, the grin he had been trying to suppress finally lighting his face brighter than the sunrise. 'She did it!'

'She certainly did.' Stefan's hand rested for a moment on the boy's shoulder. Then, 'No good resting on your laurels,' he said. 'That little old thing won't feed many. We promised your mother at least two for the pot – she probably won't let us back into the house without.'

Mark's grin widened.

Stefan lifted his head. 'More coming. There –' He reached into his leather pouch for cartridges.

Mark did the same. 'Dad?'

'What?'

'This time, why don't you try a shot?' The boy's face was alight with mischief. 'I'm sure you could hit one if you tried. And you could always borrow Fly if you needed to –'

Stefan cuffed him. 'Cheeky little sod!' Their laughter was quiet. Above them the clear sky glowed with light and around them the water glittered and swirled as the tide ran in.

They walked through the Sunday-quiet village street in companionable silence, the dogs at their heels, Mark carrying his bag with a slightly self-conscious nonchalance that brought a smile to more than one face. Mary-Anne Beckett, who lived in the cottage next to the shop and who sat next to him in school, was swinging on her garden gate. 'Hello, Mark. Mr Anderson. Hello, Fly.'

Entirely unnecessarily Mark hitched his gun a little higher on his shoulder, thus displaying the two mallard he carried.

'Bin down the marshes?'

'I reckon so.'

She wrinkled her nose exaggeratedly, 'Pooh! Smells like it!' Her eyes were admiring. She scooted the gate with one foot and swung again.

A woman's voice called from the house. 'Mary-Anne, how often must I tell you? You get off that gate!'

The girl pulled a face and stuck out her tongue, but she jumped from the gate, clicking it shut. 'My uncle and aunt came yesterday. They brought me ever such a big bag of sweets. The biggest you've ever seen, I bet. You can have some tomorrow, if you like.'

Mark shrugged. Stefan had strolled on.

'Would you like?'

'Wouldn't mind.'

'Can I coach Fly?'

'If you like. She's muddy, though.'

'I don't care.' She put her small hand through the gate and stroked the dog's smooth, wet fur.

'Mary-Anne! Come on in here!'

Mary-Anne muttered under her breath. Mark's eyes widened. The girl turned and scampered off up the path. Mark rejoined his father. 'Girls!' he said.

The back door to the cottage stood open. The wireless was playing. They rubbed the dogs down and kennelled them, divested themselves of muddy boots, overtrousers and jackets in the tiny lean-to porch, walked through in stockinged feet to the warmth of the kitchen.

Danusia was at the stove, and the delicious smell of frying bacon was in the air. 'I didn't think you would be much longer.' She turned from them, smiling. 'Stephen, *kochany*, do clear those things from the table. I've asked you a dozen times.' The words were addressed to the small boy who sat at the long kitchen table, tousled blond head bent, wire-rimmed glasses perched on the end of his snub nose in gravity-defying fashion. He was earnestly studying a diagram in an open book; beside him an extraordinary contraption of wood and wire was under construction. He greeted the newcomers with an absent smile, rubbed a hand through already wildly disordered hair and went back to his diagram.

'Daddy!' A little girl of perhaps four or five years threw herself upon Stefan. 'You went out before I was awake again! It isn't fair! I wanted to go! Have you brought our dinner home?'

'I certainly have. Or rather Mark here has.' He swung her from her feet and settled her on his arm, straightened to look at Danka, smiling a little.

'One day, can I come? One day, will you take me on the marshes with you? Can I have a gun like Mark?'

'Don't be daft. Girls don't go fowling.' Mark was dismissive. He reached into the pan with his fingers for a piece of bacon. Danka gently but firmly slapped his hand away.

The child's lip quivered. She put her arms about Stefan's neck. 'Please, Daddy?'

'We'll see. We'll see. Now, my pretty Isadore, why don't you help Mummy lay the table?' He set her on her feet. The little mouth set stubbornly. The child went to the table, dragged a chair closer to her brother, climbed up on it and pretended, frowning ferociously, to study the diagram with him. He patted her small hand absently, rubbed his chin, leaving a large dirty mark.

Danka ducked her head and laughed quietly.

Stefan shook his head. 'Why do other people manage to produce daughters who lay tables and play with dolls when I get one who won't do a thing she's told and wants a gun?'

'Do you think it might be something to do with her parentage?' Danka asked, mild and amused. She pushed her swinging hair behind her ear, scraped at the bacon. 'And now, you two, you needn't think you're sitting down to breakfast in that state. Off you go and clean yourselves up. Ten minutes. And Stephen, how many times do I have to ask you to clear the table? Do you expect us to eat breakfast on the floor?'

Isadore giggled.

'Sorry.' Stephen pushed his glasses more firmly on to his nose and left another dirty smudge on his face.

'Here. I'll help you.' His mother came to him, stood behind him, reached towards the Heath Robinson contraption he had been building. 'There's no need to break it up.'

He turned his head to smile at her – a smile that lit his small bespectacled face to radiance. A smile that anyone who had known Marek Anderson would have recognised. Stefan, watching from the doorway, saw Danusia still for a moment. Then, in a gesture of infinite tenderness she rested a hand on the boy's untidy hair. 'You can finish whatever it is later.'

'It was going to be a machine to feed Isadore's guinea pig. I'm not sure it will work, though.'

'Whether it works or not it's bound to be more reliable than Isadore is.' His mother's voice was gently amused. She lifted a finger to his smudged face. 'For goodness' sake, look at the state of you. You're almost as scruffy as the other two, and you haven't set foot outside the house!' There was nothing at all of reproof in the words, nothing but the warmth of love in her voice.

Stefan turned, closed the door quietly behind him and went upstairs to change for breakfast.

THE ITALIAN HOUSE

Teresa Crane

Secretly treasured memories of her grandmother's Italian house, perched high upon a mountainside in Tuscany, are very special for Carrie Stowe; for not only do they recall and preserve the happy childhood summers of the golden years before the devastation of the Great War, they are her only escape from the mundane and suffocating routine of her life with Arthur, her repressive and parsimonious husband.

When she discovers that she has unexpectedly inherited the house Carrie sets her heart upon going to Tuscany alone to dispose of effects of Beatrice Swann, her eccentric and much-loved grandmother.

Arriving late at night and in the teeth of a violent storm she discovers that she is not the only person to be interested in the Villa Castellini and its family connections. A young man, an enigmatic figure from the past, is there before her: and as the enchantment of the house exerts itself once more, Carrie finds herself irresistibly drawn to him . . .

<u>INTIMATE LIES</u>

Maria Barrett

TWO WOMEN, ONE MAN, AND A DECEPTION
THAT HAS NOTHING TO DO WITH LOVE . . .

Jill Turner is devastated when her beloved husband Alex is
reported missing – a suspected suicide.

Holly Grigson's response to her own husband's death is
less conventional. She reacts with guilty, shameful
relief . . .

Yet both women, strangers until now, greet the next piece
of news with the same appalled disbelief. If the evidence
can be believed they were married to the same man.
But can it be?

'Barrett is at her best when she is writing about her
characters' feelings and her description of the
confrontation between the two women is quite compelling.'
The Times

	The Italian House	Teresa Crane	£5.99
☐	The Italian House	Teresa Crane	£5.99
☐	Intimate Lies	Maria Barrett	£5.99
☐	Dishonoured	Maria Barrett	£5.99
☐	Deceived	Maria Barrett	£4.99
☐	Dangerous Obsession	Maria Barrett	£5.99
☐	Elle	Maria Barrett	£5.99
☐	Half Hidden	Emma Blair	£5.99
☐	Hester Dark	Emma Blair	£5.99
☐	Nellie Wildchild	Emma Blair	£5.99
☐	The Princess of Poor Street	Emma Blair	£5.99

Warner Books now offers an exciting range of quality titles by both established and new authors. All of the books in this series are available from:

Little, Brown and Company (UK),
P.O. Box 11,
Falmouth,
Cornwall TR10 9EN.
Telephone No: 01326 372400
Fax No: 01326 317444
E-mail: books@barni.avel.co.uk

Payments can be made as follows: cheque, postal order (payable to Little, Brown and Company) or by credit cards, Visa/Access. Do not send cash or currency. UK customers and B.F.P.O. please allow £1.00 for postage and packing for the first book, plus 50p for the second book, plus 30p for each additional book up to a maximum charge of £3.00 (7 books plus).

Overseas customers including Ireland, please allow £2.00 for the first book plus £1.00 for the second book, plus 50p for each additional book.

NAME (Block Letters) ....

....

ADDRESS ....

....

....

☐ I enclose my remittance for ....

☐ I wish to pay by Access/Visa Card

Number ☐☐☐☐☐☐☐☐☐☐☐☐☐☐☐☐☐☐

Card Expiry Date ☐☐☐☐